EMERGENCY CONTINUED

RICHARD RIVE

Emergency Continued

readers international

First published in 1990 outside Africa by Readers International, by arrangement with David Philip Publishers (Pty) Ltd, Claremont, Cape, South Africa.

Editorial enquiries to Readers International London office at 8 Strathray Gardens, London NW3 4NY England. US/Canadian enquiries to the Subscriber Service Dept., P.O. Box 959, Columbia LA 71418–0959 USA.

Cover design by Jan Brychta
Printed and bound in Malta by Interprint Limited

ISBN 0-930523-87-3 Hardcover
ISBN 0-930523-88-1 Paperback

CONTENTS

CONTENTS

PART ONE

THE MANDELA MARCH

Wednesday 28 August 1985

By 9 a.m. a crowd of almost four thousand people has gathered outside Athlone Stadium. They are intent on marching from there to Pollsmoor Prison to deliver a message of solidarity to Nelson Mandela and other political prisoners. There is a heavy police presence with many Casspirs and vans in evidence. The stadium is completely sealed off. Policemen and soldiers line the whole of Klipfontein Road on the stadium side, from central Athlone to Vanguard Drive. Just before 10 a.m. the officer in charge gives the crowd five minutes in which to disperse. When the order is ignored the police move in.

Andrew Dreyer
Eastridge Secondary School
A. Z. Berman Drive
Mitchell's Plain
7785
Cape Town
South Africa
August 1988

Professor A. G. Hanslo
22 Barkwood Court
Scarborough
Ontario
M1W 3V1
Canada

Dear Abe

How pleasant for me to have received two letters from you in such quick succession. I must apologise for my cursory reply to your first letter which I received at the end of July. I realised that mine was no more than a mere acknowledgement of receipt, but I was then in the middle of an almost untenable situation at my school, and, by the time your second letter came, I was in the middle of an almost untenable situation at my home. I hope that this letter makes up for my having been such a bad correspondent and fills you in with all the latest events.

I was really astonished when I received your first letter after the long freeze. The last letter I had received was twenty-four years before. You are lucky that I am still alive. Fifty-four last birthday rapidly going on sixty. Fortunately Mrs Carollissen's boy (remember Eldred?) still lives in their house in Grassy Park (where I boarded) to which you sent that letter. His conservative and starched parents are now both dead. Eldred teaches with me at the same school so he brought me your letter. You could have bowled me over. For a few minutes I had to ask myself, "Now who on earth is Professor Doctor Hanslo?"

So you are now an Associate of York University and teach African literature? What happend to your B.Sc? What a change in direction in one so versatile. I always knew you would end up that way. You were never really a scientist. Do you, in any of your courses, teach my one published novel or my four published short stories? Or at least tell your students about your friendship with a famous black writer before and during the 1960 Emergency? Yes, it is twenty-five years ago. A quarter of a century and almost a lifetime ago. Long time ago. When de little black bull went down de meadow. Long long time ago. Remember?

3

You mean that after all those years you still had some concern for me? Nevertheless you are quite correct, we have had hell here for the last few weeks, in fact ever since the State of Emergency was declared in certain areas on 21 July. This State of Emergency is very different from the one we knew in 1960.

The situation itself is so paradoxical. You can avoid the worst if you are privileged enough, as I am, to live in a quiet suburb like Elfindale. Then what is happening in the township and ghettoes might as well be ten thousand miles removed.

For weeks now we have been subjected at school to police surveillance, raids and searches. Pupils and teachers have been shot at with rubber bullets, tear-gassed, arrested and detained. This happens almost daily for weeks on end.

A typical day will start quite normally with the expectation of lessons. Then the pupils decide to have a mass anti-apartheid rally at the school or at some other venue. The end of any teaching for that day. Posters, chanting, slogans, toyi-toyiing and speakers exhorting the crowd to action, any action. On any one such day we might have up to four thousand pupils in our grounds drawn from all over the Peninsula. Then the police arrive in Casspirs and armoured trucks and give the crowd a few minutes in which to disperse. They usually ignore the order. Then follows either a baton charge, the police flaying with quirts and sjamboks, or the shooting of tear-gas canisters. The pupils retaliate with stones and any missiles they can find. We stand by angry and impotent, trying to reason with whoever is prepared to speak to us. By midday I have had enough and get into my car and drive home. Once in Elfindale people are walking their dogs, washing their cars or shopping in the main road. They are not unconcerned about the happenings but are ten million miles away from the action which they read about in their newspapers or see on their television screens.

For the past number of years, as I mentioned in my brief reply, I have been deputy principal at Eastridge Senior Secondary School which has twelve hundred pupils (very large even for the townships). I teach English to the Standard Nines and Matrics.

When I compare the time now with those heady days in 1960 I find that this situation is far worse, on a far bigger scale and far more protracted. The battle is grossly uneven. On one side we have the people's movements, community organisations, workers, and students armed with stones, petrol bombs and moral and political rights. On the other side they have the entire might of the State, soldiers, policemen, Casspirs, armoured cars, guns and limitless powers of arrest and detention.

Yes, of course I felt resentful about your leaving the country so soon after your mother's death. That's why I did not reply to your letters. I resented it when you wrote that you were thinking of becoming a Canadian citizen (although not

4

necessarily a Canadian as you were at pains to point out). However, I am well past that resentment now and pleased that you have also become a littérateur. What on earth caused it? A real renaissance man, eh? I suppose it is easier and more rewarding to be teaching African literature quietly on a Canadian campus where your main concern is discussing Ngugi's theories of the decolonisation of the African mind. Maybe it is easier to be able to take your wife shopping in downtown Toronto or send the children to a summer camp in Minnesota or go with the entire family on a jaunt to Miami and Disneyworld. Yours is a very different world and in a way I envy it. I confess that after so many of my friends left for Canada and Australia I was also sorely tempted.

I have been married for twenty years now and have a pleasant wife, Mabel, who tends at times to be over-religious and over-insistent. (For goodness sake don't mention it in any of your letters.) She worries about me, the children and our lack of spiritual reverence. My only son is Bradley Abraham (guess where he gets his second name from). Bradley is a second-year physical education student at Hewat College, but has lately been the source of much worry and anxiety for us. He is an executive member of the Western Province Students Representative Council and up to his ears in politics. Whether he will ever qualify as a teacher is speculative. He and I disagree politically on most things and I feel that he resents the fact that I am not more active than I appear to be. He is most probably correct. After all the years of knocking my head I am tired and just want to creep into myself and teach my pupils and write my books and stories. I have never told my children about my political past, about our political past, about what happened to us in 1960 and before that. I don't think I mean to either. Not at this juncture.

The police have been after him and he is now on the run. I have not seen him for the last week. My daughter Ruth (guess again?) is in Senior Certificate at our old school, Steenberg High. She is the quiet member of the family. What with her mother ranting religion, her brother ranting politics, my seeming indifference, she has a hard time of it but bears it stoically.

I have had a desperate urge to write about 1985, to document it as a personal history. I have started to get it down in novel form, which I do best, so that no-one can say afterwards that they didn't know, and so that no children can say afterwards that they weren't told.

I am jotting down my experiences daily as well as those of others, and keeping copies of all the local newspapers. It is not going to be easy to write as I find that things are happening which are so shocking and unbelievable that they verge on the melodramatic. They cannot pass for truth except that they are the truth. I mean to tell the truth through fiction, taking incidents directly from experience, embellishing them a bit and then passing them off as fiction, or faction. Someone must do it. But why me? Why must I suffer from the Hamlet syndrome? O cursed spite, that ever I was born to set it right!

5

I am beginning to doubt whether I am able to distinguish between truth and fiction. The line is sometimes so hazy that I cannot tell the difference. But I must persevere and maybe send the results to you as Brutus did with his Letters to Martha, *or hide the pages under the linoleum as La Guma did with* A Walk in the Night.

I am sending you an account of some of my experiences during July and August, especially of my somewhat unpleasant altercations with Brad. I am also including a few chapters of the novel. Maybe I should start with the happenings of today, 28 August, since it is still vividly in my memory. Please let me know whether you receive these. I would also welcome any criticism you may have.

The Minister of Law and Order, Louis Le Grange, had warned that the march would be illegal and that he had instructed his police to do all in their power to stop it. But the leaders decided that the march must go on.

1

Andrew cruised very slowly down Thornton Road, driving his way carefully through the heavy crowd moving towards the stadium. He pulled off into Hewat College. A few cars were parked there but otherwise the college wore a deserted look. There were no students in animated groups sprawled out on the lawns or smoking on the steps of the Arts Block. He pulled up at parking-lot outside the Men's Gymnasium, looking around for anyone from whom he could make inquiries. Maybe he should go to the secretary`s office. A lecturer or student might be able to tell him where to find Bradley.

It was now two weeks since the boy had last been home. The argument that evening, the last of a series, had been the worst and possibly the most decisive. And that scruffy girl-friend of his, Lenina, who was always hanging around him, an angry activist daughter of an angry activist father. He was sure that that was the root cause of the problem, Brad's relationship with Lenina. Trust her father to give her a name like that. Her influence over his son must be considerable. Love and politics were a powerful combination. She had also unsolicitedly offered him some of her political advice.

"Mr Dreyer, you must understand that we are all in this together. You are as oppressed as any of your pupils although you don't seem to acknowledge it."

Comparing him with her father to Andrew's discomfort and humiliation. Turning his own son against him. What a bloody cheek, and from a first-year university student just out of her teens. After that last encounter Brad had taken his clothes and left without even greeting. Disappeared with her just like that. Of course he had left for short spells before, but this last departure had a note of finality about it. Usually after a day or two he would phone from a public callbox or get a message through just to say that he was safe. But now for two weeks, nothing but silence. He could be detained, for all they knew, or out of the country receiving military training somewhere. Maybe he was over-reacting and Brad was staying with one of his friends, sulking but still attending college. He hoped against hope that that was so, that the boy was dutifully attending lectures — that is, if there were any lectures to attend.

Andrew sat in his parked car not sure what to do next. He glanced at the newspaper headlines.

"Boesak Detained at Bellville Road Block Last Night." The situation was certainly deteriorating. "Zola Budd Set to Break New Record." He had no desire to read further.

Maybe Brad was right. Maybe the boy had a point. The two of them had never really spoken intimately. Maybe he was afraid of intimacy because it might reveal too much or hurt too much. He had provided his family with everything they needed, seen to their material welfare, because he was determined that the children should never experience what he had experienced in District Six. Andrew had never spoken about the past, about his past. He had watched with growing anxiety as Brad became more and more politically aware. Too young to understand in 1980 (he was only fourteen then) but since that time he had become very much involved. And with that awareness, no doubt egged on by his girl-friend, more critical of his father's attitude, what he interpreted as political indifference. Indifference or withdrawal? Maybe a cultivated withdrawal. A refusal to get involved yet again. 1960 had been more than enough for one lifetime. He knew that Brad had put it down to his father's protecting his position as deputy principal of a High School, protecting his personal interests, his relatively high salary and his housing subsidy. But the boy was so wrong. Or was he? Maybe it would have been better had they sat down and talked? Or would that have aggravated the situation?

Andrew had not deliberately set out to cultivate this attitude of neutrality over the years. It had just grown as he became more and more withdrawn. It had started soon after 1960, even before he was married and the children were born, very soon after his experiences during the Langa and Sharpeville Emergency. And now, twenty-five years later, on 21 July to be exact, emergency in some areas. Normal emergencies and special emergencies. Special emergency ends. Normal emergency continues.

He did not want to admit even to himself, that he had come to Hewat, instead of going to his school in Mitchell's Plain, in the hope that he would find Brad. He hoped desperately that he would meet some student who would reply casually, "Oh Brad Dreyer? Yes of course, I saw him a few minutes ago in the Men's Gymnasium. Go along the main corridor and turn left just before you get to the hall."

A car pulled up next to his. A precise and trim lady got out, obviously a lecturer. Andrew also got out of his car. He was about to formulate his question, but before he could do so, she remarked, waving her arms over the deserted campus, "Not a student in sight, how pleasant."

"Excuse me, madam?"

"Oh, good morning."

"Good morning. Do you think there might be any students inside?"

"Not a chance. They're all down at the stadium straining at the leash to free Mandela. What is certain however is that there'll be no lectures for today, and that at least is a blessing."

"Do you know Mr Bradley Dreyer? He is a student."

"What year?"

"Second."

"I'm afraid not. I lecture only to third-year Junior Primary. You looking for him?"

"Yes, I'm his father."

"Oh, I see. Well, if he is anywhere he'll be at the stadium. Is anything the matter?"

"No, not really."

"Why don't you try the secretary's office? They might be able to help you."

"It's not so urgent. I think I'll take a walk to Klipfontein Road to see if he's there. Is it all right if I leave my car here?"

"No problem. But be careful. I have just come through Athlone and it's going to be very rough."

Andrew joined the crowd walking down Thornton Road. At first just a trickle which grew to a huge swell. At Klipfontein Road his way was almost blocked by thousands of milling people. Armoured cars and Casspirs cruised up and down pinning them to the near-side of Klipfontein Road. As far as the eye could see there were police and soldiers lining the stadium-side of the road, from Central Athlone to Vanguard Drive. On the other side, separated by the slow-moving armoured vehicles, massed the prospective marchers and spectators. Hundreds of children, many in school uniforms: Athlone High, Alexander Sinton, Spes Bona. Here and there a South Peninsula blazer all the way from Diep River or a Livingstone High badge from Claremont. Andrew was searching for the distinctive blue Hewat blazer or tracksuit top. Older political activists mixed surreptitiously with the crowd. Determined boys and girls, some barely out of their teens, wore the distinctive Gadaffi scarves wrapped around their necks, and clutched stones, or wet handkerchiefs in case of tear-gas.

Housewives tried to get through the human barrier to do their shopping. Businessmen, shopkeepers, anxious teachers keeping an eye on their pupils. Andrew was searching faces, faces, faces, looking for Brad. But in the milling, pressing, jostling crowd this proved impossible. And what if he did spot him? Would he be able to say, "Let's go somewhere quiet, Brad, and talk"?

Andrew found himself surrounded by University of the Western Cape students who were relating how their train from Bellville had been stopped, how they had eluded the railway guards and managed to get to Athlone by other means. Here and there posters of Mandela were brandished aloft to taunt the police. Other groups were singing freedom songs in praise of the leader. The crowd was growing larger by the minute and the atmosphere was becoming more and more tense. It waited for the spark to ignite.

Andrew weaved, bumped and pushed his way until he found himself on a shop stoep opposite the stadium, which was by now sealed off by police and soldiers. He saw an officer with a megaphone standing on the roof of an armoured car but he could not make out what was being said.

Then the spark ignited. An order was shouted over the megaphone, and the atmosphere became charged with electricity. Police with quirts and sjamboks ran across the road and started lashing out. The crowd jostled and pushed to avoid the blows, and some were trampled underfoot. Andrew darted into the café, which was already crowded with frightened people. The owner hastily bolted the doors. Through the plate-glass window he could see people outside being chased and whipped; young and old, men, women and children, students, workers and housewives.

Trapped in a bloody shop. Like being trapped in a bloody urinal twenty-five years before. The irony of the situation hit him and he even managed a wry smile. But in 1960 he was a young teacher searching for his friend Abe after a baton charge. Now he was a 47-year-old deputy principal of a High School searching for his son Brad during a quirt and sjambok charge. Promotion over twenty-five years from a urinal to a café. Abe was most probably lecturing at his quiet Canadian campus, thousands of miles away from this inhuman beating and flogging. What different paths they had taken. Andrew wondered whether he had taken the right path.

With a splintering crash the door collapsed and people tumbled in, some being cut by the broken glass. People inside fought and screamed. There was the strong acrid smell of tear-gas in the air.

"Keep calm and let's get the hell out of here!" Andrew shouted above the noise.

"Where to, mister?" an old lady asked, indicating the confusion outside.

"It will be better outside than inside!"

He squeezed his way past people, avoiding the broken glass and found himself back on the stoep. People were roaming around bewildered and frightened. The police were again lining up on the opposite side of Klipfontein Road.

Andrew saw a group of clergymen walking up to the commanding officer to level their protests. A heated exchange took place. Then a police van drew up and the clerics were unceremoniously bundled into it. The van pulled away with a screech of tyres.

An elderly housewife, beside herself with shock, walked up and down in front of the police brandishing a Bible and screaming at them, "You are supposed to be Christians, but look what you are doing. God will punish you for beating us like this!"

People were sullenly regrouping after the intial panic. The word spread rapidly. "Assemble at Hewat. Get to the college as fast as you can. The march will still take place. We march from Hewat."

Andrew felt the tension leaving him and a weariness taking over. He was sweating profusely. In either case he would have to go to Hewat to get to his car. He might even spot Bradley there.

2

It was on the evening of Wednesday, 14 August, that Andrew came home after a lengthy, protracted and frustrating staff meeting at school. Trouble had once again broken out. The president of the school's S.R.C., Trevor Petersen, a Standard Ten pupil, had been raided at his home during the early hours of the morning. His place had been searched but he himself had not been detained. When he came to school he gave the news to his fellow-pupils and they decided to organise a placard demonstration along A. Z. Berman Drive. Soon the Casspirs came rolling in.

The mood turned ugly. The principal, Mr Langeveldt, went out to reason with pupils and police. The officer in charge ordered him to get his pupils off the road immediately and dismiss the school or there would be trouble.

Andrew and the rest of the staff stood next to the principal as he addressed the pupils. He noticed that Joe Ismail was not present. When Mr Langeveldt instructed the pupils to go home quietly he was roundly booed. Trevor Petersen then rushed forward and took over the mike. He exhorted pupils to refuse to move from the school because an outsider, a policeman at that, had demanded it. This was their school and they were staying right where they were. A whistle blew and the police moved in. The first tear-gas canister exploded.

Andrew ran for cover to avoid the gas. He found himself in the Domestic Science room with a crowd of frightened girls. From a vantage-point he could see a group of Standard Sixes being chased up a staircase. They sought refuge in an end-classroom and bolted the door. A group of policemen, in hot pursuit, smashed one of the windows and lobbed a canister inside. Soon the door burst open and the pupils came out coughing and spluttering. Then they ran the gauntlet of blows from the batons. Andrew watched, stunned and helpless.

At last they managed to get all the pupils off the premises, and the Casspirs and vans also moved away. The staff meeting which followed went on and on and became more and more acrimonious. How to trace detained pupils. Collecting bail money. Protest delegations to the Education authorities. The possibility of legal advice. Joe Ismail, a senior English teacher, was bent on baiting the principal and the deputy. He always claimed to have been an activist in his younger days and had indeed been detained twice during the 1960s. He spent most of his time quoting the classics as a reminder of his Unisa B.A., and revelled in his political past. The head student and the S.R.C. were completely under his influence, as were some of the younger teachers. Andrew disliked and distrusted him but nevertheless treated his barbed comments as civilly as he could. At six o'clock the meeting was finally adjourned. Andrew drove back to Elfindale with a raging headache, his nerves scraped and raw.

He found the house locked and in darkness but this was not unusual. Mabel was most probably at a prayer meeting and must have dragged a reluctant Ruth with her. Brad was goodness only knew where. At some political rally or other. He must have seen the boy twice during the last two weeks. Sooner or later they would have to talk. Maybe sooner than later. It seemed as if he was becoming a stranger to his own son. Or had he always been a stranger?

Andrew let himself in and poured a whisky. He had no appetite for food. Not that he and Brad had ever been really close. He wasn't really close to anyone. Found difficulty becoming too intimate. He had a few friends, one or two teaching colleagues, and knew the odd writer. He spent more and more time in his study reading and writing the stories that seldom found a publisher. His greatest success was his one novel, which had received moderately favourable reviews, and a few short stories in the literary journal *Contrast*. He had been introduced to a few well-known writers. But he was reluctant to become part of the literary establishment, or the teaching establishment, or the political establishment, or any establishment for that matter.

When his only novel was published it brought him temporary recognition as well as criticism. Most people he knew congratulated him and then either did not read it or forgot all about it. Joe Ismail had made it known that, had Andrew Dreyer not been black, he would never have been published. His was a case of apartheid in reverse. If one is black and shows the slightest signs of literacy, then white liberal publishers will pounce on one. But really would it be good literature? Andrew had heard these remarks in the staff-room on more than one occasion but had chosen not to rise to the bait. The Standard Tens, encouraged by Mr Ismail, felt that his novel was climbing on the protest bandwagon. He did not reply to those accusations.

Andrew took off his jacket and tie and decided to listen to music. He had not listened to Smetana's "The Moldau" from *Má Vlast* for years. It had always been a favourite of his. He found the record at the back of a pile and put it on the turntable. His white girl-friend, Ruth, of the 1960s had given it to him as a present so many years before. He switched off the lights and settled back with his drink.

Two solo flutes, the river Moldau high up in the mountains, take up the motif, which once established is taken over by the strings. Then country folk revel at a wedding feast on its banks. The symphony broadens as the river sweeps its leisurely way through Prague to Vysehrad, flowing wide and majestic, while he is waiting for Ruth in a Rondebosch flat a quarter of a century before. Where could she be now? Could she also hear the gentle flow of the Moldau, wherever she was? Did she still remember him in the way that he remembered her? He still remembered her over all the years, tended to live in a past he shielded from everyone, lived for that past. Then an increase in vigour and tempo as the Moldau shoots over the St John's rapids. A sudden eruption, startling and ominous like a crowd suddenly turning dangerous. Like school children clutching bricks and stones and turning ugly. From Sharpeville and Soweto to Rocklands and Eastridge. From Langa, a long time ago. When de little black bull went down de meadow, long time ago. The sharp acrid smell of tear-gas, like the sharp ammonia smell of the dark menacing water of the Hanover Street swimming-baths. A long, long time ago. Sharpeville. Mitchell's Plain. District Six. Má Vlast. *My country. The music becomes enriched harmonically and methodically, and passes into a long coda as it is carried forward to a last view of the distant river sweeping relentlessly down to the sea. Down to de sea. Long, long time ago. When de little black bull went down de meadow, long time ago.*

Andrew sat in the dark sipping his whisky, not wishing to spoil the moment. He heard someone at the door and reluctantly got up. Then it opened and all the lounge lights were unceremoniously turned on.

"Oh, it's you, Dad? I was worried when I found the door unlocked and all the lights off. I didn't realise that anyone was home."

"Yes, it's only me. I was listening to music."

Bradley was tall and athletically built. He had inherited his father's good looks, the firm chin and dark eyes with heavy dominating brows. He had in tow a young girl. She was fair, quite good-looking, but there was a hardness about her mouth. A female Lady Macbeth, Andrew thought. She seemed to cultivate a deliberate scruffiness by wearing a nondescript blouse covered with political badges. She also wore carefully torn jeans. There was something hostile and challenging in her.

"Oh, and this is Lenina, Dad. She is a first-year student at U.W.C. Lenina, this is my father."

"Pleased to meet you," Andrew said, rising from his seat. The girl did not respond.

"Lenina is also on the Western Province S.R.C. with me."

"I see, another member of the politburo."

"No, Dad, merely someone who is heavily involved in the struggle."

"Well then, good for her."

Bradley ignored the remark. "Is mother home or busy Jesus-jumping?"

"I won't allow you to speak about your mother like that in my house."

"Sorry, Dad, no offence meant. I don't really need a fight at this juncture. What I desperately need however is a change of clothing."

"And something to eat," Lenina said, speaking for the first time.

Andrew turned to her and she met his gaze coolly.

The two young people went into the kitchen.

Andrew refilled his glass. There was something familiar about the girl in spite of her attitude. He knew he had seen that face somewhere before. He recognised it through the hard looks, the same hard looks that the Eastridge activists had, pupils like Trevor Petersen, the questionable and fanatical followers of Joe Ismail. Strangely enough Joe's own son, Neil was different. A quiet boy, respectful and a loner. Not a very good student. Maybe deliberately so because of his father. Andrew had heard that the boy and his sister had been adopted. Yes, there was something familiar about Lenina.

After a time Bradley reappeared freshly dressed and munching. Lenina held a plate of sandwiches. Andrew watched them still standing.

"Care for a slice, Mr Dreyer?"

He ignored her and turned again on Bradley.

"Am I allowed as a parent to ask where you have been the last few days? Your mother is worried sick."

"Of course you are allowed to ask, though I am not obliged to reply."

"I take exception to that."

"I do appreciate your concern, Dad, but it is not wise that anyone should know where I am. I am being watched, so it is better in case . . ."

"In case what?"

"In case they come and ask questions. You can then genuinely say that you don't know."

"So not even your parents are allowed to know where you are?"

"Not even my parents."

"Is this a game you people are playing?"

"No, it is not a game. Look Dad, these days it isn't safe to confide in anyone. In any case you either don't know or don't care what happens to me. Why the sudden concern now?"

"You really believe I don't want to know what happens to you?"

"I think you want to know only as much as you allow yourself to know. For instance you do know what's happening at your school. You cannot avoid knowing that. But do you ever stop to think why it is happening?"

"And you really believe that I don't care about you?"

"Maybe you choose not to care."

"Mr Dreyer," Lenina intervened putting down the plate of sandwiches, "you must understand that we are all in this together. You are as oppressed as any of your pupils although you don't seem to acknowledge it."

15

The remark cut deep but Andrew chose to ignore it. She continued.

"Brad is doing important work for the Front. The system will be happy if they can lay their hands on him."

Andrew listened but his concern was with his son. He felt bruised and hurt.

"You still haven't answered me. You really believe that I don't know and I don't care about you?" he persisted.

There was a long pause.

"Yes, I do."

"How much do you know about me, about what I do and how I think?"

"Look, Dad, I have never known you to get politically involved like Lenina's father for instance. I have known you to read the newspaper, to grumble about the news, to speak about what is happening at your school — and nothing else. I know that what is happening at Eastridge affects and hurts you. But that is only one school, your school. I have heard members of your staff discussing you and the remarks were embarrassing. You have written a book and I am proud of you but it is not enough. You have never taken a definite political stand."

"I see Mr Joseph Ismail has been speaking?"

"As well as some S.R.C. members."

Andrew tried hard to control himself.

"And you believed all that?"

"Dad, I didn't come home to hurt you. But you must face the truth some time or other. We belong to different generations. Your one did little other than theorise and accept their Coloured status and humiliation. You people were Coloured and allowed yourselves to be treated as such. You left us the mess we are in now. That was your legacy. Our generation is different. We are fighting back but not as Coloureds. We are fighting back as the oppressed breaking the shackles you should have broken. We are taking the political stand you should have taken. And in our case we are doing something positive about it."

"Like running away from the Special Branch?"

"Yes, that is also part of it."

The irony of the situation hit Andrew and he smiled wryly.

Lenina took up the cudgels. "He is right, Mr Dreyer. Your generation did little other than talk, talk, talk."

"All of us?"

16

"Not all of you. There were exceptions but they were very few. Cissie Gool and after her Joe La Guma, Reg September, my father, Johnny Gomas. They were few then but we are many now."

Andrew turned towards her. "I don't remember soliciting your advice and I don't remember being told who you are."

"Her name is Lenina, Dad. I told you so."

"Lenina who?"

"Lenina Bailey."

"And your father?"

"You might have read about him. He spent twelve years on Robben Island and is now at home, in bad health and, even worse, very disillusioned about the past. I grew up for twelve years without a father. Do you know what it is like to grow up without parents, Mr Dreyer?"

He did not answer her.

"You mean you haven't heard of her father, Dad? He was of your time."

"Yes," Andrew replied softly. "I have heard of him."

"Well, good for you. There's some hope yet," Lenina said sarcastically.

"O.K. Dad. No ill feelings, I hope. We must be off now in case the bully boys come. Will phone when the heat is off. Give Mom and Ruth my love. Ask Mom to pray for me. Come on, Lenina."

And they were gone.

Andrew poured himself another drink, a stiff one this time. He knew he was drinking far too much lately. He stood in the middle of the room holding the glass, his mind reeling with events of the 1960s, the years before that, the years after, District Six, Mitchell's Plain, Brad. Then he switched on "The Moldau" again, dimmed the lights and sank back into his chair as the music started.

Lenina Bailey. Lenina Bailey. So that was who she was. Justin's daughter. A sad smile played around his lips.

3

Andrew walked briskly up side streets to avoid the crowd but found he still had to weave his way through some of the thousands hurrying to Hewat. He entered the college through the Belgravia Road gate and walked across the overgrown sports field to the Men's Gymnasium. A group of lecturers were standing on the steps. He recognised some of them, and stood discreetly at the back as they watched the growing masses.

Those who were not streaming through the gates were climbing over walls and creeping through holes in the fences. Every minute the crowd was increasing, congregating on the athletics track. A furious argument was developing between those in favour of marching and those against it. A car pulled up and two men ran across the field with arms full of poster blow-ups of Mandela's face. The crowd by now numbered nearly four thousand and many more were still coming.

In the middle of the field the debate continued. A well-dressed man, probably a teacher or lawyer, was addressing the group. He had a slightly affected accent. Foreign television crews filmed the incident.

"You have made your point. The whole world will know by tonight what happened down at the stadium. To march now is not only unnecessary but absolutely suicidal."

A teen-age girl took up the challenge. "We cannot call it off now. We said we would march and we are going to march. We will look stupid if we don't march!"

There was ragged applause.

"It's not a case of looking stupid or not. Lives could be involved. You mustn't allow your emotions to run away with you. It is important to keep cool. Think of the consequences if we march."

Andrew had moved nearer and was listening intently to the argument. Another girl, unable to contain her emotions, moved to the centre of the circle. Andrew thought it was Lenina but was disappointed when he looked more carefully.

The girl spoke loudly and rapidly. "Some of you don't realise that every day in Mitchell's Plain they raid our schools. They beat us with quirts and sjamboks. They fire tear-gas at us. And this has been happening for weeks and weeks and the newspapers say nothing about it. This cannot go on. We must march so that the world can know what is happening to us daily!" She was led away crying.

A young boy wearing an Arafat scarf, he couldn't have been more than sixteen, confronted the well-dressed man. "There's no time now for your theory and armchair politics. If you haven't got the guts then go back to Fairways where you belong. But we will march. An injury to one is an injury to all." He shot his balled fist into the air and the crowd responded with the salute. The man shook his head sadly and left the circle.

Andrew noticed that the campus was almost completely surrounded except for the Thornton Road entrance. Through the trees and houses he could spot armed police on top of Casspirs surveying the crowd through binoculars and filming it.

He felt someone nudging him in the back.

"I didn't expect to find you here, sir."

He turned round to see Trevor Petersen, president of his school's S.R.C.

"So what brings you here, Mr Dreyer?"

"I may as well ask what brings you here?"

"I'm going to march to Pollsmoor. Are you?"

"No, I'm here to look for my son."

He never had liked Trevor, one of Mr Ismail's loud and vociferous specials. He and his cronies were always challenging the principal or anyone else in authority. The staff of course knew that Joe Ismail was the *éminence grise*, the schemer behind the scenes, but were either too intimidated or too indifferent to do anything about it. In fact some of the junior staff members seemed to agree with him. Joe used the youngsters to feed his own ego, to undermine discipline, to get at those he disliked for political or other reasons. He impressed the radical students with his Bachelor's degree and his political past. Spoke about both all the time whether in the classroom or staff-room. Andrew realised that the news would soon spread all over Eastridge that when others were marching to free Mandela, Mr Dreyer was also there but searching for his son.

"Well, good luck to you, sir. I hope you find him," he said sarcastically and the boy disappeared back into the crowd.

Andrew wanted desperately to leave. But how? The place seemed surrounded except for the Thornton Road gate which was now manned by teachers and lecturers. If Trevor was there, other Eastridge teachers and pupils could also be in the crowd. If he left now and was spotted he might have a lot of explaining to do.

In the centre the argument still continued. It was obvious that

19

most of the crowd were in favour of marching regardless of the consequences.

A young man was speaking. He seemed more mature, and looked like a graduate student. He had a pronounced Afro and sported a jaunty earring. He spoke in Afrikaans. "O.K. O.K. We all know we are here because we want to march to Pollsmoor. But why do we want to march? The object is to focus the attention of the world on the position of Mandela and other detainees. At the stadium this morning we did so. It will soon be on television screens and in newspapers throughout the world. We have already achieved our purpose. So why must we march now?"

"Are you scared?"

"Of course I'm not. I just can't see the reason for marching after all that."

There was derisive laughter from the crowd.

A senior college student took over. "If you people feel we must march, then we must march. We will need marshals to maintain discipline. Will volunteers please go over to the trees?" Quite a few people left. "And please remember that we must be dignified. There must be no unnecessary provocation on our part. The eyes of the world are upon us."

More television crews were converging on the campus. A priest who was recognised immediately and who was obviously very popular held up his hands for silence. There was brief applause. He took off his heavy-rimmed spectacles, wiped them and then put them back on.

"We have amongst us priests, imams and nuns who are prepared to lead the way. We will march in front." Then he added with a slight laugh, "We don't think they'll dare beat up nuns in front of the television cameras, will they?"

Marshals hastily organised the crowd into an untidy crocodile. Andrew watched from the sidelines. He realised that emotions were running high and appreciated the reasons for that. He tended to agree with the speakers who emphasised the futility of the march, but something inside him responded to the desperation of the situation. It was the same gut reaction he had felt in 1960. The absolute danger of an encounter with police armed with whips and guns.

The singing started as the clerics linked arms in front. A huge banner appeared from nowhere and was unfurled. It read "A Nation That Loves Martyrdom Cannot Be Enslaved". Then the march began.

Andrew watched, uncertain whether to join it or not. From the corner of his eye he spotted Trevor marching past. The youth tried to attract his attention by indicating loudly that Andrew should join the demonstration. As a group of chanting students passed he thought he spotted Lenina and Brad. He hastened forward but was quickly shoved into line by a young marshal.

He managed to move up alongside the column, desperately peering into faces. Maybe it was only an illusion. What with the happenings down at the stadium, being seen by that Trevor Petersen boy, the arguments on the field, he found his mind so confused that he was now unsure whether it had been Brad and his girl-friend or not. Half a dozen times he thought he spotted them and half a dozen times discovered that he was wrong.

Andrew had worked his way up near the head of the column when they reached Klipfontein Road bridge. Police stood shoulder to shoulder blocking the entire road. Behind them Casspirs and police vans were waiting. Those in front stopped and got down on their knees. The remaining marchers followed suit bowing their heads. Then someone started singing "The Lord's Prayer".

It happened suddenly. An order was given and the police broke ranks and ran across beating the marchers. Those in front received the full impact. Andrew watched horrified and sick to this stomach. All he could think of was the priest who had assured them, "We don't think they'll dare beat up nuns." They were now beating up nuns. He saw the same priest being flogged. The crowd was running wildly, attempting to get back to Hewat. Andrew stood mesmerised, unable to move. "A Nation That Loves Martyrdom." A quirt narrowly missed his head and he galvanised into action and started running and ducking. He managed to reach the college and leaned against a wall wanting to vomit. People were pouring back into the grounds and angry students started pelting police vans with stones.

From the open field between Hewat and Sinton tear-gas canisters were shot into the grounds. Some landed in the middle of milling groups, injuring a few. Other people ran around gasping for air and looking for water. Andrew reached his car and got in. He would have to get back to Eastridge. If only he could get back home instead. He drove slowly to the Belgravia Road gate which was surprisingly open. A policeman stopped him and peered into the car.

"I'm a teacher and I'm trying to get out."

"O.K. But see that you get right away from here."

What was it that was written on that banner again? "A Nation That Loves Martyrdom Cannot Be Enslaved." He wondered how true it really was.

4

I am writing this letter to you two days after I sent a fairly detailed one as well as some chapters from my new novel. So there is much material right now over the Atlantic winging its way towards you.

It is Friday evening, 30 August, and I am sitting in my study totally depressed. The only pleasing things lately are the two letters I received from you. Of course I am happy for your maple-leaf bliss in the wilds of Toronto. You must tell me more about yourself, your wife and your children. Where it is possible, I will fill you in with snatches of my uneventful life during the in-between years. But, I must warn you that I have lost contact with most of our mutual friends of the 1960s and earlier, as effectively as if I were living in Canada. We are indeed a lost generation. We are yesterday's men. We are the hollow men, the stuffed men, leaning together. I mean to contact Justin quite soon. I now have his address in Manenberg and I will dutifully send you all the details.

The new novel which I am writing is not going to prove easy. In terms of purpose and intention it falls between two or possibly three stools. Maybe I am too ambitious. It begins last month when I had a row with Brad and his girl-friend. My intention is to write this novel as seen through my eyes. To that extent it will be autobiographical. But then all serious creative writing is autobiographical, or is it not? As the omniscient narrator I suppose I am allowed to show how the happenings affect me or anyone else for that matter. What makes it worse is that I am casting this personal history into the novel form. But this has a distinct disadvantage. I do not have the supremacy of the long view. I have no perspective. In fact I am so close to my subject that I am practically in the middle of it.

I have the dubious experience of having written only one book and a few short stories. The novel was written in 1961 and published a year later. It dealt with the emergency of 1960, Sharpeville and Langa, and was played out around Cape Town. Of course it had autobiographical elements, although it was not altogether so. You appear in it, and Justin and Braam and of course it concerns a character like me who grew up in the squalor of District Six, experienced a terrible childhood, and then pulled himself up by his bootstrings. He qualified, became a teacher and then became involved in politics. Does it ring a bell? I've had people asking me whether this was my life and whether my mother died in that manner in a slum tenement in Caledon Street? Was I ever accused of being a mother-killer? Of course not. It was a work of fiction with factual elements, or a work of fact with fictional elements. I felt it had all the ingredients of excitement. It was a young man's first novel, full of uncontrolled enthusiasm and bursting with green excitement. It received modest reviews however and did not sell well. And soon after it was banned. It has now been unbanned (without my approval or pre-knowledge) and is freely available in bookshops. Of course it was autobiographical as most writings are. In a way I was trying to record our dreams and hopes against the canvas of political repression. I will gladly send you a copy of the book if you have not come across it yet.

Now as for the present work, if ever it gets done, it will be a very different novel. It deals with a situation twenty-five years later, written by an author nearly twenty-five years older. Although some of the characters are different, the situation they find themselves in is not all so very different.

How can one really exercise the sublime detachment of the novelist if one is directly involved in the situation one is writing about? I cannot plan what happens next since I myself must wait to find out what is going to happen next. I cannot predict what my characters will do or say and thus have no control over the direction they will take. So much for the writer's sublime omniscience and detachment. All I am able to do right now is to wait, observe, transcribe and garnish here and there. This might prove a futile exercise. I can but try. Please keep writing letters encouraging me.

I work in the evenings and most mornings before school. At night I record happenings. In the mornings and over weekends I fictionalise them. I spend hours locked up in my study. Sometimes I experience that occupational hazard, the writer's block, then I merely diarise. At other times I get dreadfully snarled up. Very often I cannot tell the difference between what I have experienced and what I have invented.

If ever you meet her, I think you will like my wife, Mabel, although she tends to be enigmatic. Even after twenty years of marriage, there are times when I feel that I don't really understand her. She is kind, pleasant, accommodating, but can also be obstinate when she chooses to be.

I was going through a terrible time after Ruth and I parted. We both realised that it was the best thing to do. In any case Mr Talbot, stockbroker, came to fetch his daughter, snatching her out of the arms of her presumptuous Coloured lover and dragged her back to Vereeniging. We don't use the word Coloured *here any longer. If we have to write it we use inverted commas, and if we have to say it we twitch two fingers of both hands at the side of our heads to simulate inverted commas. We have a genius for being unoriginal.*

I met Mabel at a church function of all places. You can deduce from that how depressed I must have been. Yes, I was as depressed as all that. It was a musical evening given by the Anglican Guild and Mabel was in the choir. I was desperate, longing for Ruth, worrying about Ruth, worrying about myself. So when I met Mabel and we started going out, I poured out my story to her. She was most understanding. We married in 1964. I love Mabel, and in a way she tries to make me forget. But I still love Ruth in a different sort of way. One can love differently, can't one.

I have no idea what happened to Ruth and where she could be now. Our break was a clean one. She might have married a Johannesburg financier and be living now in Houghton. She might be living up the road from me, in Constantia, on the other side of the tracks. She might be married to a dull husband who is something in the city. Her children might be at exclusive private schools and she the doyen of a riding club in Tokai, holding gymkhanas in aid of worthwhile charities. She might even be out of South Africa for all I know. In fiction we could meet again, but in real life this is unfortunately highly improbable. Why cannot life be fiction? Why cannot life imitate art as Wilde is reputed to have said?

When Bradley was born, two years after our marriage, I thought it would put an end to all our problems. What Mabel and I needed was a child to mould us into a single unit. I gave Brad everything I never had; love, attention and security. I did not want to spoil his childhood so kept my past away from him. In fact I think I was really keeping it away from myself. Of course as he grew older he asked the usual questions, but although I answered as truthfully as I could, I always kept the answers as vague as possible. I don't know how much he got out of his mother but she took her cue from me. But then she also doesn't know much about my life before 1960. No, I am not hiding my past, I am deliberately forgetting it. When Ruth was born two years after Brad, Mabel raised no objections to my choice of name for our daughter. Maybe my decision to call her Ruth goes to show just how successful I was in forgetting my past.

Brad was fourteen years old and in Standard Seven at Steenberg High, when the 1980 school boycotts took place. He marched with the rest and attended mass meetings but I think saw it more as a game than anything important. But after that he began to read seriously, joined community organisations and got more and more politically involved. I neither encouraged nor discouraged him. But once he had matriculated and was at Hewat College he began to question what he felt was my indifference. My book made no impression on him. He saw it purely as a work of fiction. Our arguments became more frequent. I wrote to you about one of them before, but the altercation on Monday, 19 August, was the worst. It was not the most violent but certainly the most decisive. I felt afterwards that it was the turning-point in our relationship, that now we were definitely moving along different paths.

I had come home from school, late as usual, when I found him in the kitchen chatting to his mother. Ruth was sitting at the table working on some assignment. I was exhausted and all I wanted was a hot cup of tea. I kissed my wife and daughter and said very sincerely how relieved and happy I was to see Brad.

5

"Evening my dear, evening Ruth. Brad, this is indeed a pleasant surprise."

"Evening, Dad," Brad said breezily.

"I'm very glad to see you. Are you home for good this time or only a brief spell as usual?"

"Not for good, I'm afraid. I dropped in to say that I will be away for much longer. I have already packed my case."

"Why for much longer, if I may ask? We miss you." Andrew removed his jacket and tie and sat down next to Ruth.

"Things are turning ugly, Dad. The emergency will be extended to Cape Town. There will be many more raids and many more detentions."

"And you may be picked up?"

"Well, they don't need a State of Emergency in order to pick up people." He attempted a smile. "I just wanted to warn you that they will most probably come here looking for me."

Mabel bustled over with a cup of tea for her husband. Andrew fought against his weariness.

"Why, why, why?" He asked looking down at the table as if the answer could come from there.

"Why what, Dad?" Bradley asked.

"Why must it happen to us? Do you consider yourself a great political leader or do you see yourself as a great martyr?"

"Neither. I merely consider myself as part of the oppressed."

"And that, let me make it very clear, is not your monopoly."

"I never claimed it was."

"Tell me, why do you cause us so much worry? It might not seem apparent but we are concerned about you."

"I know mother is concerned and I do regret the trouble I cause her."

"And what about me?"

25

"Are you concerned, Dad?"

"I can't believe that you can ask such a question."

Mabel could see the direction things were taking and did not like it. She busied herself washing up with her back to them, but she was listening intently. Ruth gathered up her books and hurriedly left the kitchen.

"Sit down, Brad," Andrew said. "I think it is time we talked frankly."

Brad took the seat vacated by Ruth.

Andrew's tone was quiet and controlled. He lowered his voice to a whisper. "Your mother and I realise that you are your own man now. You are nineteen and have your own ideas. We accept all that and make allowances for it. But do you make allowances for us? Do you in turn ever consider your mother and your sister? Do you ever consider me?"

"Dad, the way I see it, my responsibility is far greater than one merely confined to my immediate family."

"Your responsibility? Now don't bullshit me!"

Andrew realised that he must control himself. Mabel turned round and looked sharply at him.

Brad continued. "I sincerely believe that the future of many more people than this family is at stake."

"So we must be sacrificed for your ideals? Does every other family in South Africa have to be sacrificed for some individual's youthful ideals?"

"Come now, you are being absurd."

"Am I really being absurd?"

"Have you made any sacrifices?"

"I don't know. Maybe you can tell me."

"O.K. If you are prepared to listen, I will tell you."

Mabel felt she had to intervene. "You are going too far, Brad. Of course your father has made sacrifices. And in addition we are now expected to give up our only son."

"There are many only sons in this country, Mom. Only sons and only daughters. Lenina is an only daughter."

"I knew that name would crop up sooner or later," Andrew remarked.

"And why not? Both she and her father have sacrificed."

Andrew wanted to know more but covered any signs of curiosity. Bradley however continued without prompting. "Her mother left her

26

father two years after she was born. Mr Bailey was then in and out of jail for political reasons. On one such occasion her mother merely dumped her with an aunt and uncle in Manenberg and disappeared out of her life. Her aunt then had the job of rearing her. After a long-drawn-out trial her father was sentenced to Robben Island for twelve years. Lenina saw him twice during that time. Now he is a diabetic and under house arrest in Manenberg with a sister-in-law who doesn't want him and a daughter who doesn't know him. But he has not given up in spite of restrictions and ill health. He is still involved."

"I appreciate all that, but what is its relevance?"

"That is Lenina's story. She is an only daughter. What is my story? I am an only son."

"But I can't see what all this has to do with us."

"It has everything to do with us, Dad, everything. Mr Bailey has given up his life for the cause."

"While I sit back comfortably in Elfindale? Is that what you're saying?"

Bradley remained silent.

"What your father did, was for you children," Mabel said reproachfully.

"Yes, maybe for myself as well."

Bradley stood up. "May I be allowed to ask a question?"

"No-one has stopped you up to now."

"Why did you never become involved, Dad? I mean, really involved? Ever since I can remember, you have seldom been to any meeting, never joined any community organisation or attended or spoken at a rally?"

"How do you know that I was never involved?"

"I don't know, so you tell me."

"Tell you what?"

"Dad, I really know very little about you except what I see and sometimes overhear."

"What do you want to know?" Andrew asked wearily.

"How involved you are."

"Don't be silly, Brad," his mother intervened again.

"But you people tell me nothing. In this house I am told as much as you want me to know. I might as well be living on the moon."

"Your father has had a hard life and he doesn't like speaking about it."

27

"Leave this to me, Mabel. All right, son, since you want to know. I was born and grew up in Caledon Street, District Six. My mother died as I was doing Senior Certificate at Trafalgar High. My sister, your late aunt Miriam, took me in. After matriculating I went on a scholarship to the University of Cape Town, where I obtained a B.A. degree in English and a teaching diploma. Later I got a B.Comm. degree through part-time study. I met your mother in 1964 and we were married in St Mark's Church, on Clifton Hill, a year later. I am at present the deputy principal of Eastridge Senior Secondary School, where I teach English. I have one published novel and five published short stories. Now, does that satisfy you?"

"No, it does not satisfy me. You have told me what you are but not how you think. What are your political commitments? What organisations do you belong to? Where exactly do you stand?"

"Nowhere that would satisfy you."

"No-one can afford to be neutral in this situation."

"I assure you that I am not neutral."

"Stop it, you two," Mabel said, her eyes swimming with tears. "Brad, I think it's sin that you should talk like that to your father."

"I will talk to my father the way I have been wishing to talk to my father for a long time. I have a right to certain answers. My comrades ask questions. They pass snide remarks. What has your father done for the cause other than writing an obscure novel, teaching ghetto kids and drawing a fat cheque at the end of every month?"

"And how do you answer that?" Andrew asked, genuinely interested.

"I don't know. I really don't know. I have no answers."

Andrew looked sharply at him. "Are you ashamed of your father?" Something went hard inside him.

"I am ashamed of my father's lack of commitment."

"But you nevertheless allow your father to feed and clothe you, to look after you and care for you?"

"Dad, you have no alternative. I suspect that you do it out of a sense of duty. You and I have nothing any longer in common."

"You believe that also?"

Brad himself was close to tears. Ruth had come in and was listening at the door. Mabel stood over the sink, crying softly to herself.

"Yes," Andrew said after a long pause, "yes, maybe we don't have anything in common."

"I think so."

28

"Yet you are prepared to benefit from the material things your non-committed father can provide?"

"If that's what you are getting at, then maybe I should now get the hell out of this place."

"Please, Brad," his mother said anxiously.

The silence was intense. Brad stood up. "O.K., Dad, O.K., Mom. The discussion is now over, and I assure you it will never be repeated. I'm leaving home now."

"Cut out the melodrama and sit down."

"I am leaving right now."

He turned abruptly and went to his room to fetch his suitcase.

Mabel and Ruth followed him. Andrew could hear their heated discussion, but was no longer interested. He was very, very tired, and the confrontation had enervated him. He was too tired even to fight back.

Brad reappeared with his case. "O.K., Dad, no hard feelings." He put out his hand to shake and Andrew took it without saying anything or showing any reaction.

"I'm off now. So bye, Mom. Bye, Ruth. And good luck, Dad."

He kissed his mother and sister and, without a further glance at his father, was gone.

Andrew remained alone in the kitchen for some time, after the two had gone to bed, then got up. He felt very, very old. He went into his study, shutting the door firmly behind him. He poured himself a whisky and put on a record. Then he started jotting down notes for his new novel.

6

After witnessing the aborted march, Andrew tried to concentrate on his driving but his mind was bewildered. Why was he still going back to Eastridge? Everything seemed so confused, what with those events at the stadium, being trapped inside that claustrophobic café, the march, the beatings at Kromboom Road. How did that banner read again? "A Nation That Loves Martyrdom Cannot Be Enslaved." Was that fatalism or deliberate masochism?

As he turned into the school's grounds, he saw that there were very few parked cars and hardly any pupils around. The juniors would most probably have been kept at home, and some of the seniors would have gone to the march or some other rally. As he parked he felt no desire to face either the principal or the staff. Best if he went straight to his office. If they wanted him they could find him there.

He was on his way when he heard his name being called. Miss Russell, needlework mistress, oldest spinster on the staff and most experienced gossip.

"Oh, Mr Dreyer, Mr Dreyer!" She came panting after him. "I'm so sorry that I must call you like this, but they've been searching all over for you this morning."

"I was temporarily off the premises."

"Without permission? Naughty, naughty." She wagged an admonishing finger playfully at him. Andrew felt that he had to get rid of her or burst. Miss Russell was determined not to let him go.

"Why were they looking for me?"

"The principal wanted you in his office urgently. It was announced several times on the intercom."

"You know his reason?"

"No, unfortunately not, Mr Dreyer."

"All right. I'll see him as soon as I'm ready. Thank you for the message."

He just had to get away from her.

"There's so much trouble around, you know, Mr Dreyer. Half the staff is not here. I suppose the only thing one can do nowadays is to mind one's own business."

"You're so correct, Miss Russell, so very correct. One should mind one's own business, shouldn't one?"

"Now don't keep the boss waiting."

"Thank you very much."

"He left her standing. She obviously wanted to continue the conversation but he wasn't going to allow that.

Andrew sat behind his desk in his office trying to gather his thoughts. What could the principal want that could be so urgent? That Russell woman was prone to exaggeration. Most probably routine work like getting the summary register up to date or checking the requisitions file. Mr Langeveldt tended to panic over trifles.

The principal was a nervous, ineffectual man who was balding rapidly. He had applied for the position and was then amazed when he actually got it. Only afterwards had he realised what he had let himself in for. He was required to get the school to run smoothly. He found it almost impossible to get it to run at all. The pupils were difficult, the S.R.C. was demanding, the teachers proved uncooperative, that Mr Joe Ismail was always out to humiliate him, especially in front of other staff members, and then, there were the hosts of inspectors and subject advisers. If he could resign his position he would do so at once, in spite of the cut in salary.

Andrew felt no sympathy for him. Mr Langeveldt had applied for the principalship and must therefore accept the consequences.

His phone rang and the school's secretary was on the line. "Mr Dreyer, the principal wants to see you urgently in his office. I also have a telephone message for you." Andrew got up wearily.

Mr Langeveldt was very worried. "Mr Dreyer, we have been looking for you all morning."

"Yes, I have been told so. I wish to apologise for my absence. I meant to phone you this morning but found it impossible. I was searching for my son."

"I am sorry. Is something the matter?"

"I'm not sure. He left home the middle of last month already and we haven't heard from him since."

"He's not in some sort of trouble, is he?"

"I hope not."

"So did you find him this morning?"

"No."

"Mr Dreyer, I appreciate your concern, but you are the number two man here. If I have to go away for any reason, you must be around to take charge. If you can let me know beforehand when you cannot be in, I'm sure we can make the necessary arrangements. I can always get Mr October to act."

"I am indeed very sorry."

"The reason I was looking for you was that I received a letter from Head Office about two weeks ago, that two subject advisers would be at the school next Wednesday, 4 September. I'm afraid I misplaced the letter and completely forgot about it. Then they phoned this morning. Now why must they come at such an inconvenient time, I really don't know. It makes absolutely no sense to me."

"So why are they coming?"

"A routine visit, I was informed. English and Human Ecology."

"Will they want to see any teaching done?"

"I suppose so."

"But there will hardly be any pupils to teach."

31

"I warned them about that. I told them that I cannot guarantee anything. I cannot guarantee teachers, I cannot guarantee pupils, I cannot guarantee the safety of any advisers or inspectors."

"It is extremely short-sighted of them."

"And put me in an awkward spot. So then, for what it's worth, they'll be here tomorrow morning. I'll call a meeting of all English teachers at 1 p.m. in the 10a room to inform them of the visit."

"The notice is somewhat short."

"I will have to explain to the teachers that it is my fault, and apologise for misplacing the document. I cannot imagine where I put it. I phoned the Department back this morning but they were not interested in my request. I would appreciate it if you did not leave the premises today without my knowledge."

"I assure you that I'll be at the meeting."

"And by the way, the secretary has also been trying to contact you. She has a telephone message."

He went straight to the secretary's office.

"Oh, Mr Dreyer, some woman has phoned three times for you this morning. Let me see? Where did I write it down? Oh, here. A Miss Lenina Bailey. Does that ring a bell? It sounded urgent. You must please phone her back as soon as possible. This is the number."

"Thank you. I'll phone from my office. Could you let me have an outside line, please?"

The phone rang on the other side for some time.

"Hallo?" It was a man's voice.

"Could I speak to Miss Lenina Bailey, please?"

"She's not in at the moment and I don't know when she'll be back. Would you like to leave a message?"

"No, that won't be necessary."

"Who shall I say called?"

"A friend. Just a friend. Tell her I'll phone again later."

"O.K."

Could that have been Justin? The voice did not sound familiar? But what voice could sound familiar after twenty-five years? Why would Lenina have phoned? He thought she disliked him. Brad? And here he was forced to attend a bloody meeting about a bloody visit by a bloody subject adviser. He heard the principal making the announcement over the intercom system.

Mr Langeveldt did a rapid count.

"There should be eight teachers. Who's missing, Mr Dreyer?"

"Mr Cloete."

"Yes, he phoned this morning that his wife wasn't well."

"Mr Evans and Miss Petersen."

"I haven't heard from them. Did you get any message, Mr Dreyer?"

Andrew nearly remarked that the principal was fully aware that that was impossible since he had been away all morning.

"No, Mr Langeveldt."

"So let's see who's present. Mr Dreyer, Mr October, Mr Ismail, Miss Toefy and Mr Carollissen. Let's get on with the business."

The principal informed them briefly that Head Office had written some time before to inform him that two subject advisers would be coming for English and Human Ecology the following week. Unfortunately he had delayed telling the teachers concerned. But he had already informed the Human Ecology people and was now informing the English teachers. Mr Langeveldt sounded nervous.

"Are there any questions?"

"Yes, the notice is somewhat short. What is expected of us, Mr Langeveldt?" Mr October asked the question. He was middle-aged, but looked far older than his years. Rather quiet, not very efficient and a bit of a plodder. Pupils found him weak and lack-lustre.

"I suppose they'll want to speak to you and listen to some of your lessons. I will suggest that you have your record books, preparation books, essay books and so on, ready in case they wish to see them. I presume these are all available. Mr October?"

"Yes, my work is in order, but I cannot guarantee that I'll have any pupils to teach."

"When they wrote, didn't you phone back and tell Head Office about the situation here?" Miss Toefy asked. She was an enthusiastic follower of Ismail's.

"Of course I did. I explained the circumstances and suggested the postponement of their visit. But Head Office was adamant that my request came too late. Arrangements had already been made. So the advisers will be here tomorrow."

"And you accepted that? You meekly accepted all that?" Joe Ismail spoke for the first time. He was a dark, brooding, square-faced man.

"I had no choice in the matter."

"You could have refused to allow them to come," Miss Toefy said.

"It's not as easy as all that."

33

"You could have argued that their notice came too late."

"I'm afraid I am at fault. It did come on time."

"And you are only informing us now?" Joe demanded.

"I must apologise. It's my fault."

"Have you told them that you misplaced their letter and never informed the staff?" Joe asked.

"No."

"That could prove awkward for you, couldn't it?"

Mr Langeveldt remained silent.

"And are you able to guarantee their safety when they come?" Miss Toefy took over.

"I explained that but they insisted on coming."

Joe Ismail spoke slowly and deliberately. "Mr Langeveldt, with due respect to you as principal, it is ridiculous of the department to arrange this inspection, and it is ridiculous for you to have agreed to their coming." He was in his stride. Mr Langeveldt winced.

"It is not an inspection, Mr Ismail," he said feebly.

"Well then, call it what you will. I repeat that it is ridiculous to arrange their coming at a time when feelings here and everywhere else are running high. I heard that at a school in Bishop Lavis they burnt out an inspector's car last week. What will happen once our pupils learn that departmental officials will be on the premises tomorrow?"

"Pupils can only learn that if they are told that, if the information is given to them." Andrew had deliberately not spoken until now. He looked directly at Joe.

The latter returned his stare. "I'm not sure what Mr Dreyer is getting at."

"I'm getting at the fact that certain pupils at this school seem to know too much about what happens at staff meetings, about who says what. Sometimes they know more than some of us do. Information gets around, Mr Ismail, and I would suggest that the source must be at staff level. That is what I'm getting at."

"And you are suggesting that some of us are passing on information to pupils?" Joe rose to his feet.

"Yes, I'm suggesting that."

"Then let us know who they are. Let us have the names," Miss Toefy added.

"I am not prepared to do so. I am merely stating that information leaks out and the source seems to be some people on the staff."

Joe took over the attack. "Mr Principal, I take the greatest

34

exception to such an accusation. If Mr Dreyer has any information he must be prepared to state publicly whom he is accusing."

Mr Langeveldt threw up his hands in despair. "Please, gentlemen and lady, let us control our tempers. Mr Ismail, could you please sit down? We cannot afford such divisions on the staff. Certainly not at this time. I'm sure that the deputy principal was not getting at you personally. But we do know that some pupils, especially S.R.C. members like Trevor Petersen, know far too much about confidential staff matters. But let's remain calm and get back to where we were. I regret the lateness of the notice, but am now informing you what I have been instructed to do."

Miss Toefy put up her hand. "Mr Langeveldt, you still haven't answered Mr Ismail's question. If the advisers come as they state they will, and the pupils demonstrate against them, are you going to protect them or do you expect us to do so?"

"We are expected to offer protection to any visitor to our school. The advisers are no exception."

"They are not visitors," Joe added. "They represent the state department and all it stands for."

"Call them whatever you wish. We owe them the courtesy we would extend to anyone else."

Eldred Carollissen indicated that he wished to speak. At just over forty, he was still attractive with a bronze complexion and striking green eyes. He had gone to University of Cape Town, where he obtained a Bachelor of Arts degree in English. He had then won a British Council scholarship to University of London, where he obtained a Masters degree. He was married and the father of a teen-age son and daughter. He was still very close to Andrew and had matured into a level-headed and independent thinker. Joe Ismail disliked him because he was not malleable or easily influenced.

"Yes, Mr Carollissen?"

"We all realise that the information has been given us at the last moment. But with all the trouble around we cannot really be too hard on the principal for having misplaced it. However, what we would all have preferred was that the advisers would not come on Wednesday. Is there any possibility, even at this late juncture, of deferring their visit?"

"Mr Carollissen, you must believe me. I have been on the phone all morning. I have tried my best to do so. Why they are so obstinate, I do not know. Lady and gentlemen, I trust that all your work is in

35

order. We will try and arrange what pupils are present, into classes. Are there any further questions?"

"I wish to make a statement," Joe said, rising again. "I wish to have it recorded that I am completely against this inspection. If they do come, I, for one, cannot guarantee their safety. Nor do I see that it is my duty to protect them. Under these circumstances I refuse to teach for them. My books will also not be avilable for inspection."

"That could be interpreted as insubordination."

"Interpret it any way you like."

"I'm sorry about all this," Mr Langeveldt said, "but I am not happy with your attitude, Mr Ismail. I have my orders from Head Office."

"Then I would suggest you should tell them to go to hell with their orders."

"And I would suggest that you control your language. There is a lady present." Andrew remarked.

Miss Toefy sneered.

"So, Mr Dreyer, will you then carry out the department's instructions?" Joe challenged.

"If I must teach tomorrow, I shall do so." Andrew said quietly.

"Then you have finally turned full circle. Are you now an apologist for the department?"

"I have never been."

"You sound like one now."

"Please, gentlemen and lady, let us control ourselves," Mr Langeveldt pleaded yet again.

"And you," Joe turned to the principal, "are you going to tell them that you forgot about their ridiculous instruction?"

Mr Langeveldt remained silent.

"Have you no loyalty towards anyone?" Andrew asked rising.

Joe also got to his feet. "I have no loyalty towards the authorities and I have no loyalty towards their inefficient lackeys. My loyalty is towards my pupils."

"You mean towards selected members of the S.R.C.?"

"I take exception to that."

"You certainly have no loyalty towards your principal. Then what about the staff? Have you any loyalty towards your colleagues?"

"That doesn't concern you."

"It does concern me. In case you don't know it, I am a member of the staff."

"You are the last one to speak about loyalty. For how long have you remained loyal to your former political friends?"

"I'm not sure what you are getting at."

"I repeat, for how long have you been loyal to your former comrades, your erstwhile political cronies?"

What the hell do you mean?"

"I am asking when last you showed any loyalty towards people like Mr Justin Bailey? Remember him? You were comrades once." There was a sneer on Ismail's face.

Mr Langeveldt was unsure what the argument was about but did not like the direction it was taking. He shuffled to his feet.

"Please, gentlemen and Miss Toefy, this is all so unnecessary. All I'm asking is that you hold yourself in readiness for a possible visit tomorrow. I will try my best to postpone it, Mr Carollissen, but if they insist, then we must do the best we can under the circumstances. This meeting is now closed." He left, a very lonely man.

Andrew was angry and confused. He realised the need to stay calm and collected. Joe and Miss Toefy were in heated argument with Eldred.

Mr October came over to Andrew. "Don't take that Ismail chap too seriously. He's mad."

"And very dangerous," Andrew added.

7

On a mellow Wednesday morning, two days after Brad had left home, Andrew was having his tea in the staff-room, sharing a table with Eldred Carollissen and Mr October. He was reading the *Cape Times*. And half-listening to the discussion the other two were having. Joe Ismail and Miss Toefy were sitting on a couch near them needling Wilfred Evans, who was a young, bland, English teacher. Andrew picked up snippets of their conversation, which seemed to be about evidence of colonialism in *The Tempest*. Wilfred seemed completely lost and bewildered. Eldred and Mr October were discussing the consumer boycott of white businesses which was about to be launched in the Western Cape. Or rather, Eldred was talking and Mr October listening.

Andrew was still thinking about Bradley and, although he gave hardly any indication of it, he was very worried. He was sleeping badly and drinking far too much. But today he seemed more at peace than usual. Maybe it was because he had taught his first lesson in weeks. Admittedly the class was only half full, but at least he had taught. The classroom boycotts were becoming more and more frequent, with pupils refusing to be taught the formal lessons and demanding alternative programmes.

His novel was also coming on, though in fits and starts. He wrote whenever he found the time, but found it impossible to work at school in spite of the fact that hardly any teaching was taking place. The atmosphere was nerve-wracking. One could do nothing and it proved more enervating than a full day's work. He was brutally frank in his book, especially about his disagreements with his son and his despair over the worsening educational situation. He meant to keep one copy of everything he wrote safely stored away, and send another to Abe in Canada for criticism. He knew that Abe would reply promptly.

Mr October spoke the way he thought, slowly and a trifle nervously. "What, Mr Carollissen, do you then see as the immediate demands of this consumer boycott?"

"Well," Eldred replied, also carefully measuring his words, "it revolves around many things."

"Such as?" Mr October asked.

"Such as lifting the State of Emergency, releasing all political prisoners, and getting the Defence Force out of the townships. These are immediate demands."

Andrew had a suspicion that Eldred was a strong sympathiser, if not already a member of the United Democratic Front. Although they discussed many things they had never discussed that.

The staff-room was not particularly big, so that without straining too hard it was possible to overhear most conversations. Miss Russell always sat and knitted where she was able to hear everything, her ears finely tuned. The rest of the staff who were present, about twenty members, were reading, chatting and attempting the *Cape Times* crossword puzzle.

"I'm not so sure how you expect those demands to be met," Mr October ventured. "Surely if you are hitting at white shopkeepers and businessmen, you may very well be antagonising some who might be in agreement with your demands. Also, isn't there something racial about boycotting only white businesses?"

"Not really. If the white businessman has ever agreed with any of our demands, he has never shown it. So hit him where it hurts most, his pocket. And then let him declare where he stands on these issues."

"But surely," Andrew said, looking up from his newspaper, "there are positive and negative boycotts. How would you class this one?"

Joe snorted from his couch. "Some people are still living in the good old 1960s. Positive and negative boycotts, I ask you."

Andrew looked hard at him. Joe continued, addressing anyone who chose to hear. "The boycott is a tactic, not a principle, therefore you make of it what you wish. You decide whether it is going to be positive or negative. If it is a principle, as some so-called politicians believe, then it is not negotiable."

"I'm not sure whether you are addressing me," Andrew said, struggling to control himself.

"I am addressing anyone who is sufficiently open to listen."

Most of the other teachers stopped what they were doing. Miss Russell mumbled "Oh dear, oh dear" to no one in particular but it was obvious that she was enjoying the altercation.

"I don't recall your asking anyone else their opinion."

"My opinion is given unsolicited and free of charge. If necessary, even for you, Mr Dreyer."

"Stop behaving like a bloody spoilt child," Eldred said angrily.

"Oh, what have we here? The sorcerer's apprentice? So I presume that to advance any opinion in this staff-room one must be invited?"

"Mr Ismail," Mr October said and he twitched nervously, "Mr Carollissen, Mr Dreyer and I were having a discussion when you interfered. I wonder whether you could restrict your remarks to those whom you think might benefit from them."

Andrew slowly folded his newspaper and got up. His cup was still half full of tea. He left and as he passed Joe's couch the latter sneered. Andrew looked straight ahead and refused to be baited.

He was sitting in his office wondering just why Joe was so antagonistic towards him. Maybe it was Andrew's treatment of him, which was negative and strictly professional at the best of times. Maybe Joe resented something. But then he seemed generally against anyone other than his immediate circle. The man was eaten up inside. Yesterday's man? A hollow man?

Eldred came in still visibly upset.

"I'm sorry about all that, but one day I'm going to hit that Ismail chap. He is nothing but a trouble-maker, an *agent provocateur*. I sometimes wonder whose side he is really on."

"Most probably his own. He has so many chips on his shoulder. One must realise that he is looking for a platform and searching for a following. The best thing to do is to ignore him."

"Which he then accepts as a personal victory," Eldred added. "You should have heard him once you had left. He is over fifty and has never recovered from his B.A. degree. He is alway name-dropping. He is always speaking about a letter Luthuli is supposed to have sent him commending some turgid poem he had written about the Chief. His most serious ailment is that he is a congential, egotistical bore."

"It is true that he was involved in the Congress Movement. For a brief period he was a member of the South African Coloured People's Congress. He was an activist of sorts in his time."

"Who has faded now through lack of attention."

"Who are we to judge?" Andrew suggested.

He then deliberately changed the subject. "I believe that you are connected with the Western Cape Consumer's Action Committee?"

"I'm on the executive, if that's what you mean." Andrew's question perplexed him.

"Are you people calling any public meetings soon?"

"We are having one at the Rocklands Civic Centre this evening."

"And I suppose you are going?"

"I have to since I am an official."

"Could I come along with you?".

"Of course you may."

"All right then. Let me pick you up at your home at about 7.30 p.m."

"See you then."

Eldred left Andrew's office somewhat mystified by this sudden display of interest. Andrew himself was just as puzzled. He wasn't sure what had prompted him to decide to attend his first political meeting in more than two decades. He hoped that the experience would not be too traumatic.

He knew where Eldred lived in Second Avenue, Lotus River, having boarded there himself for many years with Eldred's family. Mr and Mrs Carollissen. Mrs Millicent Carollissen. What a woman.

"Mr D.," (she always called him Mr D.), "Mr D., do you read all those books in your room? Surely not all of them?"

She was Afrikaans-speaking, but for social purposes spoke English with a heavy Afrikaans accent.

"They must cost you a lot of money. But we Coloured people must be prepared to pay for our learning if we want to get anywhere."

How things had changed. *Coloured* was acceptable in the 1960s. Then in the 1970s *Black* became more fashionable. Now it was *So-called Coloured* or one was merely non-racial. *Coloured* itself was anathema in political circles. The unpredictable march of the ethnic label.

Mrs Carollissen died in 1975. Her ineffectual husband, realising that life was no longer worth living, did what he had done all his married life and followed her example the following year. Andrew wondered what had become of the other children. Now that he thought of it, Eldred seldom mentioned them. Vincent, Paul, Jeremy and a nasty little girl called Charmaine, the family horror who spitefully took after her mother. And a maid called Minnie or something like that.

He pulled up outside the house and was let in by Eldred's fourteen-year-old daughter, Candice, who showed him into the lounge. The feeling of familiarity came on strongly. Fortunately Mrs Carollissen's huge, ugly pieces of furniture had been relaced by a modern, more elegant suite of Swedish pine. Mrs Carollissen however still dominated the lounge from her huge, mounted photograph perched strategically on the mantelpiece. Andrew had a suspicion that she was disapprovingly watching his every move from her vantage-point. The room had lost its dour, Dutch Reformed Church look of the Mrs Carollissen era.

Eldred came in putting on his jacket.

"Sorry to keep you waiting."

"I've been revelling in an absolute orgy of nostalgia. Waves and waves of it. Your mother seemed somewhat displeased that I've come," he said looking respectfully up at the photograph. "I saw her frowning disapprovingly at me. What has happened to my old room? The one that had all my books?"

"Chesney uses it now, but please don't go and look. It is top-heavy with disco stuff and the room itself is dedicated to the Bee Gees or Jaluka or something like that."

"I miss those reproductions we had up here. Remember, Christ holding his bleeding heart and Queen Elizabeth, the Second."

"Mercifully Vincent took them away when I renovated the house. I know that somewhere up there, the old girl is unhappy about it, but I'm sure that Vincent would have found some use for them. He has

41

her taste. They are most probably on his walls in Mandalay skirted by flying porcelain ducks."

"Your wife home?"

"No, Lucille's at her mother's place this evening. The old lady's lonely and getting on in years. Well, then, shall we be off?"

"Yes, I'll drive if you direct."

"O.K. We're leaving for the meeting now, Candice. Tell your mother when she comes home."

Andrew drove down A. Z. Berman Drive. Along the way they passed Eastridge Secondary School."

"So tranquil and so peaceful in the moonlight. Yet so deliciously deceptive," Eldred remarked.

"Except for the ghost of Mr Joe Ismail, B.A., which doth within those confines, with a monarch's voice, cry *havoc*!"

"And let slip the dogs of every kind of subterfuge and intrigue imaginable."

"Let's not be nasty."

They turned right into Spine Road. As they neared the Civic Centre they were aware of a heavy police presence. A road-block was set up about 200 metres from the hall. They joined a long queue of cars waiting to drive through. Warning lights flashed *Police, Polisie*, and armed and uniformed men were clustered menacingly on both sides of the road.

"Well, this is a foretaste," Eldred remarked.

"What do you mean?"

"It looks like trouble tonight. This is the preliminary intimidation, the softening-up process."

They waited for twenty minutes until it was their turn. Torches flashed into the car.

"Where are you going?" a policeman asked.

"Rocklands Civic Centre."

"To the meeting?"

"Yes."

"Pull up over there."

"Why?"

"I said, pull up over there!"

They did so and joined the many other cars taken off the road. Two policemen ordered them out and conducted a brief body search. They went through the car, taking their time, but could find nothing incriminating. They took down the registration number and de-

42

manded names, addresses and places of occupation. Then the two were allowed to go.

You know, Abe, it all came back again, that time in 1960 when we were also stopped at a road-block on Prince George Drive. Remember? Ruth, you and me. The intersection swarming with policemen armed with stenguns, the torches flashing in our eyes. You pretended to be White and Ruth's husband, and I was your Coloured boy who had been beaten up by skollies. You were taking me home to Grassy Park. I remember how you even offered a policeman a cigarette which he refused?"

Because of the number of other vehicles, outside the hall, including buses, displaying registration from all over the Western Cape, they were forced to park some distance away.

Inside, the Centre was humid and heavy with noise and activity. Eldred, as an executive member, was ushered to a seat on the platform. Andrew was given one at the back of the hall. Behind the speakers was a huge banner, "U.D.F. UNITES" with the logo at its side. At the end of the platform a burly man was waving an enormous A.N.C. flag of black, green and gold. The hall was festooned with slogans. "State of Emergency or State of Terror." "Viva Mandela." "Buy Right to Forward the Fight" and "Happy Second Anniversary, U.D.F. — The People's Movement." The hall was packed and Andrew estimated that there must be more than 4 000 people inside and outside. The atmosphere was tense and there was a spirit of defiance, with singing and dancing interspersed with the shouting of slogans. There was no visible police presence. To find Bradley in that mass, assuming that he was there, would be a minor miracle.

Lynne Davis of the Clothing Workers Union was introduced by the chairperson and started speaking. "White business, especially white big business, has been a big supporter of the government for a very long time. The consumer boycott draws attention to this fact and links big business with the government. It makes the oppressed people see who are their friends and who are their enemies."

She spoke above the incessant hubbub, the singing of freedom songs and the occasional shouting of slogans. Her voice was powerful and carried well over the mike.

"The boycott draws the attention of the oppressed people, that they are the only people who can save themselves. And they must begin to do so right now. The consumer boycott is a real way of beginning to take that little step forward which can eventually prove to be a giant leap."

This was somehow different, Abe. It was different from our meetings in the Fifties and Sixties. There was more tension so that in a way it was more frightening. The audience seemed more aggressive, more determined and, strangely enough, more optimistic. This is a young person's revolt and it contains more energy, more controlled energy. The participants, and most of them are far younger than we were, are less cautious and more reckless. I dread to think what will happen when all that energy will be fused, controlled, directed and then let loose.

With a series of clenched-fist salutes, "Viva the people", "Viva the U.D.F.", "Viva the consumer's boycott," Lynne finished her speech. She looked so terribly young and fragile. A man sitting next to him told Andrew that she came from Lansdowne and was a University of Cape Town graduate who had gone straight from university into the trade union movement where she was now a full-time organiser.

The next speaker brought greetings from the Eastern Cape, where a consumer boycott had been in progress for quite some time. He told them that the mayor of Port Elizabeth had described the situation there as "desperately urgent". Dozens of small shops had been so hard hit that they had been forced to close down. A supermarket owner in Commercial Road said he was going on holiday. With only R2 takings on the first day of the boycott, there was no point in his remaining open.

Abe, while I was listening to the speaker, I suddenly felt lonely, desperately lonely in a hall crowded with thousands of people. I felt the way I did when I spoke on the Grand Parade after I had seen Justin go off to jail during the Defiance of Unjust Laws Campaign. I remember you were rather hard on it and described the campaign as puerile political exhibitionism. I also remember that I did not reply to you but deep down I disagreed with you. I remember that you also had reservations about my speaking at the protest meeting, as you felt I would be identifying myself with Congress politics. I did not reply on that occasion also but deep down I knew that I was identifying myself with any movement that was against people like Justin being jailed for their political beliefs.

The Port Elizabeth speaker continued. "As a result of the boycott in the Eastern Cape, the Chamber of Commerce and Industry has desperately called upon the President to meet them. There is no doubt that the consumer boycott has had great effect there. It can have as great an effect here in the Western Province."

Yes, Abe, the mood of fierce optimism and aggressive challenge I felt in that hall was different from our mood in the 1960s. Don't misunderstand me. We had both optimism and challenge then, but they were not of the same calibre. We were challenging because we were desperate. These youngsters, many still at high school, are challenging, not because they are desperate, but because they know that they will win in the end. Maybe not now, maybe not next year, but they know they must win. The future is on their side. They are the future.

A black trade unionist from Guguletu spoke next. He was small, fierce and a ball of verbal fire. He had the audience eating out of the palm of his hand. "Until now all our struggles have been contained within the townships and locations where the oppressed live. The rest of white South Africa is entirely happy to have it that way. The defence force and police appear to them to have the situation under control. Their life goes on as normal. They make money as usual. They go to bed as usual. They go to parties as usual. What the consumer boycott does is to extend the struggle from the township to the city, to the length and breadth of South Africa. No corner of this country must remain untouched. No corner of . . ."

There was a scuffle two rows in front of Andrew and a man was pushed into the aisle. People were shouting and remonstrating. Youthful marshals rushed up from all parts of the hall. The man was led struggling to the back door amid a chorus of boos. The chairperson announced that an informer with a tape-recorder had been uncovered and had been summarily evicted.

More and more speakers. The hall was now uncomfortably hot. "It is possible the workers may lose jobs, but haven't workers already lost jobs?" Loud cheers and shouts of "Viva Mandela." Andrew spotted a noisy group of Eastridge Senior pupils at the far left-hand side with Trevor Petersen in vociferous control. "Suddenly we find the bosses very concerned about blacks losing jobs. What the oppressed people are doing is taking a step in the direction of a new society in which unemployment, loss of jobs, bad housing, starvation and gutter education will come to an end." On and on and speaker after speaker.

So, Abe, after two hours of haranguing and rhetoric my ears were singing. All the time I was trying to work out why I had really come. There must be a complexity of reasons both conscious and subconscious. Of course I wanted to find out what these meetings were all about. I wanted to find Brad. I wanted to find myself. And I ended up mentally confused and incoherent. My intellectual self rebelled against the apparent disorganisation, the sloganising, the political clichés, and the populist nature of the meeting. But my gut reaction was that this was all me. That was me speaking on the platform, me shouting slogans, me challenging the authorities. My being there did not have much to do with the consumer boycott. Maybe it was because Justin had gone to jail as a Defier more than thirty years before. I also felt

like pushing my balled fist into the air and shouting "Viva!" with the youngsters.
I knew I was a political cliché and did not for the moment wish to be anything else.

After the meeting he waited a short time for Eldred at the car. After the humidity inside the hall he thankfully sucked in the cool, crisp, night air. There was not a policeman or police vehicle in sight. Eldred arrived and they climbed in and he pulled away. The road-block was gone and only the empty macadamised length of Spine Road stretched in front of them.

"So did you get what you had come for?" Eldred asked.

"I think so. Yes, I think so. I think I am beginning to find myself," Andrew replied.

8

An hour later, almost completely enervated by the staff meeting, he phoned Lenina again. The same voice answered. This time Andrew identified himself as Bradley's father and gave his home number. The voice on the other side assured him that the message would be passed on to Lenina as soon as she came home.

Half an hour later, Lenina herself phoned the school and the secretary put her through. Almost everyone else had left but luckily Andrew was still there.

"Is that you, Mr Dreyer?"

"Yes, Andrew Dreyer speaking." He hoped he didn't sound too matter-of-fact.

"This is Lenina, Lenina Bailey. I've been trying to contact you all morning."

"Yes, I got your messages and phoned back. Weren't you told?"

"No, I have not been home yet. I'm calling now from a public phone in Athlone."

"Is it about Bradley?"

"Yes, I have a message which he wants me to pass on to you. No, there is nothing wrong. He is safe at present and in no danger. But I prefer not to discuss anything over the phone. Is it possible to meet somewhere, Mr Dreyer?"

"Of course, if you think that's best."

"When are you free?"

"I can be free any time from now."

"Can you suggest a place? A restaurant or something?"

Andrew thought quickly. "O.K. What about The Traverna in Long Street?"

"Anywhere but Long Street."

"Then you suggest somewhere else."

"There's a quiet tea-room in Kenilworth Centre. I will be in Claremont later this afternoon. It is upstairs, near the car park. I can't remember the name but you can't miss it. How about four o'clock?"

"All right, I'll meet you there then."

She had stated that Brad was in no immediate danger. That was some consolation. Maybe Brad himself would be at the tea-room. Maybe Lenina was merely acting as a go-between. Maybe Brad was in more trouble than could be admitted over the phone. What a strange girl. Still her voice sounded more matter-of-fact and business-like than aggressive.

When he was ready to leave he found the school deserted. Everyone else had gone except for Mr October who was himself now leaving. They walked together to the car park.

"Terrible day it has been, hasn't it?", Mr October said, pulling a wry face.

"Well, I hope it is all over. I've had enough excitement to last for some time."

"And now we have that subject adviser tomorrow."

"Goodness, I almost forgot about it."

They reached their cars.

"Well, Mr Dreyer, don't prepare too much. I doubt whether there'll be any children to teach for them."

"I doubt it. Have a good afternoon, Mr October."

Strange fellow, October. He was seldom perturbed but, if so, showed it. Not good in a crisis, but dependable otherwise. Lived a quiet, dull life with his quiet, dull wife. All their children were grown-up and married and had most probably left home through sheer boredom. He read widely, watched television and listened to classical music. He and his wife had no real social life. He did his job according to the syllabus. But it was obvious that he did so to avoid controversy. Andrew had realised earlier on that Mr October could crack, and when he did so, would be pathetic. Over the years he had cut a deep groove between his home in Steenberg and the school in Eastridge. However, things didn't pass him by.

Kenilworth Centre was not as busy as usual, possibly because it

47

was mid-afternoon. Andrew preferred to park in the open lot and then take an escalator to the first floor. He found the neglected restaurant hiding in a corner with only one middle-aged couple having tea and a surly waitress immersed in a Mills and Boon romance. Now what time did Lenina say? 3 p.m. or 4 p.m? He really was becoming very forgetful. Andrew enquired from the waitress whether a young lady had asked for him and received a negative, disinterested answer. In case she did come, could the waitress tell her that Mr Dreyer had called, was somewhere in the Centre and would be back at 4 p.m. She hardly bothered to look at him when he spoke.

Andrew decided to go down to the Central News Agency in the main foyer. What a hell of a day. These people shopping, the Kenilworth housewives and Rondebosch school children, behaved as if nothing was happening just down the road from them. The trouble at the stadium, that dreadful café in which he had sheltered, the abortive march to Pollsmoor, the beatings in Kromboom Road, the staff meeting — he must not forget about that English adviser — and that difficult Joe Ismail. How the devil did he know of Andrew's connection with Justin? How much did he really know? And now Lenina's phone call. Was Brad in serious trouble or not?

He was half-peering at titles in the shop window with all these thoughts milling around inside his head, when he heard someone behind him saying "Hello?"

He spun round quickly expecting to see Lenina and looked into the face of an elderly man grinning toothlessly at him.

"Oh, hallo?" Andrew replied completely puzzled.

"Are you Mr Andrew Dreyer, the author?"

"Well, yes?"

"You don't know me, but I recognised you from your photo on the back of your book. I got it out of the library. My name is Mr Samuels. I also originally come from District Six."

"Oh, yes?"

"I liked parts of the book. I'm always proud when one of our Coloureds show just what we can do. What I didn't like were the mistakes."

Andrew was in no mood to discuss a novel he had written more than twenty years before, in a busy foyer, with a person he did not know.

"For example, if you don't mind my saying so Mr Dreyer, you state that Ayre Street ran off Seven Steps. Now that's not correct. It was

William Street, not Ayre Street." He chuckled at the point he thought he was scoring.

Andrew knew that the man was wrong, but was in no mood to start any argument. He remained silent searching for the chance to get away.

"Writers also make mistakes. I told my wife so. I haven't got much education myself but I like my reading and I can quickly spot any mistakes. My wife always says that I should have been a detective or a school teacher."

"I'm sure that you're correct, Mr . . ."

"Samuels, the name."

"Mr Samuels. Now if you will excuse me, I have to be off. I'm expecting someone upstairs."

Mr Samuels was not to be put off so easily.

"You busy writing another book, Mr Dreyer, if you don't mind my asking?"

"Yes. But I really must be off now. Thank you for the advice."

"About our Coloured people?"

"It was nice meeting you, Mr Samuels."

"I must tell my wife that I actually spoke to you. Of course she won't believe me. Mr Dreyer, we used to live in Ashley Street in the good old days, but now . . ."

Andrew mumbled some greeting and left Mr Samuels grinning toothlessly.When he entered the restaurant, Lenina was sitting at a far table waiting for him. The first few moments were formal and uncomfortable and they spoke neutrally. He roused the reading waitress and ordered tea. Then Lenina came straight to the point.

"Mr Dreyer, you must wonder why I phoned."

"Yes, is it about Brad?" he asked anxiously.

"Yes, it is, but there is no cause for alarm."

"He is in no kind of danger?"

"Not that I know of. He would have mentioned it to me."

"So where is he now?"

"I don't know, Mr Dreyer. I saw him last, a week ago, but yesterday we spoke on the phone. He sounded a bit worried but assured me that he was in no immediate danger. He asked me to contact you to say that he was all right. That's why I phoned."

"Yes?"

"He also wants me to tell you that he is sorry for what happened the last time you met. The fact that he did not come home to see you personally was not because he didn't want to, but because it would have been risky. He suspects that he is being watched. Have the police been to your place yet?"

"No."

"Well that's a relief anyway. I'll tell him so. It is wise for him to stay out of circulation for a time."

"Is it possible that I can meet him somewhere safe?"

"I'm afraid not, Mr Dreyer."

Andrew felt his temper rising. He struggled to control himself but nerves felt raw and exposed.

"But everything is so vague. Where is my son? He is my son, you know. What is happening to him, Miss Bailey? As his father I have a right to know."

"It's not as easy as all that."

"Are you people playing cops and robbers? Is it games you are playing?"

"No, we are not playing games, Mr Dreyer."

"But why are you withholding information from me?"

Andrew raised his voice and an elderly couple two tables away looked curiously at them. The waitress brought the tea they had ordered, slopping it down.

"Mr Dreyer, I'm sorry if I am upsetting you. I do not mean to. Brad is in no danger at present. But he is sure to be detained if they can find him. The system is out looking for him. Fortunately he has managed to elude them so far. We don't know how much they really know about what he is doing."

"And what is he doing?"

"Let's leave it at that. Even if I knew where he was, I couldn't tell you. And I give you my word that I don't know. But what seems to worry him, and he mentioned it to me a few times on the phone, was his relationship with his family. You might not realise it, but Brad is very fond of you. He insisted that I contact you and make things right. You must not be too hard on him. He sincerely regrets what he has done."

While she spoke Andrew listened intently. A young girl, a very young girl, still in her late teens. They were all so very young to be playing with dynamite. Too young to take on such enormous responsibilities.

"And you, Miss Bailey," he said at last, "are they after you as well?"

"Please call me Lenina. I suppose I'm still suspect, but thank goodness, they don't seem to be very interested in me at present."

"Were you followed here?"

"No, I don't think so. I have been in Athlone and Claremont all morning. Don't worry, I don't think they have anything on you."

"How do you know?"

"I don't know."

"Will you tell me the moment anything happens to Brad?"

"I certainly will. He said he would phone me this evening, and I will then tell him that I have met you. Is there anything else you would like me to add?"

Andrew thought for a while. He was slow in answering. "Tell him that we all miss him. Tell him that we are all behind him. Tell him that I believe in . . . yes, tell him that . . . that I believe in what he is doing."

They sipped their tea. There was an uncomfortable silence. Andrew had difficulty looking Lenina in the eye. He felt he had revealed too much of himself to this girl he hardly knew.

He felt that he had to ask the question. "Was that your father who answered the phone?"

"Yes, it must have been."

"I know him."

"I know you do. He has mentioned you quite a few times."

"So he does remember me?"

"Of course he does. He still remembers you. He likes you and respects you. The two of you must meet again. You must visit him in Manenberg."

"Won't he object?"

"Why should he?"

"But is it possible? Isn't he under house arrest?"

"Yes, but he is allowed out weekdays between the hours of 7 a.m. and 7 p.m. But he is not well at present and seldom goes anywhere. He is restricted to the magisterial district of Athlone."

"When you see him, tell him that I would like to meet him again. Tell him that it has been a long time."

"I certainly will. I'll tell him this evening."

"And what about your mother?"

A steeliness came into her eyes.

"I suppose she is all right."

"Where is she now?"

"Are you really interested?"

"Not if you do not wish to speak about it."

"She dumped me with an aunt when I was barely two years old. Father was in jail then. I saw her again for the first time last December. She sent for me sixteen years later."

Abe, you must remember Florence, Justin's wife. She was a friend of your late mother's, and was often at your home in Grand Vue Road where she went to complain about Justin and his politics. Remember the evening in 1960? Justin had just been arrested and they were after us. We went to their home in Arundel Street, District Six, to fetch a parcel of pamphlets Justin had left for me, and found her sitting on the bed painting her toenails and listening to pop music on the radio. It was then we heard over her radio that the State of Emergency had been declared. How he could have gone back to that woman and stayed with her for so many years longer, and have a daughter like Lenina from her, I find hard to imagine.

There was something indefinable but frightening in that girl's eyes. Her face suddenly became hard and inflexible. It was as if I was seeing someone ageing in front of me, from eighteen to sixty in a flash. Although she seemed hesitant to speak, I realised that she had to get it out of her system. She had to tell her story to someone. She could not tell it to her aunt, or to her father. But it had been smouldering inside her waiting to explode. She found in me someone sympathetic. I got the impression that in reliving her meeting with her mother she was speaking to herself rather than to me. Her story was very disconcerting.

9

Lenina glanced down at the address on the paper in her hand. Upper Long Street was shabby and congested with second-hand shops, cafés, sleazy restaurants, and mouldy buildings which were standing cheek by jowl. She was searching for 210, but couldn't see the number. Where it should have been was a large, ugly Victorian tenement with peeling brown paint covering its walls. A bottle-store had its number, 206, displayed in prominent letters on its plate-glass window. Then a vacant lot layered with refuse. A narrow, dingy lane and the brown-painted building. Wide balconies, fenced off with wrought-iron railings, ran the entire lengths of the second and third floors. She could make out the grandiose name fading at the top, "Long Street Mansions".

That must be 210. She could find only one entrance. It was

cluttered with overflowing bins of refuse. Two scarred and beaten-up derelicts, who frequented that part of the street, peered suspiciously at her from the gloom of the doorway.

Lenina climbed a rickety staircase and reached the first-floor landing. Although it was late afternoon, and the sun was brilliant outside, her eyes had to accustom themselves to the darkness. A long, dank passageway, with doors spread evenly on both sides disappeared into the gloom. Permeating everything was the smell of mould and rot.

She chose a door behind which she could hear music and laughter. She knocked hesitantly. The laughing stopped and the door inched open. An eye looked through at her.

"Yes, what you want?" a female voice asked.

"I'm looking for a Mrs Bailey. Mrs Florence Bailey."

"Who's there?" a man's voice shouted from further inside.

The woman at the door shouted back at him, "It's someone for Florrie."

"Well, tell them to go upstairs."

The door opened wider. A scraggy, white woman in an open blouse and dirty, faded jeans stared Lenina up and down.

"What do you want with her?"

"I'm looking for Florence Bailey."

"Tell them to go upstairs," the man shouted impatiently.

"You a friend of hers?" the woman asked.

"I wish to see her."

"Why?"

Lenina was annoyed at this unexpected interrogation. She was about to leave when the woman was pushed aside and the man himself stood in the doorway. He was stripped to the waist and his thin, pale body bore crude tattoos. He was barefooted and an unlit cigarette dangled from his lips.

"Why don't you tell the blarry lady, Florrie lives upstairs? Next floor, beautiful, third door on the same side. If she's not there, you can always come back here. You don't want to come in for a quick drink, do you?"

Lenina was about to retort when he pulled the woman back and banged the door shut. From the passage she could hear them laughing.

Lenina climbed to the next floor and knocked at the third door. At first there was no response. She knocked again and the door was opened.

A woman stood smiling in the doorway. "Hallo, Charley." Then her face froze. "Sorry, I thought you were Charley."

She looked over fifty but might have been a bit younger. She might also have been quite good-looking but that must have been a long time before. Heavy and badly applied make-up could not hide lines and tell-tale wrinkles. She had a battered look. Her body was still shapely although running to fat. Her prominent feature was the bunch of rich, bushy hair dyed a rich red. She was wearing a thin, cotton blouse above a soiled skirt. Cracked polish was unable to hide the rinds of dirt under her toenails. Lenina was appalled at the sight.

"I'm looking for Mrs Bailey."

"Come again?"

"Mrs Florence Bailey. You know where I can find her?"

"What do you want?"

"I wish to speak to her."

There was a puzzled look in the older woman's eyes and she screwed them to see more clearly. Then bewildered recognition shot into her eyes and she began to blubber uncontrollably. Hot tears started to course down her face mixing with the stale powder. A thin grin spread incongruously across her face.

"So you are my little girl, my little Lennie."

She tried to embrace the young girl but Lenina stiffened and put out her arms to prevent it. The older woman swallowed tears and mucus.

"I don't suppose I can blame you, can I? But please come inside."

The room was cluttered and dirty. Lenina searched for a clean place to sit. A large, unmade double bed and a soiled studio couch. In the middle of the room was a table on which were thick, empty glasses and two half-filled bottles of wine. Four cane chairs around the table. In a corner a hot-plate, and a sink overflowing with dirty dishes and cutlery. A transistor radio blared loudly.

"Hell," the woman said, wiping her eyes with a used tissue which she took from an overfull ashtray, "Hell, when I phoned I never expected you to come. You mustn't mind me crying, I'm so happy. I just can't tell you how happy I am. This is a surprise. It's been years and years."

"Sixteen years," Lenina said coldly.

"You mustn't be too hard on me. I'm your mother, my child."

"Yes, I realise that."

"Your mother who hasn't seen you for all those years."

Lenina felt her initial anger giving way to coldness. "Could you please switch that radio off!"

"But first we must celebrate our meeting. Do you take a little something? She indicated the bottles on the table. Lenina shook her head indignantly.

"I hope you don't mind if I do. Just a little drop to celebrate my little girl who has come to visit me." She poured herself a full glass. Her foot involuntarily tapped in time to the pop music coming over the radio.

"You like the music?"

"No, I don't."

"Then I'll make it a bit softer. I see you can be just as headstrong as your father."

"My father is not headstrong."

Justin had always told Lenina about her mother's addiction to trashy music on Springbok Radio. It seemed that things had not changed since then. Only now it was the same sort of music on Radio Good Hope.

"Tell me, Lennie," she said hesitantly, unsure of herself and what sort of answer to expect, "How is Justin? Is your father happy?"

"He is as happy as can be under the circumstances." Lenina looked steadily at the woman opposite her. Maybe it was a mistake to have come, or was it? The phone call. Fortunately she was home and had answered the call. The lipstick-coated, slurred voice at the other end, giving name and address. The repetition of the same sickly, sentimental rubbish. "Your mother longs to see her daughter."

She came so that the mother could see her daughter. She came and found this. Was it morbid curiosity? Sadism? In a peculiar way she was satisfied and happy with what she saw, but showed no visible reaction except cold hostility towards that cringing, ingratiating, blubbery caricature that was her mother.

"I've waited for years and years and I couldn't wait any longer so I phoned you. I hope you don't mind. I didn't know what to expect, how you would receive me. I would have been happy only to have heard your voice."

"Why? You never treated me as your child."

"I wasn't in a position to."

"Why did you abandon me? I was barely two years old and my father was in jail. Why did you give me away?"

"I've never forgiven myself for it."

55

"Why?"

"Because I had to."

"Why?" Lenina persisted.

It came hesitantly at first and then tumbling out as if blocked for decades. Lenina listened.

"There was another man, a white man from Jo'burg. His name was Tom. He said he loved me. I couldn't take what Justin was doing to me any longer. He kept getting picked up. Now for this sort of politics, then for that sort. He spent four years in Jo'burg at the treason trials. I went up to visit him and met Tom there one night at a party in Fordsburg. The few times I went up afterwards was as much for Tom as for Justin.

"Did my father know about this?"

"Tom was one of those who floated on the fringes of the Congress Movement but was really there for the girls he could get and use."

"If you knew all this, then why did you insist on going out with him?"

"I was a woman and I was alone. What could anyone expect me to do? I didn't want to be lonely. I couldn't make love to my transistor radio."

"And all this time while you were married you were unfaithful to Justin?"

"No, he was just as unfaithful to me. He had another mistress, politics. He was married to politics. We were never really man and wife."

"Did you try to make things easier for him, knowing his political commitment?"

Perhaps Florence did not hear the question. Perhaps she chose not to hear it, but she seemed to be speaking more to herself than to Lenina.

"We had no money and were forced to move from our nice house in Eden Road in Walmer Estate, near Mrs Hanslo, to a dirty, two-roomed place in the backyard of an Indian Congress sympathiser. I just couldn't take that."

"Arundel Street in District Six?"

"And I was left almost friendless. Yes, of course there was Tom, but he was in Jo'burg. I used to visit Mrs Hanslo in Grand Vue Road, but now that I was living way down in District Six, I couldn't get there so often. And then they raided her house looking for her son, Abe, who was on the run, also for politics. The poor woman was alone at home, and after the police left she died of a heart attack. My only friend was now dead. Soon after Justin was arrested again. I no longer wanted to live alone. I didn't want to die alone like Mrs Hanslo."

Lenina was listening, piecing together the information. "Did you know Andrew Dreyer?"

"Why do you ask?"

"Daddy used to mention him."

"Old Andy? Yes, of course I knew him. We went to school together. I believe he is a big-time teacher now and doesn't speak to his old friends. He had a white girl at the time, I can't remember her name, Ruth or something, and they got caught under the Immorality Act. Justin told me the whole story. But her father had lots of money. He came down from somewhere in the Transvaal and I don't know what he did or how much he paid, but he took his daughter home and Andy was set free. Lucky bastard. Now he is a great, big, respectable man teaching other people's children. Those were bad days for all of us in 1960." She attempted a smile.

"Go on."

But Florence needed no prompting. "For years I led one hell of a life. When you were born — I remember it was March 7th, in 1967 — I thought all our problems were now solved. We could be one happy family if Justin could give up his politics. But it was even more difficult with a baby. I was getting on in years. I was just over thirty, and Justin was even more involved in politics. Then they arrested him for sabotage and he was sentenced to twelve years on Robben Island. That was the last straw. I phoned Tom, and he came down from Jo'burg to fetch me. He offered to make up for everything I had gone through. I could go back to Jo'burg with him and we could live together as white. It was fair enough. But he wouldn't allow me to come with my baby."

"So you abandoned me?"

"No, I wouldn't put it that way. I cried a lot, and then I took you to your aunty Hester in Manenberg. She was married to Justin's younger brother and they had no children of their own. I knew they would be happy to have you."

"Were they really?"

"Of course they must have been, otherwise I would not have taken you there. If you don't believe me you can ask your aunty Hester or your uncle."

"My uncle died eight years ago."

"I'm sorry about that."

"So then you went off to Jo'burg?"

"Yes, for twelve long years while Justin was on the island. Hell, I must have another drink. You don't mind do you?" She poured herself a large one. "I'm sorry I don't have any coffee or tea or a cool drink to offer you. If I knew you were coming . . ."

"What happened in Jo'burg?" Lenina persisted. She was determined to know the full story. Her father had always been vague, maybe deliberately so. How would he react if he knew that she had contacted Florence? Was now sitting in her mother's room in Long Street? Need he ever know? Was he really an innocent in all this? Had he not also abandoned his daughter as much as Florence had?

"Tom was a procurer, a pimp. He soon forced me how to make money for him. He lived off me. I was attractive enough."

"Then you worked for him?"

"Yes, but you mustn't blame me. I had one hell of a life. But what could I do? This man beat me and used me for twelve years, all the time that Justin was on Robben Island. I had nowhere else to go, no friends anywhere. Then I read in a newspaper that Justin had finished his sentence and had been released. I ran away and came back to him in Cape Town. Justin refused to see me."

"Did you blame him?"

"I wanted so much to be a wife and a mother, but he wouldn't give me a chance. I went to Manenberg where you people were living, but your aunty Hester shut the door in my face. I was just over forty and an old woman, beaten-up and scarred, living how and where I could. I lived here, there and everywhere. And then I came here. I've been in this room in Long Street for the last few years."

"Making money for yourself, this time?"

"Yes, because it's the only thing I can still do. And it becomes more and more difficult as time passes. I dye my hair but it doesn't help." She tried to look coy and pouted her lips, but Lenina was not amused.

There was a knock at the door.

"I'm sorry," Florence said confused, "I didn't realise it was so late already, I am expecting a customer."

"All right , I won't disturb you. I'm leaving now."

"You must come and see me again."

"I'll think about it."

"I have been talking all the time and have not given you a chance to tell me anything about yourself. I want to know everything about you."

Lenina got up as the knocking was repeated, a look of abhorrence on her face.

Florence shouted, "Coming!" to the person at the door. She struggled with what she wanted to say next. "Do you mind if I kiss you?"

She moved over but the smell of wine and stale sweat was too much. Lenina turned her back to avoid any contact.

The door opened and a Taiwanese seaman stood grinning in the entrance. He saw Lenina.

"Florrie home?" he asked loudly. He had a bottle of wine in his hand.

"Oh, it's you, Charley?" Florence said coming forward. "Lenina, this is Charley. Charley, this is my daughter."

"Oh, oh. You have very pretty daughter. Just like mother."

Lenina slipped past him and hurried out of the building. She did not wish to look back.

10

In spite of all the happenings on that one day, on his way home from Kenilworth Centre, Andrew kept thinking of the conversation he had had with Lenina in the tea-room. She had spoken most of the time and he had listened. Her account of the meeting with her mother was rendered even more poignant because there was a minimum of histrionics when she related it. He had sat transfixed, allowing his tea on the table to get cold. That depressing room in Upper Long Street. The decay that permeated the room and was part of her mother. The experience must have hurt her deeply but she showed an admirable control well beyond her years. What was happening to their children? What was happening to Lenina and Brad and Trevor Petersen and Ruth and even Neil, that bullied son of Joe Ismail? What were they doing to their children?

It was almost six o'clock. Elfindale was quiet and the street where he lived was deserted except for three of the neighbour's children who were playing on their bicycles. The suburb bore a deserted, bored, middle-class look far removed from the working-class hustle and bustle of the Cape Flats.

Andrew garaged the car, as he did not intend going out that

evening. He found Mabel in the kitchen, kissed her, and then sat down at the table to read the *Argus* which had just been delivered. Banner headlines about the riots at the stadium and the march on Pollsmoor. Twenty-nine people arrested. One priest has to have an eye operation after a baton blow to the face. Teachers at a Bellville South School are appalled at police action in that area where a matric pupil was shot dead. The U.W.C. Staff Association calls for talks between the authorities and the authentic people's leaders.

"You look very tired, Andrew," she commented quietly. "Was it a busy day?"

"Yes, lots of happenings." He tried to concentrate on the newspaper.

Mabel poured him a cup of tea, put it down next to him, and then sat heavily on the opposite chair. She was patiently waiting for him to tell her any news about Bradley. As if reading her thoughts he put the newspaper down.

"No, I have not found Brad yet. But I did get a message that he was safe."

She did not comment but the relief showed on her face.

Andrew told her briefly about the events of the day, the incidents at the stadium, the march — he indicated the newspaper headline — the staff meeting. He told it as factually as he could as if he himself had been a mere onlooker. She listened, commenting only when necessary. But when he described his meeting with Lenina, she noticed his rising enthusiasm.

"You mean to say that Lenina Bailey actually phoned you at school?"

"Yes, three times. With the last attempt she got through and we arranged to meet at K.C. She told me that Brad had phoned her yesterday and had asked her to contact us to say that he was safe."

He did not add any more. He did not wish to discuss Brad's plea for reconciliation with him. He felt it was too intimate even for his wife to share.

"So we still don't know where he is?" Mabel asked, disappointed though relieved.

"No, Lenina also doesn't know. At least that's what she says. It is best for all of us not to know."

"I pray all the time that our boy will not get into serious trouble."

"It's a risk we must take. We have to stand behind Brad and believe in his cause and in what he is doing."

She was lately becoming aware of his subtle change in attitude towards his son's politics. He was not only saying that they must stand behind Brad, but that they must also identify with Brad. Andrew's attitude was changing from one of indifference to one of understanding his son's involvement. Over the last few weeks she had noticed this greater awareness in the way her husband expressed himself about their son. Maybe it had always been there but he had never allowed it to reveal itself. She knew from the years of their married life what a private person her husband was. There were things he kept even from her.

Andrew had told her about the meeting he had attended with Eldred in Rocklands, but she had presumed it was one called by the teachers' association or the Senior School Sports Union where he was the Eastridge delegate. Lately she noticed he attended political meetings and rallies and had even discussed some of them with her. He had asked her to go with him to the most recent one in the Athlone Civic, but she could not because she had to help with the refreshments at the church youth meeting that same evening.

Andrew had shown little interest in her church activities. He never interfered and never involved himself. Even when the children were growing up, he had not gone to any service with the family. Then when Bradley was fourteen or fifteen the boy had refused to accompany his mother any longer. When Mabel complained to him, Andrew had merely shrugged his shoulders, but secretly he was pleased that the boy was asserting himself. Ruth still went with her mother on occasions, but then she was quieter and less rebellious. Maybe it was only a matter of time before she too would raise objections.

Andrew seldom went out in the evenings. He spent much of his time in the privacy of his study, reading, writing and preparing for school. But lately he was going out a few times to political meetings and rallies, sometimes with Eldred but more often alone. Mabel never asked questions since she presumed that he was searching for Bradley. If he found the boy he would be sure to tell her.

Andrew said slowly, "Lenina proved to be very different from what I had expected."

"Yes?"

"I had no idea she was the daughter of an old school-friend of mine."

"You mean Justin Bailey?"

"Yes, How did you know?"

"Brad told me when he first mentioned Lenina. That was before he brought her here."

"So you knew all along and never told me?"

"I thought you knew."

"What else did Brad tell you about Lenina?"

"That they were in love."

"So it isn't only politics?"

"I suppose it's a bit of both." She smiled slightly. "Are you angry with them?"

"No, not really. I am a bit annoyed that I am never told about these things, but I am not angry. In fact I am rather happy for them."

"I'm very glad."

"If I had known they were in love when he first introduced her to me, I would not have been quite so happy. But I am, now that I have heard her story. She is a remarkable girl. Not once today did she mention to me that she and Brad were lovers. I thought that they were merely comrades."

"You must have noticed that there was more in it than that."

Mabel was far more perceptive about some things than he, and discreet about her children's relationships.

"So what was Lenina's story?" she asked, busying herself with setting out the table.

"I'm sure you know that she has had a very hard life. She gave me some of the details, entirely unsolicited. Justin was in and out of jail for politics. Her mother, Florence, dumped her with an aunt when she was barely two years old, and ran away to Jo'burg to her white lover. And last December Lenina had a traumatic meeting with her mother, for the first time after all those years . . ."

"Yes?"

". . . in a filthy room in Upper Long Street . . ."

Mabel listened intently.

". . . where she was earning a living as a whore." For the first time Andrew showed a hint of anger in his voice.

"She told me this horrifying story. Lenina had gone to meet her mother not knowing what to expect. Florence had phoned her, pleading with her daughter to visit her. They then met in that dingy room. It must have been a terrible experience for both. When Lenina left, a Taiwanese seaman was at the door."

Mabel shook her head sadly and started putting out plates and cutlery.

Andrew continued. "Florence has only herself to blame. She neglected her husband and her only child."

"There must have been other reasons as well, Andrew. No mother neglects her child deliberately. It's not natural. Does Justin know about his wife? Did Lenina tell him?"

"I don't think so. I get the impression that I was the first person she confided in. I don't think she would have told Brad. She is strong enough not to."

"Will Justin be angry when he learns that his daughter has met her mother?"

"I don't really know. I don't really know Justin and what the years have done to him. We haven't met for twenty-five long years."

Mabel spoke to herself more than to Andrew. "There are problem parents and there are problem children. We are all part of one great problem. We are all part of one great guilt."

"I don't think I understand what you are saying."

"Lenina is in rebellion against her parents because they gave her nothing. Brad is in rebellion against his parents because they gave him too much," Mabel said.

"Is it wrong for us to have given our children too much? Don't we love them?" he asked.

"But we should also have given them understanding."

He wasn't sure of her reasoning. He understood clearly what she was saying, but found it strange coming from her. Wasn't it she who had shown lack of understanding? Didn't she insist that Brad must accompany her to her interminable church services? Was she so self-righteous that she was unable to realise her own lack of understanding?

As if to answer his question, she said, "I often blame myself because I know I am also guilty. Somewhere I realise that I, that we have gone wrong. Brad and I drifted apart when I insisted on his going to church with me. When was it that you and Brad drifted apart, Andrew?"

"Did I drift from Brad, or did Brad drift from me?"

She seemed to ignore the question. "I really don't understand what is happening to our children. I don't understand what is happening to us. I will pray harder for understanding."

He felt his annoyance coming back and buried his head in the newspaper but knew he would be unable to read. The two ate their dinner in silence. Ruth was away studying at the home of a classmate down the road.

Mabel hurried with washing up the dishes so that she could attend an urgent meeting in the church hall.

Andrew decided to spend the evening in his study jotting down the day's events and integrating them into his novel. Or maybe he should write a long letter to Abe to get the gall out of his system. Thousands of miles and twenty-five years removed. Abe would have a better perspective. Twenty-five years removed. He thought of Justin. Being physically removed and uninvolved, Abe would be better able to understand. Writing a letter to Abe, he realised, would in fact be no different from writing a letter to himself.

11

My dear Abe

Hearing you on the telephone last evening was quite an experience and quite unexpected. Mabel and Ruth were very thrilled to hear your voice for the first time. After all these years you had no trace of a Canadian accent. I am so pleased that my letters and the completed pages of my novel are getting through to you. I am very impressed with your prompt replies and grateful for your detailed criticism.

Lately I have had experience piling up on experience. So all my mind is clouded with a doubt. This evening I am seeking asylum in the quiet of my study, away from the shootings and beatings, the problems I come across at school, my missing son, his girl-friend, Justin's daughter Lenina whom I wrote to you about, and so on and so on. I meant to work on the novel this evening, but decided instead to write this letter to you and in the process to sort out my scattered thoughts and impressions. In a way I am evaluating the happenings today and trying to formulate them in terms of a better perspective and a global view.

Canada and South Africa exist on different planets. Peace, calm and security in the one place and tumult, unrest and instability in the other. I often long for your world of literary debate which you describe so enthusiastically, and to be involved in researching papers such as those you kindly send me. Protest and Challenge. Commitment and non-commitment. Engagé literature. If only I could be personally involved.

I read with interest the Ngugi wa Thiong'o article, in which he pushes hard the thesis that African writers must use their indigenous languages in the fight against neo-colonialism, since their potential audience and readership are an indigenous one. I appreciate his sentiments and admire the tenacity of his argument, but

64

question the practical application of such a proposition. For instance, in what language must I write? I consider myself a black South African. My home language is Afrikaans. I grew up speaking the racy, bastardised Afrikaans of the District Six slums. My pupils at Eastridge are mostly Afrikaans-speaking. But I write in English, not as a political gesture but because it is my reading and writing language. I cannot read and write Xhosa or Zulu. I am the contradiction that is Africa. I was bastardised by colonialism in such a manner that I have one foot in Europe and the other foot on this continent. And there are Blacks like me who know English better than Tswana, French better than Wolof, and Portuguese better than Chokwe. This is our linguistic legacy. How exciting that it is so.

The irony implicit in such a situation was shown in the Soweto riots of 1975. It started as a language issue. Black children took to the streets because the white authorities insisted that Afrikaans should be a language of instruction in black schools. The children revolted not because they wanted to study through indigenous languages such as Xhosa or Tswana, but because they wanted English to remain as a medium of instruction in secondary schools. Then the insurrection spread to Cape Town, where the "Coloured" pupils also took to the streets. But ironically, those pupils were mostly Afrikaans-speaking. So that unfair language imposition was no longer the main criterion. What was the chief grievance was the brutal, naked discrimination in education and elsewhere. The Afrikaans language issue merely sparked off the much wider and deeper felt resentment against apartheid.

If I were to decide to write in Afrikaans or Xhosa, I would deny accessibility to at least some groups who do not read Afrikaans or Xhosa. Not that I am making a special case for it, but English and French are the lingua franca of Africa, the most universal languages on this continent. English is a non-indigenous African language. All protest meetings I attend in Cape Town are conducted in English, the rhetoric is English, and the slogans and banners are in English.

Maybe you should break your self-imposed exile and come home to see for yourself. When some of "our" people who have emigrated to Canada or Australia return to pay a visit, it seems as if it is to substantiate how judicious they were to have left when they did. The wife of a once-prominent physical education instructor, now living in Toronto, told me on her last visit here, "In Canada they treat us just like white people." She said this without batting an eyelid and looked as if she were pronouncing a great truth.

Why do such people leave South Africa in the first place? I suppose that in every age some people somewhere are bound to leave their countries and adopt new ones. That was one of the features of colonialism. The Dutchman picked up his roots and settled in South Africa. The Frenchman picked up his roots and transplanted them in Algeria. Sometimes, as in the case of colonialism, the motive was profit. At other times it was necessity such as land hunger or political and religious persecution.

One thinks of the 17th century French Huguenots or the 19th century Irish peasants.

The "Coloured" exodus is a comparatively minor one. It has little to do with colonialism but much to do with neo-colonial attitudes. At first they went to England, then to Canada and now Australia. One can argue that those people leaving (and I do not include people like yourself who were forced to go for political reasons) are doing so in order to escape apartheid as well as for reasons of upward social and economic mobility. Of course they are entitled to opt for a life free from discrimination. But it becomes a pathetic exericse when they start apologising and employ the "I-did-it-for-the-sake-of-my-children" excuse.

The exodus of "our" people which I am writing about is essentially a brown, middle or professional class phenomenon. The black workers and peasants are not involved since they can scarcely afford to get from their "homelands" to the industrial centres in search of work, far less of trying to emigrate to Canada or Australia. Which first-world country today will take in the illiterate, unschooled, unsophisticated black wretched of the earth who has no money or skills? The wretched refuse, the homeless, tempest-tossed? Give me your poor? It has a hollow ring about it and the liberty torch is flickering more and more faintly.

I suppose that one must concede that choice may be individually exercised and should in most circumstances not be curtailed. I accept that, as long as the subsequent substantiation, if it is ever proferred, does not degenerate into pathetic excuses. Most of our emigrants don't even bother to offer any reasons for their leaving or for what purpose they went. Some even develop into vociferous anti-apartheid spokespersons from the safety of their adopted countries.

Interestingly enough, it is not the young who are leaving as happened during the Irish potato famines. I happen to know quite a few families where the younger members refused to accompany their parents. Those who go are solid, middle-class browns in mid-career who claim they are tired of battling against colour and class discrimination.

The black youths of today, and I include all who are not White in this category, are different from what we were yesterday. We were a generation that grew up in a climate of less overt discrimination which was more institutionalised than constitutionalised. What we wanted was a reversion to the pre-1948 status quo. We actually believed that under the Smuts and the United Party there was far less discrimination and that things were better. Certainly political movements were not banned then, we were allowed to hold protest meetings in the Drill Hall and on the Grand Parade, and we could ride anywhere on the suburban trains in Cape Town. District Six was allowed to exist. The Cape Corps marched off to free Ethiopia *from discrimination which they experienced in their own country. When the National Party won the white election in 1948 we were subjected to a spate of added discriminatory legislation. Segregation was entrenched even deeper as part of the constitution. We fought to regain the past. We were yesterday's children who looked back even further.*

The black youths of today are the apartheid generation. They have never experienced anything else. They have nothing to look back to. But far from this creating a docile, submissive generation as intended in the Verwoerdian dream, the white government spawned a monster it now realises it cannot control. Because black youths had nothing to lose, they reacted with the zeal of those who have everything to gain. They are confident of the future because they are the future. They have reached the stage where guns, imprisonment, detentions and bannings no longer hold any fear for them. Such people can never be contained or conquered. I see this attitude expressed in my pupils at Eastridge, in Brad and in Lenina. They are willing to listen to our theories; they display interest in our views; they sometimes even ask us questions; but finally they know that they will do their own thing.

I have seen young boys, mere teenagers, with wet scarves wrapped around their mouths and noses in case of tear-gas, face armoured trucks with nothing but stones. I have seen young girls raising their clenched fists defiantly at armed policemen. I am not romanticising. They have paid a terrible price for their opposition, sometimes they have lost their lives. But their faces are hard and set and they are prepared to sacrifice. Apartheid has spawned this frightening generation that refused to be frightened.

At other times I have seen those same children behaving as normally as any other children anywhere else. They cry, they love, and they date. They go to bioscope and put up posters of Prince and Michael Jackson on their walls. They play soccer in Mitchell's Plain and swim in the municipal pool in Manenberg. But they also face armed policemen with nothing but bricks and raw courage. What will happen when the stones are replaced with guns? These are tomorrow's children who look forward and not backward.

I am holding back this letter so that I can include a few extra pages of the novel. The frustrating thing is that I cannot progress any faster than events are happening. I do not know which characters will appear next on my pages and what they will do. In art one does know. In life one doesn't. The novelist's absolute control and omniscience are missing from my book. This is first-person reality written as third-person narrative. Many times I cannot distinguish between fact and fiction. I often wonder whether they are different. Instead of being in control and manipulating, I am being controlled by events and am being manipulated by happenings. It is a very stange experience for a novelist. And I am not sure whether I understand what I'm doing or not. You must write and advise me.

PART TWO

OPEN THE SCHOOLS

Tuesday 17 September 1985

After pupils and students have been spasmodically boycotting educational institutions for almost six weeks, the Minister of Culture and Education in the House of Representatives, on 6 September, closes by decree 465 schools and colleges in the Western Cape because in his opinion the safety of pupils can no longer be ensured. After eleven days of being forced by law to remain off their school grounds, a decision is taken to defy this order publicly. On the morning of 17 September, parents, pupils and teachers assemble inside many schools waiting for either eviction or arrest.

OPEN THE SCHOOLS

Professor Abraham Hanslo
Department of African Studies
York University
Keele Street
Ontario
M3J TP3
Canada

Dear Abe

I find it almost impossible to describe to you some of the events of the past few weeks. A few of course I have already written about in previous letters, but the worst I have not sent off. I just couldn't at the time. I am doing so now because I feel I have to get these off my chest. Any would-be chronicler cannot afford to be too queasy.

For example, I found Thursday, 5 September, so traumatic that I am at a loss how to write about it as objectively and unemotionally as possible. But of course I must make the attempt.

It proved to be a day of violence, burnings and bloodshed during which, miraculously, only two people died and twenty-two were arrested. I certainly expected far more deaths. Belgravia Road was, at times, a kilometre-long battleground as high-school pupils with petrol bombs and stones battled against armed riot policemen. In Retreat, quite near my home, things were almost as bad. Surprisingly again, only one man was wounded during police action, after stones were thrown and burning roadblocks set up. One of the tactics the pupils employ is to place used car tyres and other rubble across the road and then set these alight.

From outside my house or school, I can often from a distance make out the course of events. The first sign is usually smoke from barricades which I can see trailing up beyond house and tree tops. Soon after I hear the wailing of sirens as police vehicles move in. Sometimes a government helicopter will hover overhead. Then I hear the staccato of rifle fire mingled with screaming and shouting, and finally I observe smoke from tear-gas spiralling up to mix with the smoke from burning tyres. What a scenario. And I watch glossy-eyed. I then feel that I cannot hate too much.

On the same day, on 5 September, at a high school near Hewat, about 2 000 pupils assembled. They had a coffin in which they were symbolically going to bury apartheid in a mock funeral ceremony. I was in the area and stopped to watch. It was soon after that the inevitable police Casspirs arrived and started firing tear-gas into the grounds. Who informs them so that they always arrive promptly? Pupils hurriedly dispersed, but some of the braver ones regrouped at the corner of Veld and Belgravia Roads and spread out along the road next to Hewat. A barricade of ten burning tyres was set up. Most of the police left and a Casspir, seen circling the area, withdrew when half-bricks, stones and petrol bombs rained down on it.

Such scenes are repeated daily all over the Western Cape, from Steenberg to Scottsville, from Retreat to Elsies River, from Bonteheuwel to Bellville South.

The following day, on 6 September, by a decree of the minister, over 460 "Coloured" schools and colleges were closed indefinitely. Half a million pupils and students were directly affected. In Mitchell's Plain all 60 primary and secondary schools, including Eastridge, were officially closed. To be found on the premises of your own institution was considered a criminal offence.

At our school we had, up to now, had more than our own share of trouble. Besides having to contend with the daily boycotts, we had the nasty incident when the subject advisers came, a heated joint staff–S.R.C. meeting immediately afterwards, and then we were shut down with all the other schools. After our closure we held Staff–Pupils liaison committee meetings in a nearby church-hall since we were forbidden by law from being on our premises.

Such a situation would obviously prove to be untenable.

1

Andrew was still somewhat unsure about the turn taken by his renewed political involvement. It seemed as if he were getting more and more involved. Whether some pupils and staff members now trusted him politically seemed irrelevant to him. Of course there would always be those who would say that he was merely trying to establish his own credibility, that he had never really shown exactly where he stood, that his appearance as a speaker at the protest meeting in the Athlone Civic was pure opportunism. They also claimed, he had heard, that he put the interest of his family before that of the struggle. Andrew remained non-committal when these accusations were put to him. Only once had he openly discussed his personal involvement and that was with Eldred on that evening after the terrible events of the adviser's visit, when Eldred had come over.

While shaving and dressing on the morning of 17 September, he speculated just how much his colleagues really knew about him. Was it his fault that they were wrong? Joe Ismail, it seemed, was onto something, and must have discussed it with his cronies, but he was no longer around now. And how much did the authorities really know? They might have been satisfied with his behaviour during the visit of the subject advisers. They might have been dissatisfied with his speaking at a public protest meeting. These two actions could seem to be contradictory. They could certainly have confused some of the staff, although that was not the intention. Confusion could be a powerful and dissipating weapon, but he had never used it as such. And would he today again be exposing himself? Endangering his position? Brad's position? Lately he felt a numbness when he thought of his son. And now this action. Civil disobedience. Deliberately breaking the law and courting arrest. How would his wife ever understand? How would she ever agree with it?

The three of them had spent the evening before quietly sitting around the television set, Mabel, Ruth and himself. This was not usual. Normally he would have been reading and writing in his study, Mabel would have gone off to some church service or other, and Ruth would have escaped from the loneliness and boredom of the house to study with a friend. Mabel and Ruth were watching a soap opera on TV1. Ruth seemed more tense and fidgety than usual. Andrew was sunk into the evening newspaper. "Mandela gets medical treatment for enlarged prostate". "Stevie Wonder, whose songs were banned after he dedicated an academy award to the jailed A.N.C. leader, is heard again on SABC." "The Teachers Union of South Africa urges the government to reopen schools."

Andrew wondered when the authorities would take the sensible decision to open the schools again. The situation was reaching breaking point. Thousands of children aimlessly roaming the streets and thousands of teachers doing nothing at home. This had been going on for almost two weeks.

He looked up at Ruth. "So what is happening at Steenberg High tomorrow? Have you people decided on anything?"

She glanced nervously at her mother. "Yes, we are also joining in the protest and going to classes."

Mabel was astonished. "What's that you're saying?"

"I said that we are going to protest. We are meeting outside the school at 8.30 tomorrow, and then we are going into our classes."

"But that's against the law. You will be asking for trouble."

"We are going nevertheless."

"You will be arrested, my girl."

"That's a risk we are prepared to take."

Mabel turned to Andrew in desperation. "Do you hear what the child is saying?"

"Yes, I heard," he said looking up from the *Argus*.

"Are you not going to try and stop such foolishness?"

He put down the newspaper and explained to her slowly and patiently.

"It is a decision, Mabel, taken at most primary schools, secondary schools and colleges, including Steenberg and Eastridge. Tomorrow morning we are meeting outside our respective schools, parents, teachers and pupils, and then we are going onto the premises. We know we will be breaking the law, but we have no alternative. Our patience has run out." He picked up the newspaper and continued reading.

"But you can all go to jail."

"As Ruth has explained, that's a risk we are all prepared to take."

"Look, Mom," Ruth intervened, "we are tired of sitting at home and being prevented from going to our own schools. So tomorrow we are asserting our right to be there and to have classes."

This was a new Ruth, an assertive Ruth quite in control of herself. Ruth sounded more and more like Bradley. Mabel did not understand what was happening to the child. And her father seemed absolutely indifferent to it all.

"I'm afraid I have to agree with Ruth," Andrew said quietly. "They cannot deny us the right to continue with education in our own schools, no matter how distorted and twisted that education is."

"Then what are you doing tomorrow, Andrew?" Mabel almost pleaded.

"I am going to Eastridge," he said patiently. "I'm going to park in my usual spot. I will then go to the 10a room and I will teach literature to whoever is present, as I normally do. If that is a crime, then I am prepared to be arrested and face the consequences of doing what I am supposed to do."

It still made no sense to her. Mabel turned again to Ruth. "And you?"

"I am going to Steenberg."

First Bradley and now Ruth. The sudden change from pliability to stubbornness, happening almost overnight.

"Did you say that parents will also be there?"

"Some will," Ruth answered tersely.

"Then I'm coming with you."

"I would rather you did not. I don't want you there. I don't need your protection."

Andrew knew that the split had come and was irrevocable. The umbilical cord was finally severed. He appeared to be reading his newspaper but was in fact listening.

Mabel was visibly upset at the rebuff. "But it will be dangerous, my child. I am still your mother."

"I know it will be dangerous, but I can manage on my own."

Mabel got up and went out into the kitchen, crying. Ruth did not follow her but remained seated. Andrew looked quickly at his daughter and their eyes met for a brief second. There was something which he had not seen before, something hard. He gave no sign of approval or disapproval. Then he buried his head yet again in the newspaper. He knew what Mabel would still have to learn, that the split was a permanent one. Parent and child had drifted completely apart. He wasn't able or willing to intervene.

The following morning he behaved as naturally as he could, asking routine questions about appointments and bills to be paid. Mabel was tight-lipped while she prepared breakfast, and answered in monosyllables. Ruth, also ill at ease, toyed with her porridge. The phone rang sounding louder than usual in the silence. Ruth jumped up. "All right, I'll get it," then shouted from the passage, "It's for you, Dad. A woman on a public phone."

Andrew took over the receiver. "Dreyer here."

He recognised the voice at once. Lenina did not introduce herself but said quickly, "Meet me at Hewat this morning between 8 and 9, outside the Arts Block."

"Have you any news about him?"

"I'll tell you when I see you."

"All right then, I'll be there."

The phone rang off immediately.

Mabel looked enquiringly at him without saying anything.

"Nothing's the matter," he said reassuringly, "just a routine call."

He hoped that Mabel would not offer to pray for them. This time they would need more than prayers.

She nevertheless made a last effort. "Don't you want me to go to school with you, Ruth?"

"No, I don't," the girl said firmly.

He sat in his car and was about to switch on the engine when he realised that if he went to Hewat, he would not be at Eastridge for their demonstration. That could be misinterpreted in certain circles. He wasn't able to see himself going around afterwards explaining why he had not been there, telling who ever would listen that he had been asked at the last moment to go off somewhere to meet with someone who would give him some information about his son. It just wasn't worth the effort. Should he first go to Hewat or Eastridge? The numbness was ever present when he thought about the boy, as if he were trying to blot out his anxiety. It was almost six weeks now since they had last met. He hoped Lenina would have something more positive to tell him this time. Even bad news was more assuring than this terrible silence. Not being at Eastridge on this morning of all mornings, was a risk he would have to take. He only hoped that nothing serious would happen. Why did the authorities insist on this ridiculous closure of schools? Why not reopen them all and allow normal classes or boycotts to resume? Normal chaos? It might be wiser to skip the meeting with Lenina and go straight to Eastridge. She would be sure to contact him later. But then his curiosity? Or was it his anxiety? Whatever information she had could obviously be delayed for a short time. He had gone so long without any news that a few hours more could hardly make any difference. Yes, it would probably be wiser to go to Eastridge to prevent the embarrassment of explanations afterwards. He debated for a few seconds longer and then switched on the engine and drove straight to Hewat.

2

The crowd was growing in Thornton Road, especially around the main gate of Alexander Sinton High School. As Andrew neared, his car was held up temporarily by a young marshal in school uniform, as a crocodile of parents, pupils and teachers weaved across the road and deliberately entered the gates. There was a grimness and determination about this act of civil disobedience. No police presence as yet, although a helicopter buzzed ominously overhead. Once the file had entered the grounds, Andrew was allowed to drive through.

He parked inside Hewat where he could clearly see the entrance to the Arts Block. No Lenina yet. A group of lecturers and students were gathering, also in defiance of the closure. He walked over to join them, scanning the faces. One lecturer who recognised him greeted. Lenina was not amongst them. He returned and got back into his car and sat reading the *Cape Times*, glancing up continually in case she had arrived. The Hewat group was also swelling every minute.

Andrew heard a commotion and saw the lecturers and students rushing over to the wire fence on Kromboom Road. Beyond it was an open sports field, then Camberwell Road and then Alexander Sinton could clearly be seen. Something was happening at the school. The helicopter was hovering very low over it. He got out of his car, locked the door and hurried to join the group at the fence. There was now a heavy police presence opposite. Casspirs were parked on the sports field and police vans were driving in and out of the gates. The crowd had by now swollen dramatically. Andrew walked quickly up Thornton Road to get a closer look. Sinton was cordoned off and a number of uniformed men were preventing members of the public from entering. Those inside were trapped and piled into vans. Two of those vehicles, crammed with parents and teachers, screeched past him, heading for Manenberg police station.

A high wall opposite the main gate was manned by pupils displaying banners and posters. "Viva COSAS. U.D.F. Lives. The Doors of Learning Shall Be Open." The crowd was now so heavy that

Andrew was forced to watch from its fringe. A driver, directed by some youths, manoeuvred a furniture van into place across the road to form a barrier. He jumped out with the ignition keys and disappeared into the crowd. A butcher's van and three other cars were also driven to add to the barrier, their drivers all disappearing. There was now a stalemate. The police would not allow anyone to enter Sinton, and the crowd would not allow the police vans inside to leave. Other vehicles were being parked to barricade the streets surrounding the school.

An old man giggled next to Andrew. "There are three vans inside the playground, mister, all full of school children. The police can't drive out because the people have blocked all the streets." He laughed hilariously and was obviously enjoying the situation.

The helicopter continued to buzz waspishly overhead. Then a chant started, slowly and almost imperceptibly at first but then rising in volume and momentum as Muslims and Christians in the crowd took it up. "Allahu-Akbar. Allahu-Akbar. God is great. God is great."

To find Lenina would be virtually impossible. The crowd by now numbered well over a thousand. The vans remained trapped inside filled with arrested children. Empty vehicles blocked the surrounding roads. Posters waving and more chants added to the original one. "Allahu-Akbar. Allahu-Akbar. COSAS Lives. U.D.F. Unites."

It was a matter of time before police reinforcements would come. The crowd became more restless and more grimly determined. Andrew heard mothers complaining that their children had been arrested and children shouting that their parents had been apprehended. A rumour spread that the principal of the school was trapped somewhere inside, arrested along with his pupils. Someone remarked that some teachers had already been taken to the police station. The helicopter buzzed irritatingly overhead.

Andrew felt many bodies pressing up against him so that he had to fight to maintain his balance. Then he felt a sharp nudge against his shoulder. With difficulty he managed to turn to see Lenina and an older man almost on top of him.

"I've been waiting for you," he shouted above the noise.

"I'm sorry," she shouted back, "I couldn't make it on time." She said something else but he had difficulty hearing her. "We can't meet under such conditions," she shouted.

The older man grinned at him. Andrew thought there was something familiar about him.

"You still know me?" he shouted in Afrikaans.

Andrew shook his head negatively.

"Caledon Street, man, District Six!"

"Oh yes," he said without conviction.

The crowd was now jostling even more and Andrew almost toppled onto the people in front of him.

"Meet me this evening," Lenina managed to say, "464B Manenberg Avenue."

He was about to ask a question when he was forced to restrain himself from falling. He heard screaming in front and then the crowd ran and scrambled in all directions. Lenina and the older man were lost somewhere in the chaos.

Tear-gas bombs landed near him and the air turned pungent and acrid. Andrew held his handkerchief over his streaming eyes and nose. Police began firing rubber bullets and youths retaliated with barrages of rocks. Pandemonium broke loose. Andrew ran into the garden of a nearby house. He found an outside tap and wet his handkerchief. Then he joined the anxious family watching from their stoep. Noise and absolute confusion. The ratatat of guns shooting and the putputting of the helicopter overhead. He saw two youths being pursued with flaying batons across the sports field. One slipped and was mercilessly clubbed.

Two tow-trucks lumbered up Thornton Road and, to the booing and jeering of the crowd, started hauling the vehicles from the barriers. The helicopter was directing the operations from the air.

Bands of youths grouped, threw rocks, were charged or shot at by the police, fled and then regrouped. The road was now cleared of major obstacles and the three police vans drove through with their cargo of arrested pupils.

The spirals of tear-gas thinned out, the police withdrew and the helicopter chugged off. An unhealthy calm settled over the area, which now wore a beaten and deserted look. Half-bricks and stones lay strewn across the road. Here and there torn posters and odd items of clothing. A bakkie filled with slogan-shouting high-school pupils, some still in uniform, pulled up. They jumped out unloading used car tyres which they quickly set alight with cans of petrol. Soon the surroundings were covered in dense, black smoke.

When it seemed safe Andrew walked quickly back to Hewat. How ironic, he thought, that he always seemed to be parked at Hewat when hell broke loose. Already twice now at any rate. What was the number again? 464B. Yes, 464B Manenberg Avenue. He found himself chanting, "Viva UDF. Allahu-Akbar" over and over again. He had better get back to Eastridge as soon as possible. His eyes were still smarting. He scribbled the Manenberg address at the back of his notebook in case he forgot. People at Eastridge would most probably have had the same experiences as those at Sinton. He wondered whether anyone had been injured or arrested. And he had not been there. There was no use worrying about it now. He would meet the accusation when it was levelled at him. He somehow knew it would be.

3

Dear Abe

I hope it doesn't sound too melodramatic if I tell you that in spite of all the unpleasant things I have experienced lately such as the aborted march on Pollsmoor and my son going missing, the worst to date was the day the subject adviser for English insisted on turning up in spite of all efforts to keep him away. I don't think I came out of the situation well at all, although I do not regret the stand I took, since I am convinced I acted in the best interest of the school. I might have been injudicious, even unwise considering the circumstances, but certainly not disloyal to the pupils or staff. I am not a collaborator nor a sell-out and have never been one. I said so explicitly to Eldred that evening when he turned up to discuss the situation with me. He either could not or would not understand. I had never in my life experienced such hostility directed against me as I did on that particular day.

It seems as if, because one is frustrated at being unable to fight the enemy outside, one invents and fights a supposed enemy inside. Why is it that people react more harshly against those they oppose within their community than those they oppose outside of it? The attitude of the Boer against the hendsuppers *during the Anglo–Boer war, or the Jews against the* kapos *who watched over them in the concentration camps? I am not suggesting that there should never have been resentment against those people. In fact I believe they deserved the retribution they received. I am merely observing a phenomenon that that resentment is much stronger towards the supposed collaborator within the community than towards the real enemy outside. I'm sure there must be a sociological and psychological explanation for it. Blacks necklace other Blacks, never Whites. And the authorities laugh and pass it off glibly as "Black on Black violence".*

Maybe I can best illustrate what I am trying to say by giving you an account of the happenings on that day at Eastridge Secondary School. It may also illustrate my theory that, if any individuals refuse to conform to the demands of any particular ideology, they fall foul of all contending ideologies. Maybe it is safer to be partisan and hide behind the most popular ideology of the day. Maybe I am becoming cynical. So let me tell you about the adviser's visit and allow you to judge for yourself. As Oscar Wilde wrote in De Profundis, *"This is not to excuse but to explain myself."*

Andrew arrived at Eastridge early the Wednesday morning, slightly apprehensive about what might happen on that day, although he was determined not to show his misgivings. Things would have been far better had the advisers been less obstinate and declined to come. Because he resented the pressure exerted by Joe Ismail and his clique, he either kept silent or deliberately adopted a contrary attitude. He knew it was a childish thing to do. Maybe Langeveldt had managed to postpone the visit. But then the man was so inept, so accommodating, that he most probably accepted his instructions without raising any objections.

As he drove in, Andrew sensed that something was unusual. The boycotts had been going on for many weeks now, and there had been a noticeable decline in attendance. The previous day hardly any pupils had been in classes, never mind being present at the alternative programmes they themselves had demanded. But today, in terms of attendance, things looked almost normal. This was ominous. Had word of the advisers' visits got around? There seemed to be pupils everywhere; chatting in classrooms and lounging in corridors. Some juniors were kicking around a tennis-ball on the tarmac. There were also angry groups of seniors bunched in earnest conversation and casting surreptitious glances at every arriving car.

Andrew greeted the pupils and was met with silent stares. He waved to a group of teachers who stood smoking outside the staff-room door and received the same response as he did from the pupils. The atmosphere was certainly foreboding.

He had put down his case and was about to consult his timetable when Eldred entered without knocking. Andrew looked up surprised.

"Morning," Eldred said curtly.

"Morning?" Andrew responded uncertainly. "Is anything the matter? You look so grim."

"I wish to speak to you as the deputy of this school."

"All right then, what is the problem?"

"Do you know whether the subject advisers are coming today?"

"No, I don't really know. I suppose they are. As you can see I've only just arrived."

"What happens if they do come? What do you expect of us? What will you yourself do?"

Andrew contemplated what had occupied his mind intermittently since the staff meeting the previous day.

"You can't say yet again that you don't really know," Eldred insisted.

"No, I wasn't going to say that because this time I do know. I have given the matter much thought and I have reached my conclusion."

"Which is?"

Andrew had indeed given the matter much thought but had only just come to a conclusion, maybe prompted by Eldred. Was he deliberately being contrary? Or was it the correct decision to take? He felt it was the correct decision. He spoke slowly and deliberately. "I will deal with the advisers today as I would have dealt with them under normal circumstances. I do not see that today is any different." He knew deep down that it was, but would not admit it, even to himself.

"What you are saying is that you will require us to teach for them? That you youself will give them your every co-operation?"

"Yes, that's what I'm saying." He was digging in his heels.

"But these are not normal circumstances. Today is different."

"I shall try my best to behave as if it were normal."

"You will be making a great mistake, Mr Dreyer."

The change to the formal address was not lost on Andrew. He realised that Eldred was deliberately placing a distance between the two of them. He did not wish to have an argument now, not with Eldred of all people. The phone rang breaking the tension.

"Excuse me, Eldred," he said, addressing him by his first name to emphasise their former intimacy. He spoke briefly and then put down the receiver. Eldred waited impatiently.

"That was Mr Langeveldt. The English subject adviser is in his office. The Home Economics one has had a diplomatic illness and will not be coming. The principal wants me to see him immediately, if you'll excuse me."

"Are you going to insist that we teach?"

"I will request you to teach if the adviser requires it. I cannot see that I have any other choice."

"Even under these circumstances?"

"Even under these circumstances."

"You are making a great mistake," Eldred repeated.

The bell rang for the start of the first period.

"Now if you will excuse me."

Eldred turned angrily on his heel and walked out of the office. Andrew picked up his timetable file, a resigned look on his face, and went to the principal's office.

Most of the pupils outside openly ignored the bell and went on doing what they had been doing. Some juniors lined up in front of the classes and went in. A few teachers, including Mr October, moved to their rooms. Most however stood bunched outside the staff-room door also ignoring the bell.

A mousy, officious, little man with a pencil-thin moustache sat silently in the principal's office, his briefcase on his lap. Mr Langeveldt introduced them.

"Mr Dreyer my deputy, and Mr de Villiers, English subject adviser." The latter nodded slightly but made no attempt to shake hands.

"Mr Dreyer, do we have a timetable for Mr de Villiers?" the principal asked officiously.

"Not yet, since we were unsure whether he would be coming or not." Andrew looked at the adviser but there was no reaction. "However I will suggest that he sees the 8E Second Language class first. Mr October is there now. While Mr de Villiers is busy, I can draw up the rest of the timetable and inform those concerned when he will be able to see them. I presume that you will stay for the day, Mr de Villiers?"

The adviser nodded tightly.

Andrew felt that that was the best he could do. If anyone would teach it would be Mr October, the nervous, twitching Mr October.

"That seems a fair arrangement," Mr Langeveldt said.

"All right, then I'll take Mr de Villiers to the 8E room and bring him the rest of the timetable at the end of the period."

Mr Langeveldt was extremely relieved. Normally he would have accompanied any adviser or inspector to the class himself. He was always willing and happy to do so, but certainly not today.

Andrew indicated to Mr de Villiers that he should follow him. The atmosphere outside had worsened. Pupils stared silently at the two as they threaded their way to the class. Andrew walked slightly ahead and the adviser made no attempt to walk alongside him. Cold fish,

Andrew thought. Couldn't the man sense the animosity in the air? Why did he insist on coming and placing their positions in jeopardy?

They reached the class without incident. Mr October was teaching a much-depleted group consisting mostly of girls. Andrew introduced Mr de Villiers and Mr October indicated an empty seat at the back of the class. As he left he whispered encouragingly, "Ignore anything outside. Just try and get through the lesson. I know I can count on you." Then he left and Mr October continued teaching.

Andrew walked to the staff-room through the hostile crowd of pupils which had grown large. The teachers on the stoep made a reluctant and silent pathway for him. Inside the staff-room Andrew found Miss Toefy reading the *Cape Times*.

"Good morning," he said hoping that she would not be able to detect the nervousness in his voice.

She stopped reading but did not return his greeting.

"What period do you have the Standard Sixes?" he asked.

The teachers who had been outside now started to filter in, and formed a rough semi-circle around him. It took on the appearance of a confrontation.

"Why?" she asked, gathering strength from the presence of her colleagues.

"Because the adviser would like to visit you. He is with Mr October now."

"I do not wish him to visit me."

Andrew was thrown off his guard although he should have expected a rebuff. It would be officious to accuse her of insubordination. But as if he had done so, she added.

"If you consider this to be insubordination, you may run to your bosses and tell them."

"That will not be necessary, Miss Toefy."

Joe Ismail was leaning against the door. He commented casually from there. "Mr Dreyer, you had better get one thing straight. We did not invite that adviser, in fact we were not even consulted about his visit. We were instructed. None of us are prepared to teach for him. I will therefore suggest that you go along to the principal and tell him just that."

Andrew looked at the group. Eldred was standing a little apart, but there was no doubt where his sympathies lay. Miss Russell sat in a corner knitting furiously.

"All right then, if that's how you want it, I will convey your sentiments to the principal."

"Why not just phone the department directly, or go straight to the special branch?"

"I am not in the habit of informing on teachers either to the department or the special branch. I never have and I never will."

Andrew was fighting hard to control his temper. He felt it best to leave. He found pupils milling around outside the 8E room. It looked like trouble there. He pushed his way through the crowd which was chanting, "October out! October out!"

He entered the class to find the teacher struggling to teach eleven frightened pupils against the background of shouting. The adviser sat poker-faced, watching from the back, Mr October was sweating and his nervousness communicated itself to his pupils. Andrew debated rapidly whether to ask Mr October to call off the lesson, when there was a crash and glass splinters showered the pupils. A stone had been smashed through the window. The pupils were screaming and one girl was bleeding from a cut on her hand.

Andrew rushed over. Fortunately it was a shallow cut. "All right, all right, it's not too bad," he reassured her, "go over to the secretary's office and ask her to fix it. The rest of you just remain calm."

The door was flung open. Trevor Petersen and three of his cronies burst into the room followed by many other pupils, mostly seniors.

"Yes, and what do you want?" Andrew asked.

They ignored him. Trevor addressed the class. "All of you, get out!"

"You can't just march into my class and take over," Mr October began feebly.

"Shut up, you damn sell-out!" Trevor snarled at him. Then turning again to the class he repeated, "I said get the hell out!"

They needed no prompting and rushed for the door where they were jostled and pushed by the other pupils.

"What is the meaning of this?" Andrew demanded, realising the absolute importance of remaining calm.

Trevor looked haughtily at Mr de Villiers. "We don't allow any inspectors or advisers on our premises. This is our school and we decide who can come here and who can't!"

"And who gave you that authority?" Andrew asked.

"We don't need any authority. Now you get out as well and take your friends with you."

"I take great exception to your attitude," Mr October said.

"Will you get out or shall we have to throw you out?"

Pupils were now crowding into the room, the seniors in front. The situation was ugly.

"There is no place at Eastridge for government stooges!"

The adviser gathered his papers and briefcase and left, walking closely behind Mr October. Andrew waited until he estimated that they were safely out.

"Who put you up to this?" he asked Trevor.

"Nobody put us up to this. Do you think we can't act for outselves?"

"Yes, I think so."

"Well, that's your problem, Mr Deputy," the youth said sarcastically.

"I am not prepared to trade insults with you. We can have this out in the principal's office," Andrew said.

"Why not here?" Trevor challenged.

Andrew walked out mustering as much dignity as he could. As he emerged from the room the catcalls changed to "Dreyer is a stooge! Dreyer is a stooge!"

The teachers grinned from where they were gathered outside the staff-room. Joe Ismail turned to his colleagues and pretended to conduct them in time to the pupils' chants. Andrew felt white heat rising. Somehow he reached the principal's office.

Mr Langeveldt was pale and his hands shook. They could hear the catcalls and shouting from outside.

"Mr de Villiers, my very deepest apologies. But if you don't mind, I will suggest that you leave at once. I can no longer guarantee your safety."

He peered out of the window. The situation was completely out of hand and a group was dancing the toyi toyi.

Andrew took the initiative since he realised that the principal was no longer in control of himself. "You stay in your office, sir, and I'll see that Mr de Villiers gets safely to his car."

"Do you think we should call the police?"

"Don't you dare do so!" he said angrily.

Andrew left with the adviser. They ran the gauntlet of dancing and chanting pupils. A stone hit Andrew in the back, but he did not turn around to see who the offender was. They reached the parking-lot followed by jeering pupils.

The front tyres of the adviser's government car were slashed. The windscreen was splintered. Andrew turned to remonstrate and a stone caught him full on the chest.

Then he heard shouting and saw pupils fleeing in every direction. Some cleared the school fences and others ran into classrooms. Police jumped out of vans lashing out with their batons and quirts, and flushing children out of the classes. Two Casspirs drove up and parked opposite the main entrance. A few teachers tried to remonstrate but were threatened by the police. The officer in charge spoke through a loud-hailer. He gave everyone, the principal, pupils and teachers, five minutes to leave the school premises otherwise his police would move in and arrest.

Andrew felt a mixture of disgust, bitterness and fear welling up inside him. His mouth felt red and raw. His chest hurt where the stone had hit him, but it was nothing like the hurt he felt at the treatment he had received. Someone must have called the police. But who? And, for God's sake, why? What a stupid thing to do. He reached his car. The word "Sell-out" was scratched in big crude letters on the bonnet. He got in wearily and drove home to Elfindale.

4

Instead of turning left at Wespoort Drive, as he usually did in order to get to Heathfield, Andrew, on the spur of the moment, decided to continue along A.Z. Berman Drive until Morgenster Road, where he turned right to Swartklip and the sea. He knew that if he went straight home Mabel would want to know why he was there so early. He would then have to explain and he didn't feel like explaining. Everything was still far too fresh and hurt far too much. The alternative was to lock himself and his anger up in his study. He didn't need any sympathy from anyone. The decision to head for the False Bay coast was an impulsive one, but he needed the breathing-space in order to collect his thoughts and pull himself together.

He drove some distance along the marine road in the direction of Macassar and parked under a clump of Port Jackson trees. He decided, also impulsively, to go for a walk and hug the shoreline where possible. Although it was cool, he removed his coat and tie to be more comfortable.

He looked at his surroundings. The wind-swept landscape, which was deserted, supported some blasted bushes and trees along its upper ridges. Below there were sand-dunes dotted with stunted shrubs, a few everlasting flowers and occasional flurries of tufted grass. A wispy sea-fog playfully wrapped itself around huge, granite rocks polished smooth by centuries of exposure to sea, wind and sand.

Yes, of course he was running away even if only for the morning. He had managed it successfully for years since 1960, even during the troubles of 1976 and 1980. So this wouldn't be the first time. It might be the first not so successful time.

I remember a cold, drizzling evening a long time ago, nearly forty years ago. A small group of Apostolics were singing on the Grand Parade, the night my mother died, a small group braving the slicing winter rains. Two weather-beaten men strummed hymns on their guitars. A middle-aged housewife. And that small boy gripping a pile of hymnbooks. I can still see it clearly. How old can the boy be now? Nearly fifty? Grown up? Maybe a father or even a grandfather? He offered me a hymnbook, which I refused. And then they prayed in their tight little group. En ly ons nie in versoeking nie, maar verlos ons van die bose. But deliver us from evil. What I remember most clearly was the boy's knuckles which showed white where he clutched the hymnbooks. The same night my mother died. Can I ever forget? Long time ago. Long, long time ago.

Andrew slowly started scrambling over rocks and walking through puddles, and then increased the pace, wetting his shoes in the process, trying through sheer physical effort to forget the incidents of the morning, incidents that refused to be dismissed and constantly crawled back to be remembered. He skirted places where huge waves smashed against rocks, sending up lashings of spray. The roaring of the waves was punctuated by the haunting calls of mourning gulls.

He sat down winded, to catch his breath.

I looked down and watched the ebb and flow of the constantly moving water below, thick with oozy, slippery, brown kelp. Thick with brown kelp. Like people marching and intertwining, now ebbing, now flowing, now softly, then roaring loudly. Demanding justice. Demanding rights. Demanding the right to demand. Banners and posters waving like fingers of kelp, helplessly defiant. Helplessly swished around by the flow of the water. And intermittently the shattering squawk of gulls. Mournful squawks mourning the dead of Sharpeville and Athlone. The massacre of the innocents. Always innocent people caught up in the crossfire. A boy wrapped in an Arafat scarf to hide his face, pushing up his thin arm to thrust his clenched fist defiantly at a Casspir. Delicate pincushion flowers peeping through tufts of fluffy grass, showing a delicacy that belied their strength. Behind, sand-dunes shifted by the wind echoing the waves of the sea which carry the dirges of gulls weeping for lost children. Lost childhood. Long time ago. No, not so long ago. Last week in fact. This very morning. When de little black bull went down de meadow. It was incongruous, the wrong time to indulge in nursery rhymes and children's games. Children could no longer play games in the ghettoes. Children got beaten with batons, got shot at and killed. This was the twilight of the gods, our own gotterdammerung. An endless, endless Ring cycle. Wagner and Swartklip. The haunt of shattered gulls haunting shattered lives. For how much longer? How much? O Absolom, my son, my son.

Andrew got up and continued his walk along the shoreline, this time at a much slower pace. Suddenly he was almost on top of the man. He saw him at the very last moment. From the distance he had looked just like another rock, then suddenly there sat this small, shally ball of a vagrant, hunched over a deep, tidal pool, concentrating so hard on his hand-line that he seemed almost immobile as blended intimately into his surroundings. His clothes were torn and salt-stained, bleached from years of exposure to sea and sun. He grinned toothlessly and greeted Andrew in Afrikaans.

"Morning, master."

"Good morning," Andrew replied.

He could have stepped straight out of the pages of Steinbeck's *Cannery Row*; he could have been one of Doc's boys; or he could have been Alex La Guma's Joe, the beachcomber in *A Walk in the Night*.

Andrew was slightly annoyed at his use of *master*, but wanted desperately to keep the conversation going.

"My name is Andrew Dreyer," he introduced himself.

"Paai," the man said grinning and pointing proudly to himself.

Andrew wasn't sure whether this was a first name or a surname.

"Catch anything today, Paai?"

"Not yet, master."

Had he never learnt not to say *master*? The man used it as if it were the natural order of things.

"You live alone around here?"

"Yes, master," he said pointing vaguely at a clump of Port Jacksons behind them.

"How do you manage for food?"

"The sea feeds me. I catch fish and small crabs, and I gather mussels and periwinkles and I boil them all up in sea water. Sometimes I add a little potatoes and onions when I got them. The fishermen, they all know Paai. I get bait for them and they always leave me a little something. Maybe a bit of food or a little wine or brandy to keep the cold out. Others times, when it is really bad, I go to my sister in Mitchell's Plain and she gives me food and sleeping-place for a few nights."

89

"Why do you live alone all the way out here?"

"It keeps me out of trouble, master."

That *master* again. He had to rid Paai of that irritation.

"You mustn't call me that. I am not your master. You may call me Andrew or Mr Dreyer, but not *master*.

The old man narrowed his eyes and squinted, amused at him.

"So you want to stay out of trouble, Paai?"

"Yes, Mr Dreyer. I've had enough trouble in my time. Here it is only me and the fish and the seabirds and the dassies. Sometimes the fishermen but they go away again. I don't know what happens in the city and I don't want to know."

"Are you contented here?" There was no sense in asking him whether he was happy.

"Yes, Mr Dreyer. It's no use complaining. There's no one to complain to. Sometimes it's cold at night when the north-wester brings the rain. Then the sea is choppy and brown and the fish won't bite."

As if this reminded him, Paai whipped out his handline, but there was nothing at the end of it. He carefully rebaited the hook and threw it back into the sea.

"Have you heard about the trouble with the school children and the police in Mitchell's Plain and Athlone?"

"No, master, I know nothing about it." Paai had slipped effortlessly into his use of *master* again. Andrew decided to ignore it, if he could.

"Don't you want to know?"

Paai appeared to concentrate on his handline. "No, master, I don't want to know."

I looked at this pathetic figure and compared his position with mine. Whose was the worse? This badly dressed, forgotten man crouching over a pool of sea water in his torn jersey and threadbare jeans hardened with salt clots? Was his position the worse? He had hardly any possessions and if he didn't catch any fish he wouldn't be able to eat. No, he couldn't be happier. More contented perhaps, but not happier. He had contentedly accepted his position of inferiority. Happiness did not come into it.

Paai now asked the questions. "What is master doing here this time of the morning?"

"I'm just taking a walk to clear my mind."

"Is master a teacher or something? Master looks like a teacher."

"Yes, I am a teacher."

"It must be nice to be a teacher. My sister Lucy's son is going to be a teacher. He is in Standard Five now in Rocklands. He has a good head on his shoulders. He always comes first in class."

"I wish him the best of luck."

"Teachers earn a lot of money. It must be nice."

"No, it is not always nice."

No, in fact it was seldom nice, especially lately. I wanted to tell Paai how terrible it could really be, how depressing, how frustrating. I was there on the beach with him because I was trying temporarily to forget a world of police and beatings and accusations. But it remained at the back of my mind and crept unexpectedly up on me, even when I was speaking to the contented Paai. What makes anyone contented in this explosive climate? One could exchange happiness for contentment, but that could imply deliberate withdrawal and non-involvement. As I had done. As Paai was now doing. I had tried it for decades but had found neither happiness nor contentment. I suppose one can reduce everything to satisfy one's most elementary needs, such as catching a fish for supper, or getting left-overs from passing fishermen, or locking oneself up in one's study, or merely teaching children English.

"Well, Paai, I must be going back now."

"Thanks for the visit." He adopted a wheedling tone. "Master got a little something for Paai?"

Andrew felt disillusioned. Did contentment demand its price? It could be demeaning. It could imply the sacrifice of pride. Andrew searched around in his trouser pocket and found a two-rand note and some small change.

"What will you do with this?" he said, forcing a smile.

"Maybe tomorrow I will get a lift to the town centre, master."

"O.K., Paai," he said. He now wanted to get back to his car.

Andrew began retracing his steps.

Was Paai really contented? Was this a game he was playing? Did he not also feel resentment? Was he even aware of that which was denied him? Should he be made aware and turned into a malcontent, or should he be allowed to retain his blissful ignorance? Would it be fair to force him to exchange his fishing-line for petrol bombs? Can the whole world always escape to some miserable existence under Port Jackson trees, sheltered from the north-wester? There would always be north-westers. Sooner or later one must leave the flimsy shelter of Port Jacksons and stand four-square facing the north-wester. For how long can one hide until events or one's own situation force one out?

From the distance Andrew could see Paai inspecting and rebaiting his hook. The man was reduced to a tiny ball of absolute concentration.

5

When Andrew arrived home later that afternoon, the house looked deserted. The door was locked and the curtains drawn. Ruth was either not back from school or at her friend's home. Mabel was most probably shopping at Meadowridge or the Blue Route Centre. It meant he could have some extra time for himself. He needed it badly.

He unlocked the door and walked into the house. He thought he heard a slight rustle in the bedroom and looked in. He was very surprised to find Mabel sitting on the bed and crying.

"What's the matter?" he asked her gently.

She had difficulty speaking.

"Shall I send for a doctor?" he asked, very concerned.

"No."

He sat down next to her waiting patiently for her explanation.

"Is it about Brad?" He forced it out. There was a hint of anxiety in his voice which he hoped she did not detect.

"No," she said, "it is not about Brad."

There was an instant feeling of relief. No matter how hard he tried, he could not force his son out of his mind. He had a premonition, and it was growing all the time, that something was going to happen to the boy. He was mentally bracing himself for it.

"Would you like to tell me?" he asked as quietly as he could.

"The phone," she said, "the man on the phone." Then it all tumbled out. She had received a phone call a short time before which had been intended for him. The person had called Andrew a government stooge and a sell-out. He had threatened that they would get him. They also threatened to strike when they were ready.

Andrew realised why she had drawn the curtains and locked the door.

"Did you recognise the voice?"

"No. I was too upset. I took the phone off the hook and came in here for safety. I am frightened, Andrew."

"That was a very sensible thing to do. Now pull yourself together. Shall we have some tea?"

"God will punish people like that. Why do they want to hurt you?"

"You mustn't worry any more. It's only some lunatic or other. I could really do with some tea, what do you say?"

"I'll make it," she answered getting up heavily.

He accompanied her to the kitchen.

"You must tell me whether you are in any kind of trouble, Andrew. I want to help. There is nothing that prayer can't do."

"No, of course I'm not in any trouble." He laughed pleasantly. "I even had time to go down to the sea today, past Swartklip. I met a funny old man, called Paai. Now let me tell you about Paai."

Her fear remained. After tea he suggested that she have a lie down until dinner. She agreed and went back into the bedroom shutting the door tightly behind her. Andrew quietly replaced the receiver back on the hook, and then sat down to read the newspaper. A few minutes later the phone rang.

"Is that you, Dreyer?"

"Yes, speaking?" He kept his voice low.

"So you're back now, you dirty bastard. You are a traitor and a sell-out. We are going to get you."

"When?"

"When what?"

"When are you going to get me?"

"Very soon, you bloody government stooge."

"Look mister, I don't know you, and I don't think I want to know you. But, for the record, I am not a traitor nor a sell-out nor a government stooge. I never have been and never will be. Now if you will get off my back I will be very pleased. And leave my wife alone. She is not involved. Good evening to you."

He gently put down the receiver. A minute later the phone rang again. This time he took if off the hook.

Andrew retired to his study where he remained till early evening trying to work on his novel although his heart was not really in it. He decided instead to start a letter to Abe.

I cannot deny that events today have upset me, and I am very easily upset lately. My tolerance span is very low. Small matters worry me and I easily become annoyed. I realise that my attitude should be far more objective and that I should be able to take matters in my stride, but lately my nerves have become raw and constantly on edge. Minor things tend to become exaggerated and receive disproportionate attention. I am writing this down in an attempt to obliterate the events of today which culminated in totally malicious and unjustified phone calls to my wife and myself.

Writing the letter eased the tension a bit. He wasn't even sure whether, when completed, he would post it to Canada or not. It seemed as if he intended it more for himself than Abe, as if he wished to exorcise those things which hurt, by writing about them. He poured a stiff whisky and put a record on the player but could not concentrate.

Mabel and he had a quiet dinner. She was still jittery and looked drawn. She said that she had hardly slept. Ruth was, as usual, out studying somewhere. Studying or attending political meetings and rallies? Was she like Brad all over again?

After the meal they watched the news on television. The announcer stated that there had been no incidents of unrest and there was calm throughout South Africa.

Andrew had a strong feeling that something was happening in the front of the house. He thought he detected faint scratchings and muffled voices. He did not want to mention it to Mabel in case it alarmed her. It was most probably the neighbours' children or some stray cats. Then the doorbell rang. They heard loud laughter and a car pulling away. Mabel jumped up pale and shaking. He motioned her to remain where she was, and then walked firmly to the door and opened it. No-one was in sight. The road stretched away empty and peacefully. They were both over-reacting and jumping at every sound.

Andrew walked out onto the quiet of the lawn. Peaceful and green like all the other peaceful and green lawns in the neighbourhood. The night was dark and spun thick with stars. He turned round to retrace his steps to the house. It sprang out at him, the large lurid, red letters spray-painted awkwardly "Dreyer You Are a Sell-out." His immediate reaction was that Mabel must not see it.

He shut the door as casually as he could, then resumed his seat and picked up his newspaper as if nothing untoward had happened.

"What was it?" Mabel asked anxiously.

"Oh, nothing much. Maybe someone trying to be funny." He tried to concentrate on the television news items. He gave it up and suggested that they both have an early night.

"You go ahead and I'll follow later. I just want to finish the paper and write a short note to Abe before I come to bed."

"All right," she said resignedly, "but don't be too long. And Andrew, please keep the phone off the hook. Ruth can get in. She has her own key." She left for the bedroom.

He switched off the television set and tried to settle down to the newspaper. Another ring at the door. He hoped she had not heard it. He got up resignedly and walked as softly as he could.

94

"Who's there?" he whispered before opening the door.

"It's me," a familiar voice replied.

Andrew opened cautiously.

"Oh, it's you?"

"May I come in?" Eldred asked.

"Yes, of course, of course. Only we weren't expecting anyone. Mabel is already in bed.

Eldred seemed a bit nervous. "I notice you have some graffiti on your wall," he said as he sat down.

"Yes. And Mabel and I have also had two abusive phone calls this evening."

"Hell, I'm sorry. How absolutely disgusting."

"Yes, I daresay it is. To what do I owe this visit?"

"I tried to ring you a few times."

"I was forced to take the phone off the hook."

"I understand."

"Firstly I want to apologise for my attitude in your office this morning."

"That's fair enough."

"Not for what I said. I still stand by that. But for how I said it."

"That too is fair enough."

"I also came because I wasn't happy about the turn of events afterwards."

"And my role in them?"

"Yes, if you wish to put it that way."

"Well, what did you expect me to do?"

Eldred was distinctly uncomfortable. "I wonder whether I could have a drink first."

"Of course. How thoughtless of me."

Andrew fetched the whisky and two glasses from his study. He poured Eldred a drink but did not pour one for himself.

"Off drinking?" Eldred asked, amused.

"Yes, for the time being. Now tell me, what did you people really expect me to do?"

"Let me put it this way. I think we hoped that you would refuse to accede to the orders of a minor government official."

"What you mean is that you refuse to teach for the adviser?"

"Yes."

"Why, if I may ask?"

"For one thing, the political climate. I don't need to explain that

95

to you. I feel that it was extremely unwise and insensitive for anyone to have come for an inspection when the situation at the school was in such turmoil. He had been warned. Did the man seriously expect us to teach for him?"

"I can't see why not?"

"But this is an abnormal situation."

"It is as abnormal as we allow it to get."

"No, it is as abnormal as they have caused it to be."

"Look Eldred, the important thing is that we must get it to be as normal as possible. We add to the disruption by reacting the way we do. Our job is to act and not to react. It is to continue teaching, to continue filling in our record-books, in fact to continue carrying on the way we would usually do. If we don't do so we play directly into the hands of the authorities, the confusionists and the alarmists."

"Are we able to mark compositions while our children are being shot?"

"Cut out the melodrama."

"But it is true. Our children are being shot if you call that melodrama. Can one pretend that it is not happening and go on teaching? What will you do if you see your pupils being shot in front of you? It has happened in other townships, you know?"

"I will try to keep my head. I will try to help the children who were shot. But I'll tell you what I will emphasise and what I will not do. I will not throw stones and ball my fist at the aggressors."

Eldred felt his temper rising. "For God's sake, Andrew, be realistic. This is not an academic exercise. This is the real thing. Just where do you really stand? Are you for us or against?"

"That is the fashionable question isn't it? Where does Andrew Dreyer stand?"

"Well, where does Andrew Dreyer stand?"

"I refuse to be forced to answer that question either to the authorities or to you."

"Do you know what that means?"

"Yes, it means that I risk being called a traitor. It means that they scratch 'sell-out' on my car and paint it on my wall. They abuse me on the phone. They drive my wife to becoming a nervous wreck. And for what reason? I refuse to be forced by you people to stand up and be counted at your command. I refuse to be forced to play the game according to your rules. My son, Brad, wants me to play according to your rules. You want me to play according to your rules. But you must believe me, Eldred, when I tell you that I cannot do so. I must fight to retain my integrity and my individuality and to remain my own man."

"Even if it is open to interpretation that you are their man?"

"I am not their man."

"Then show us that you are not."

"How? By refusing to carry out school duties assigned to me? By refusing to educate children put in my charge?"

"You are the one being melodramatic now."

"Eldred, let us not score debating points. I insist on my right to do what I consider to be the correct thing. It will be very easy to throw in my lot with you and Joe Ismail. It is a very tempting thing to do. But my disagreeing with your methods does not imply that I agree with the authorities."

"It could be seen as such."

"It has already been seen as such. I have already been condemned. But it is a risk I must take."

Eldred was becoming more and more frustrated. This smacked of sophistry, here-I-stand-I-can-do-no-more stuff. He realised that Andrew was in deadly earnest and that there seemed a vein of truth, or rectitude, of stubborn honesty running through his argument. He would have liked to believe in Andrew but the stakes were too high for such intellectual and moral displays.

"Andrew," he said after a long pause, "I have always had a high regard for you ever since I was a schoolboy in Grassy Park and you were a teacher boarding with us. But I am no longer sure of that. I think you are committing a grave mistake. Our community has a long memory and does not easily forget or forgive."

"Yes, I know, they don't easily forget or forgive, especially those within our ranks who refuse to conform." He paused for some time. "I think I need that drink now. Will you have another?"

Eldred nodded. "I understand that there will be a staff meeting tomorrow. You were gone by the time Langeveldt announced it. Some staff and students want to taste blood."

"So Langeveldt is in for a torrid time?"

"Yes, but I think it is October and you that they are after."

"Well then, we have no alternative but to face the morrow when it comes, and see what it holds. Tomorrow, bloody tomorrow. Time and the hour runs through the roughest, doesn't it? But I have already had a taste of the things to come. I have already tasted blood."

97

"I must warn you that on this issue I stand firmly with the others."

"I appreciate and respect your honesty."

"Tell me about the new teachers' organisation you people are planning," Andrew said in order to change the subject. "Has it any hope of lasting?"

For a short time afterwards they chatted, then Eldred left, still in doubt whether he had received the response he had hoped.

Andrew retired to his study with his glass and the whisky and continued his letter to Abe.

I am not even sure whether this obstinacy of mine (if that's what it is), hasn't been brought on by my detestation of any forced conformity. Maybe it is that which brought it on. I realise only too well that non-conformists are at the receiving end of things. The world is governed and controlled by conformists and South Africa is no exception. It has no room for non-conformists.

This is a country of extremes. Those who are not absolutely for are absolutely against. There are no grey areas. They have been whittled away and what are left are stark black and white. And everyone is forced to choose.

Of course I have chosen, and paradoxically I have chosen that which would make Eldred and the rest happy. But I chose long before they ever did. Because they press me, I refuse to let them know. I cannot allow them to think that I have chosen because they have forced me to choose. I have chosen because that was my free, unforced decision. I wonder whether I will continuously be allowed such indulgences in this country.

6

Mr Langeveldt looked around nervously at the teachers assembled for the emergency staff meeting. He sat at the head of the main table with Andrew, as his deputy, next to him. The atmosphere was one of loud, animated discussion about the previous day's events, the treatment meted out to the subject adviser, and the subsequent police raid. Three pupils had stitches put into their heads from blows received from batons. The moment Mr Langeveldt and Andrew entered the staff-room all conversation stopped abruptly and was replaced with a sullen, expected silence. The principal did a quick count.

"Is there anyone who is not present?" he asked trying to appear as genial as possible.

There was no response except for silent stares.

He whispered something to Andrew and then declared the meeting opened. The principal explained that he had hastily convened it at the request of a staff deputation who had seen him the day before. He was not sure whether, considering the climate, it was wise to call such a meeting, but had bowed to popular demand.

"In spite of everything else, Eastridge will still remain an island of democracy." He laughed. No-one else joined him. "Now would anyone like to set the ball rolling? After all you people asked for this meeting."

The uncomfortable silence continued.

"Any volunteer?" Mr Langeveldt asked again looking around for a response. "Mr Julies, you were a member of the delegation. Would you like to start?"

Hermanus Julies was a young teacher in the mathematics department. He had come to Eastridge straight after graduating at the University of the Western Cape where he had had the reputation of being fairly radical. Once he had started teaching he had become subdued and now floated on the periphery of the Joe Ismail faction. He was popular with the junior classes because of his pronunced Afro hairstyle and trendy clothes. Langeveldt chose him to speak hoping that such a choice would prove to be the least provocative. Hermanus Julies got uneasily to his feet.

"As we explained to you when we asked for the meeting yesterday, we are unhappy, sir, about the events that have taken place. As a fairly new member of the staff there are things that worry me. I have three questions which I feel require immediate answers. Firstly, who agreed to the subject adviser's coming? Secondly, who decided that we should teach for the adviser? And thirdly, the most important question of all, who sent for the police?"

"Are you finished, Mr Julies?"

"Yes, for the time being."

"Well ladies and gentlemen, we have heard Mr Julies. Let us deal with the points each in turn. Concerning the subject adviser's visit, as I told you yesterday, I really did try to put it off, but the man insisted on coming."

"Did you have no say in the matter?" Miss Petersen, a young member of the English department asked. It seemed that the junior members of staff were initiating the onslaught. Events were taking the shape of an orchestrated pattern.

"No, I had no say whatsoever."

"You didn't think of warning the adviser that by coming he was running the risk of physical harm to himself and to others?"

"I told him so. It is what I suggested."

"Good god, man, you say it is what you suggested. Why didn't you say so loud and clear instead of merely suggesting?"

"Miss Petersen, it is not as easy as all that. In certain circumstances one really has no say. Also how was I to know that the situation would deteriorate the way it did?"

"But you do know now, sir, in terms of hindsight. Your excuse is not good enough, Mr Principal."

"No, I suppose not."

Joe Ismail spoke slowly and delibaterately. "Could I be allowed to ask Mr October a question? Perhaps it will clear the air."

This looks like phase two, Andrew thought. The big guns are now coming into play and October is the first target. The skirmishes are over.

"Yes, I'm sure Mr October won't mind."

Mr October agreed nervously.

"Who instructed you to teach for the subject adviser?"

"No one did."

"Are you saying that you volunteered? That you did so of your own accord?"

"No, I'm not saying that. I was busy teaching the 8Es during their normal English period."

"And then?"

Mr October was becoming flustered.

"Mr Principal, I don't like being subjected to this sort of cross-examination."

"If you do not wish to answer any questions you need not. Please be fair in your questioning, Mr Ismail."

"I am being as fair as I can possibly be. I am being fair to my colleagues and to my pupils, all of whom are seriously implicated. Do you mind if I continue?"

There was a challenging silence. Mr Langeveldt nodded meekly.

"So what happened while you were teaching the 8Es, Mr October?"

"I don't think that question is relevant. You are trying to force me to say things I do not wish to say."

"Such as what, Mr October?"

Andrew had not spoken up to now. He had sat staring at some

papers on the table in front of him, seldom lifting his eyes. He now felt compelled to intervene. Mr October was sweating and dabbing ineffectually at his brow with a damp handkerchief.

"I took the subject adviser to the 8E class and asked Mr October to teach for him."

"So it was you, was it?" Joe Ismail turned on Andrew.

"Yes, it was me. Didn't you know all the time?"

"And what did you hope to achieve by that?"

"What are you implying?"

"I am merely asked what you wished to achieve? Did you hope not to become involved? To keep your slate clean as usual? To play it safe and do the correct thing by the department?

"Mr Langeveldt," Andrew said turning to the principal, "I take exception to these insinuations. In fact they are more than insinuations, they are outright accusations."

The principal looked helplessly from Andrew to Joe Ismail. He was clearly unable to control the situation. He nevertheless made a feeble effort. "Gentlemen, we must not allow our tempers to get the better of us. We must remember that we are one staff, one school."

"The deputy principal insisted that I also teach for the adviser," Miss Toefy said in support of Joe Ismail. "I had no alternative but to refuse such a ridiculous request. Apparently I can be found guilty of insubordination. I am prepared for that."

"You yourself mentioned insubordination, not I. However I do not deny the rest of what is being said. I asked both Mr October and Miss Toefy to teach. I did not, at the time, consider the requests to be unreasonable."

"You provoke both pupils and teachers. You put the position of both at risk. And then you have the audacity to say that you could not see your behaviour as unreasonable?" Joe Ismail said driving every point home.

"I did not see it as unreasonable at the time."

"You did not see it as unreasonable at the time to ask pupils who had been beaten, whipped and tear-gassed over the passed weeks, to sit obediently and listen to a lesson forced onto them by . . ."

"By whom? Please go on, Mr Ismail."

"By a man who stands condemned as . . ."

"A traitor, a sell-out and a government stooge? Is that what you are trying to say? Familiar words, Mr Ismail, very familiar. I saw them scratched on my car and sprayed on my wall."

101

Mr October struggled to speak. He remained seated, a very lonely man. "You must please stop all this, Mr Langeveldt, it is sick. We are busy destroying one another."

Mr Julies got to his feet. "And what about the police raid afterwards? No-one has spoken about that yet. Our children were beaten up. I drove three of them to the Eastridge day hospital to have their heads stitched. My car seats are still stained with blood."

"Yes," Mr Langeveldt said, and he sounded most ineffectual, "That was most unfortunate. What more can one say?"

"There is a lot more one can say," Joe Ismail remarked. "We still don't know who sent for the police. Would you know, Mr Principal?"

"No, I don't," Mr Langeveldt began. "But before we go around accusing anyone, it could have been someone not connected with the school. The police could have come the way they have done in the past without anyone having sent for them. We must not forget that our children were being very provocative and were guilty of damaging state property."

"Why attack them when they are not here? Why not let them defend themselves?" Joe Ismail asked.

"I do not understand you," Mr Langeveldt began.

"The head-student and some of the S.R.C. executive are outside. Why not invite them in?"

"But that would be most unorthodox. We have never allowed pupils to participate in staff meetings."

"Then it is time we started now."

Eldred had been listening without making any comment. He had never been close to Joe Ismail, or formed part of that circle. As usual he sat slightly apart from the main body of teachers. Now he spoke quietly. "I wish to propose that we call in any S.R.C. members who are on the premises and allow them to participate in this discussion."

Joe Ismail was taken by surprise but instantly recovered. "I will second that motion," he said quickly.

The principal was also caught off-guard by this turn of events.

"If you are unsure," Joe Ismail said addressing the principal "why don't we vote on it?"

"All right, all right," Mr Langeveldt grudgingly agreed. "All those in favour, please show."

"Almost all the hands went up. October abstained and Andrew voted against.

"Will someone please see whether there are any S.R.C. members outside and invite them to come in?"

Hermanus Julies went out and returned almost immediately with Trevor Petersen, Gertrude Thomas, who was the deputy head-student, Shaun Apollis, a fiery, aggressive Standard Nine pupil and one other senior whom Andrew did not recognise. The group looked arrogant, passed pleasantries with some of the teachers, and drew up seats to join the meeting.

"Members of the Students Representative Council, you are most welcome to this special staff meeting. We have decided to call you in to hear your side of what happened yesterday. Would you like to begin, Trevor?"

"O.K.," Trevor began. "Let us put it this way. We have three questions to ask. Number one: who asked that government man to come? Number two: who insisted that the staff must teach for him? And number three: who called in the police yesterday? The pupil mass wants the answers to these three questions."

Andrew shook his head and spoke loudly to no-one in particular. "We heard these same questions at the beginning of this meeting. The wording is almost identical." He smiled knowingly.

"So what if it is?" Trevor challenged him. "Are you saying that we were told to ask this? Are you saying that we can't think for ourselves?"

Andrew ignored him and spoke directly to the principal. "Mr Langeveldt, we heard Mr Julies posing those very questions this morning. Even the order is the same."

"What are you suggesting," Hermanus Julies said, getting angrily to his feet. "Are you saying that we connived with the S.R.C. before this meeting?"

"Do you mean we can't have our own opinions? Do you mean we are stupid?" Trevor asked indignantly.

"Mr Principal," Joe Ismail said, getting up slowly, "I wish to raise the strongest objection to the insinuations of the deputy. It is an insult to both pupils and staff. I wish to object in the strongest terms to his attitude which runs contrary to that of all progressive persons who are present. He has admitted that it was he who insisted that staff members teach for the adviser. He has in this meeting seen fit to defend that action which ran counter to the feelings of his colleagues and pupils. Also at this very meeting, he is the only one who has voted against pupils being allowed to be present. This is my question which I ask because I am not sure of the answer. What is the role that the deputy principal is playing? Only he can enlighten us."

Andrew remained silent throughout the attack.

Trevor was still on his feet. "I also want to ask Mr Dreyer a question."

Andrew chose to ignore him and concentrated on the papers in front of him.

"Mr Dreyer," Trevor continued, "last Wednesday, exactly eight days ago, we had the Mandela march from Athlone to Pollsmoor. I saw you at Hewat. Is that correct?"

This surprised those staff members who had not heard of Andrew's presence there.

"I spoke to you then. Is that also correct?"

Andrew continued to ignore him.

"I asked you whether you were joining the march to show solidarity with our leader. What was your answer?"

"You tell me," Andrew said, dropping his guard.

"I'll do better and tell the other staff members. Mr Dreyer told me that he was not there to march. He was there to look for his son. Let him deny that."

There were angry comments from those hearing this for the first time.

"And that, gentlemen, is the type of deputy principal we have. Mr Dreyer is nothing but a sell-out!"

"Yes," Andrew said quietly, "You don't need to repeat that. It is already written on my car and on my wall."

Shaun Apollis whispered something to Trevor. "Mr Principal, Mr Apollis wishes to say something."

Shaun got to his feet. He wore an Eastridge tracksuit top full of badges inscribed with political slogans.

"We want to inform the staff on behalf of the S.R.C. that we are calling a mass meeting of pupils tomorrow, Friday, outside the hall. We expect every staff member, as well as the principal and deputy, to be there. We will ask each of you to state individually what your political views are, where you stand in the struggle. The mass wants to know."

"I cannot allow that," Mr Langeveldt objected.

"I can see nothing wrong with it. It is a legitimate request," Mr Julies said. "I know of other principals in Mitchell's Plain who have allowed it."

"But I cannot subject any member of my staff to such an indignity."

"Why don't you ask the staff how they feel?" Joe Ismail asked. "All those who are not afraid of declaring their poliltical views publicly, please raise your hands." He raised his even while he was speaking.

A host of other hands went up. Eldred, Mr October and Andrew did not vote.

"You see, Mr Principal, most of us have nothing to hide. Trevor, you can tell your S.R.C. that all of us progressive teachers on the staff will be there."

Andrew got slowly to his feet gathering his papers. He looked at no-one while he spoke. He tried to keep his voice even. "My political views are my own. It is only of concern to others if it directly affects them. That is what democracy is all about, the right to have views of one's own which are private. I cannot see why I must be subjected to the public humiliation of having to declare exactly where I stand. If you don't know by now, then you will never know. I shall therefore not be present at tomorrow's mass meeting as I regard it as an infringement of my democratic rights."

He picked up his papers and, in the silence that followed, left the staff-room.

7

So much is happening to me, Abe, so much with which I must cope. After I left that staff meeting, having refused to agree to declare publicly my political beliefs, I felt totally rejected and absolutely disillusioned. If I could have resigned as a teacher at that moment I would have done so. I seemed to have lost the will to fight back. I drove straight to my panel-beaters in Rylands hoping that with their blow-torches they could also burn away my traumatic, personal experiences.

Over the past years I had gruadlly withdrawn myself physically and mentally from happenings around me. Maybe it was a defence mechanism. Sometimes I withdrew for years. At other times it was overnight or for a few days only. My study became my island insulated from the outside world. But sooner or later that world would surge back and engulf my haven. The phone would ring, the postman would deliver letters, Mabel would ask questions or supply snippets of news, the newsboy would drop the Argus and I would reluctantly be dragged back into this real world of unavoidable turmoil and enforced involvement.

This evening's headlines read "Night of Violence. The Battle of Belgravia Road (pictures page 17)." "Le Grange and Malan Flying In." The news items describe a kilometre-long battleground in which pupils from Belgravia Senior Secondary School, who were throwing bombs and stones, clashed with riot police. In Belhar, a nineteen-year-old youth was shot dead by police after a bus had been stoned and set alight. A railway policeman twice drove off a crowd of people who attacked his home in Scottsdene. Police said that one person might have been injured.

I took my car to the workshop this afternoon to have the scratches removed. Although I knew the manager quite well, I did not feel that I should explain anything to him. He also did not ask any embarrassing questions. At one stage I thought he might refuse to continue with the job as a sign of solidarity with the community. After all it is a risk to assist a "sell-out". Yes, Abe, it did hurt.

I spent the latter part of the afternoon scraping, washing down and repainting my wall. Mabel remained indoors and refused to come out until I could assure her that the markings had all been removed. I wonder whether by having the car resprayed and by repainting the wall, I am really obliterating all the pain and accusations. On the surface maybe, but not deep down in my psyche where it aches the most.

I chose not to go out this evening. No-one visited us and I took the phone off the hook. Mabel went to a church service and came back recharged and replenished. If only this could happen to me. If only I could pray my problems away. I suppose I am now paying the price for my obstinacy and agnosticism.

Tomorrow the members of staff are supposed to appear before the pupils' tribunal and individually declare their political stand. I wonder whether Eldred will agree to do this? I shall be going to school but will not allow myself to be humiliated in such a way. I am prepared for anything, even for physical assault. And as for poor Mr October, I sincerely hope that he stays absent tomorrow and develops a diplomatic illness. I have no sympathy with the principal whatsoever. The man is a pathetic rather than tragic figure. He has accepted a position for which he is totally inadequate.

I object with every fibre of my being to being forced to declare myself publicly. It doesn't matter whether the coercion comes from pupils, political activists or the state itself. I cannot be party to such an undemocratic process. I am prepared to answer only to whose to whom I am accountable and only when I have personally resolved to do so. If freedom implies absence of restraint, then I will fight for the retention of that freedom and against any form of restraint. It cannot be otherwise. So, Abe, tomorrow I shall go to school and hope to be allowed to behave as I usually do.

He used Mabel's car to get to Eastridge. He was aware of the children milling around, some displaying posters. He spotted two which read

106

"Free All Detainees" and "No Detention Without Trial". The pupils seemed indifferent to him, although some seniors passed remarks about the car he was using. Andrew was about to enter his office when Miss Russell came hurrying up to him.

"Good morning, Mr Dreyer."

"Good morning to you, Miss Russell."

"There was an announcement over the intercom that the principal wants to see you immediately in his office. Did you get it?"

"No. Thank you for the message."

She lingered on wanting to start a conversation.

"Wasn't that a dreadful meeting yesterday?"

"In some respects I suppose it was. But I've been to worse," he said neutrally.

"I told my sister-in-law, Minnie, I board with them in Westridge, I told Minnie just this morning that I was certainly not going to get up in front of all these children and talk about politics. I don't understand anything about politics, so what do they expect me to say? I told Minnie how rude they were and what they did to your car on Wednesday. That Trevor is really an impossible boy. Nothing but a *skollie* if you ask me. You know his mother was married twice? Her first husband . . .

"Thank you very much for the message, Miss Russell, I think I had better see the principal as soon as I have dropped my bag in my office."

Andrew found five others sitting with Mr Langeveldt in his office. Staff members present were Mr Hermanus Julies, Miss Toefy and Eldred. There were also two pupils, Shaun Apollis and Gertrude Thomas. He noticed immediately that Joe Ismail and Trevor Petersen were not there.

"Morning, Mr Dreyer, please have a seat. You received my message?"

Andrew nodded and sat down puzzled.

"Have you heard the latest?" the principal asked.

"No, I'm afraid not."

"There were police raids throughout the Western Cape during the early hours of this morning. More than a hundred and fifty people have been detained, including Joe Ismail."

Andrew stared in disbelief.

Shaun Apollis added quickly, "They also raided Trevor's house, but he was not sleeping at home last night, so they didn't get him."

"That's terrible news," Andrew said.

Shaun continued. "The S.R.C. will be having an emergency meeting as soon as we leave here. The mass meeting scheduled for today is called off."

Mr Langeveldt felt relieved but felt it wiser not to show it.

"There is also a public meeting organised by all regional U.D.F. affiliates. It is scheduled for tomorrow evening at the Rocklands Civic Centre, to protest against this latest spate of detentions. They want a teacher from Eastridge to speak."

"No, that won't be possible," Mr Langeveldt said shaking his head. "I cannot expose any of my teachers. We are public servants."

"Mr Ismail is also a public servant but that has not prevented him from being detained," Miss Toefy said heatedly.

"What about you, Mr Julies?" Shaun suggested. "Will you be willing to speak?"

Hermanus remained quiet. He had not bargained on that.

There was a long ensuing silence.

"Well," Eldred said speaking briskly, "I will then suggest that we ask Mr Dreyer, Mr Andrew Dreyer, to speak on behalf of the staff."

Andrew was taken completely by surprise.

"So, will you speak?" Eldred asked him pointedly, a slightly challenging smile around his lips.

Andrew took some time to answer. "Yes," he said uncertainly, "yes, all right, I will speak."

Shaun and Gertrude exchanged uneasy looks. Miss Toefy kept a tight-lipped silence. The principal stared at Andrew as if he thought his deputy had gone mad.

"I am not happy about that, Mr Dreyer."

"A colleague has been detailed without trial," Andrew answered slowly. "Many others have also been detained. You, yourself gave the figure as over a hundred and fifty. I am in principle against any form of detention without trial. My personal relationship with Mr Ismail has nothing to do with it. No-one is forcing this on me. I am volunteering to represent our school as a speaker at a public protest meeting."

"Yes, and I think it is an excellent idea," Eldred said taking command of the situation. "Now what time does the meeting start, Shaun?"

"At about eight, I suppose."

"All right Mr Dreyer, I'll pick you up at your home at seven-thirty. Is there anything else we need to discuss, Mr Langeveldt?"

"No, no. I don't think so. Not at the moment," the principal said bewildered. "If any of you wish you may leave now. Could you remain behind for a few minutes, Mr Dreyer?"

"Shaun," Eldred said in a clear voice, "you can inform the organising committee of the protest meeting that Mr Andrew Dreyer, deputy principal of Eastridge Senior Secondary, will speak on behalf of the school. Is that in order?"

"Yes," Shaun reluctantly agreed.

The rest left and Andrew remained alone with the principal.

"It could be dangerous. Are you aware of all the implications, if you speak at that meeting?"

Yes, of course Abe, I was fully aware. It was the same question you put to me when I decided to speak at that protest meeting on the Grand Parade in 1956, more than thirty years before. Remember the 5th December of that year when there were raids throughout South Africa? 156 suspects were finally picked up all over the country and flown in deadly secrecy to Johannesburg. About as many as are now detained. They then faced a preparatory examination on charges of high treason. The penalty could be death. Justin Bailey was one of those arrested. I wonder whether he has also been detained with the dawn raids this morning?

Remember also, I was invited a week later to speak at the mass protest meeting in Cape Town. There were certain uncomfortable implications which you pointed out to me. As a teacher I was vulnerable. The Special Branch would obviously be present. I might get kicked out of my post at Steenberg High, where I taught at the time, and could even be put out of the profession. You strongly advised me not to expose myself. I suppose if you were here now and advised the same thing, I would, as I did nearly thirty years ago, yet again ignore that advice.

"Yes, it could be dangerous," Mr Langeveldt repeated.

"Of course I realise that."

"Do you think the department is going to like it?"

"I am not doing this to please the department. I am doing this because I know it is the right thing to do. No-one is forcing it on me. I am doing it of my own free will. I wish to record publicly, without any coercion, my absolute abhorrence and rejection of detention without trial."

"I don't like it. I just don't like it one bit. You will be exposing yourself."

"I realise that. But I cannot wrap myself in a cocoon for ever. Sometimes the outside world does intrude and refuses to be ignored."

Andrew got up. He was about to leave when a thought struck him. It has been bothering him for the last two days. He just had to know, though he asked it almost casually, "Did you send for the police, Mr Langeveldt?"

"I don't understand what you are getting at."

"I am asking whether you sent for the police on Wednesday morning?"

Mr Langeveldt looked frightened. "The situation, as you must have realised, was completely out of hand. I had no other option."

"Then you did contact the police?"

"I had to do something."

"That was both dangerous and stupid."

Mr Langeveldt looked pleadingly at him. "You won't tell the staff, will you?"

"I'm not in the habit of telling such things to the staff. I will keep this information to myself, although I don't think you deserve my protection."

"How was I to know that things would turn out the way they did? I called the police to protect the adviser, not to hit the children. You must please not tell anyone that it was I who called in the police."

There was much that Andrew felt like saying, but he knew that whatever it was, it would hurt both him and the principal. He needed air, plenty of fresh air. The atmosphere in the office was stifling. He walked out and did not bother to look back at the pathetic figure sitting behind the desk.

8

It was early on the morning of the 7th, the day after Joe Ismail's detention, that, while still in the bathroom, Andrew heard the phone ringing. Mabel who was busy preparing breakfast in the kitchen, refused to answer it. Since that abusive phone call she had been reluctant to answer any other. His wife, Andrew felt, was becoming absolutely paranoid, especially about phone calls. He slipped into a dressing-gown and went to answer the persistent ringing.

"That you, Mr Dreyer?"

He braced himself. "Yes, Dreyer speaking."

He was relieved and annoyed when he recognised the voice. Was he becoming as paranoid as his wife?

"It's Mr Langeveldt here."

Must the man phone so early on a Saturday morning? Couldn't he allow people to have their weekends to themselves?

The principal's voice sounded eager. "Good morning to you, sir."

"Good morning," Andrew answered unenthusiastically.

"And how are we this morning?"

He felt like answering, "We are just fine, we are." How ridiculous to have to endure such banalities. He answered. "I'm O.K."

"Good, good."

There was a pause at the other end. Langeveldt was licking his lips and savouring the important information he was about to impart.

"Have you seen the newspaper this morning?"

"Not yet."

"Well, then you are in for a surprise, he said with relish. "As from today, the Minister of Education and Culture for the House of Representatives has closed 465 schools and colleges in the Western Cape and Boland."

"That's crazy. For how long?"

"Indefinitely, it would appear. Sixty schools in Mitchell's Plain alone. As from this morning Eastridge Secondary is legally out of bounds for all of us."

"What does that mean in actual fact?"

"It means that we are not allowed by law to set foot on our own school premises. I received a call confirming that from our inspector this morning. I am phoning you personally since you are the deputy. The secretary is telephoning all other staff members from her home."

"So where does all that leave us?"

"Nowhere really. If there are any further developments, I shall contact you."

"All right then."

"Just a minute before you ring off. Mr Dreyer, are you still planning to speak at that meeting at Rocklands this evening?"

"Yes, of course if it is still on. This will certainly not change my mind."

"I was hoping that you would have given it some thought and withdrawn."

"I have given it some thought. I am determined to speak."

"If that causes problems with the department, then I'm afraid I'll not be in a position to protect you."

"I didn't expect you to. Good morning, Mr Langeveldt."

"Just another small matter."

Couldn't the man get off the phone? Surely their conversation was exhausted by now. What more could there be to talk about?

"Remember the promise you made me, Andrew, that you wouldn't mention to anyone about my calling the police?"

Andrew felt like slamming down the phone. The principal's changing his address from his usual "Mr Dreyer" to the less formal "Andrew" was obviously an attempt to establish intimacy and bonhomie.

"Good morning, Mr Langeveldt," he repeated, putting down the phone without bothering to answer the principal's question.

The *Cape Times* had it on its front page "465 W. Cape Schools Closed." Above it, another headline, "Zola's Last Barefoot Run." And in a prominent position in a corner, an item which mentioned that ace Western Province rugby goalkicker, Calla Scholtz, was fit for the match against Free State since his injured ankle was mending nicely.

Andrew spent the afternoon in his study preparing for the meeting. He decided to concentrate on the closing of schools rather than the detentions. Others were sure to deal with that. As a teacher the arbitrary closure affected him directly. He took a yellowing copy of his 1956 speech out of an old file, and reread it. He was surprised at how relevant and pertinent it still was and how much of it he still remembered. It all came back so effortlessly.

You know, Abe, it seemed as if it were only yesterday and not as long ago as three decades. It was as if I were once again standing on the Grand Parade, the Congress banner fluttering behind me, facing a sea of earnest faces. I was speaking against the dawn arrest of one hundred and fifty-six members of the Congress Alliance who were to be charged with high treason. The Langa women, dressed in black, green and gold, were singing in the background, their voices rising clear of the central city traffic. Asikhathali noba siyabatshwa, sizimisel' inkululeko. *We are not afraid of being arrested, we will work for freedom. Not afraid of being arrested. We will work for freedom. It seems like only yesterday.*

Eldred picked him up at his house at 7.30 as arranged. They drove through Mitchells Plain along A. Z. Berman Drive passing Eastridge Secondary, and then turned right into Spine Road.

"Well, there they are again," Eldred remarked resignedly.

A police road-block. Red lights flashing on and off, on and off. Torches, guns and dogs. Stop, Police. Stop, Polisie. Lights on and off. Flashing on and off.

Their car crawled forward in the queue. A policeman greeted them in a friendly fashion, then flashed his torch around inside their car.

"Everything in order?" he asked.

"Yes," Eldred answered.

"O.K. then, you can go."

Both Andrew and Eldred were completely taken by surprise. This was far too easy. The policeman looked bored and seemed to be going through the routine without any enthusiasm. Others however were forcing lorries and minibusses from the black townships, off the road and searching them and their occupants thoroughly.

The hall was jam-packed and people spilt over into the foyer and onto the front portals. Some youths were shouting slogans while others were dancing the toyi toyi. The atmosphere was charged and feelings were running high. Andrew was ushered onto the platform and Eldred squeezed into the crowd somewhere at the back. People packed the aisles, sat on window sills, balanced on cupboards and even squatted in front of and behind the speakers on the platform. An enormous A.N.C. flag was unfurled against one wall. Behind the speakers was a U.D.F. banner, and posters displaying the logos and acronyms of affiliates.

Andrew recognised Lynne Davis of the Clothing Workers Union. For the rest there were faces, faces and more faces. He thought he spotted Shaun Apollis ushering people, but couldn't be sure in that mass. Mr Julies and Miss Toefy were most probably somewhere in the audience. Thousands of faces. Thousands of hot, sweating and eager faces.

Imam Salie spoke on behalf of a muslim youth organisation. Then a white, cassocked priest who ministered in Crossroads. Andrew recognised him from newspaper articles. Lynne Davis brought greeting from her trade union. Speeches and more speeches punctuated with poetry readings, political songs, and slogans. And yet more slogans. Viva the People. Viva the U.D.F. A Luta Continua. The Struggle Continues. The People Shall Govern.

The second-last speaker was Andrew. He was introduced to the crowd who applauded, as the representative from Eastridge Senior Secondary School. He started nervously and a bit unsure of himself, but as he became more confident his voice gained in strength and he was able to put aside his notes.

"Comrades, you must bear with me if I sound a bit rusty this evening. The last time I spoke on a public, political platform was in December, 1956. The situation since then has deteriorated to such an extent that it has forced me to come out of the cold and join you in Mitchell's Plain this evening."

A crowded Grand Parade, remember Abe? The Langa choir singing freedom songs in the background. Over and over again the lilting tunes, the voices blending harmoniously above the traffic noises. Unzima lo mthwele, unfunamanima. *The burden is heavy. The burden is heavy. Over and Over again.* Zibetshiwe, zibetshiwe, iinkokeli zethu, zibetshiwe. *The leaders are arrested. Our leaders are arrested.*

Even while speaking, Andrew was vaguely aware that he was searching for a face in the crowd. Eldred's? But that was absurd. Eldred was present squeezed in somewhere at the back of the hall. Brad's? Yes, it could be Brad's. He was always searching for Brad, hoping to find his son. It didn't matter where, as long as he could see him, could speak to him. Maybe it was not Brad but Abe he was searching for, the way he had searched for him at that meeting almost thirty years before. Long time ago. Long, long time ago.

"Comrades, Mr Joe Ismail, one of our teachers at Eastridge Secondary School, along with 150 others, were detained early yesterday morning. We wish to place on record, in the strongest possible way, our abhorrence and rejection of the practice of detention without trial. Those detained are supposed to represent a danger to state security. They are supposed to be guilty but are not charged. The state implies that such people are disloyal. Such people are capable of treason!"

And by treason, I told that meeting on the Grand Parade so many years before, I understand racial incitement, discrimination and political domination. It is the perpetrators of these who should stand accused. It is the state that is on trial. Already it stands condemned in the eyes of the whole of the civilised world.

If only Abe could be with him. Or was it Brad he wanted? Andrew felt isolated on the platform in spite of the huge crowd pressing in on the speakers. He remembered Justin's half-smile and thumbs-up sign at him, as he marched off to jail during the Defiance of Unjust Laws Campaign. That was a long time ago. Was Justin again in the thick of things? Or had he managed to escape the drag-net this time?

"Comrades, 60 000 women marshed into the Union Buildings in Pretoria in 1956 and shouted *Weee-e Strijdom, uthint' abafazi, wayithint' imbokodwe, uzakufa,* Strijdom, you have struck a rock. You have struck a rock. Today we can shout with those women's voices, across three decades, Weee-e, apartheid, you have struck a rock. Detentions, you have struck a rock. Racial bigotry and intolerance, you have struck a rock!"

Those who would divide us, I told the meeting on the Parade, only succeed in drawing us closer together. We must pledge ourselves to oppose all things that divide man from man, people from people, nation from nation. We are one people and we are one nation.

"And comrades, we must ask the question, why over 450 schools and colleges have been closed. Why half-a-million children of the oppressed have been denied schooling? Why this has happened to schools which are ours, not theirs, at a time when education should be a right and not a privilege? We are denied political rights and therefore have no say in any aspects of our lives, including our education. The struggle for a free, individual, non-racial, democratic education system cannot be divorced from the struggle for a free, undivided, non-racial, democratic South Africa free from racial oppression and economic exploitation!"

Weee-e Strijdom, uthint' abafazi, wayithint' imbokodwe, uzakufa. The struggle continues. You have struck a rock. Education for Liberation. Weee-e, apartheid you have struck a rock. Asikhathali noba siyabatshwa. We will work for freedom. We will gain our freedom!

The words came out of him in jerks, now trapped, now spluttering over. Andrew felt empathy with the crowd. The crowd felt empathy with the speakers. They and he were one. Yet he felt the loneliness pressing in on him, isolation in the middle of this sea of bodies. Looking for Brad? Searching for Abe?

"Our children are hounded, whipped, baton-charged, wounded, arrested and detained. Some are even killed. And for what reason? Because they protest against the education foisted on them. They protest against the brutality of the police and army. They protest against oppression and exploitation. And the state replies with their police and army, with the Casspirs and shotguns, with rubber and real bullets, with tear-gas, quirts and dogs. The state replies by closing the schools of oppressed children indefinitely!"

And then I concluded my Grand Parade speech Abe, by quoting that historic final dedication. "Let all who love their people and their country now say, as we say here, these freedoms we will fight for side by side throughout our lives, until we have won our liberty!"

Andrew as exhausted and exhilarated. He was sweating profusely and shivering with cold. He was isolated in the middle of a large, swaying, singing, chanting crowd.

"And finally, comrades, we are stating our demands here in Rocklands this evening as we have stated our demands throughout

115

South Africa for many years. But this time we are not knocking timidly at the door but banging with our fists. We demanded then and we demand now, that the doors of learning and culture shall be open. We shall not rest until they stand wide open for all South Africans, and we are able to say, with the relief of a fight well fought and a battle truly won, that we are "Free at last. Free at last. Thank God Almighty, we are free at last!"

9

It was shortly after 11 a.m. on the Tuesday morning, 17 September, after the troubles at Sinton seemed over, that Andrew drove from Hewat to his school in Mitchell's Plain. Had things been quite as bad at Eastridge as in Thornton Road? Had the staff and pupils there also marched into the school to face possible arrest? Had Langeveldt accompanied them? Had the police arrived with Casspirs, tear-gas and quirts? How would he be able to explain away his absence? Who would be prepared to listen to him? To believe him? Was Ruth safe? Maybe he should not be going to Mitchell's Plain but head straight for Steenberg High. From searching for Brad to searching for Ruth? Was he correct if he put his family before the struggle? Was it not wrong to do so? Surely his family was unimportant in the wider context? A microcosm in the larger conflict? As if to rid himself from all these perplexing questions he softly chanted "Allahu-Akbar, Allahu-Akbar" to himself.

The street outside Eastridge Secondary School looked like a deserted battlefield. A few locals stood gathered in earnest conversation on the street corner. Two armed policemen guarded the heavily padlocked main gates. Partly doused tyres were still smouldering in the gutters where they had been dragged. Broken rocks, odd articles of clothing and burnt and torn schoolbooks lay scattered all over the street. The smell of tear-gas lingered faintly in the air. Some few, torn posters flapped neglectedly from the school's wire fence. There must have been quite a battle. Inside, the school was quiet and deserted with not a single person in sight.

An old woman who lived in a council house opposite the main gate, was leaning inquisitively over her fence. Andrew parked in a side street and then approached her.

"Morning," he greeted.

"Morning, Mr Dreyer," she cackled, recognising him. "I thought you would be in jail by now."

"I've just arrived. Tell me, what's been happening here?"

"There was so much trouble, Mr Dreyer. The children and teachers marched into the school. Then the police came with their vans. Mr Langeveldt asked the children to go home but they booed him. I keep on saying that the children of today have no respect any more for older people. Then the police spoke to them over the loudspeaker thing and ordered them to leave the school at once. So they booed the police also. And then the teachers were thrown into the vans and the children were chased away."

"Where did they take the teachers?"

"To the Rocklands Police Station, Miss Russell told us. Some of the pupils and teachers who didn't get arrested also went down there."

"And Mr Langeveldt?"

"They say he's down there with them."

"When did all this happen?"

"I would say at about 9 o'clock because that's the time my daughter usually brings her baby to us. Then after the police left, some of the Spine Road children came and started burning tyres."

"Thank you very much, madam."

"There's so much trouble around, and the children are getting so out of hand."

"Yes, it's most unfortunate. Thank you again, madam."

He got into his car and sped off to the police station.

An angry, buzzing group of pupils milled around on the pavement outside the gate of the charge office. Three policemen stood guard to prevent their entering.

"Are there any Eastridge teachers inside?" he asked a wide-eyed, fresh-faced, young policeman, who was nervously watching the children. He seemed no older than some of the senior boys.

"Are you a teacher, sir?" the policeman asked in Afrikaans.

"Yes, I'm the deputy principal of Eastridge Secondary School."

"O.K., come in." He opened the gate partially to allow Andrew to squeeze through.

"Dreyer, *jou vark*!" someone shouted from the crowd.

Andrew chose to ignore the invective.

Inside, a small pocket of teachers from his school stood in the courtyard in earnest discussion. They did not return Andrew's greeting but went on with their conversation. He could sense the hostility. He tried to attract Miss Petersen's attention.

"Is the principal around?" he asked her quietly.

She did not even bother to turn around but indicated the charge office with her thumb. Then she continued speaking to her colleagues.

Inside the charge office Andrew found a very worried principal sitting with Mr October on a bench against the wall. Policemen were going about their business seemingly unaware of the two.

"Morning Mr Langeveldt, Mr October," Andrew greeted.

"Oh, good morning, Mr Dreyer," the principal answered. "Just excuse me for a moment." He hurried over to a small, dark man in a neat suit who came out of one of the rooms.

"That's Mr Cohen, the lawyer," Mr October whispered to Andrew. "He must have paid the admission of guilt fines already."

Mr Langeveldt came back to them. "Cohen says it is all right now. Fortunately it is only R50 per person, seven teachers involved so R350. It is lucky I brought sufficient money."

"Which teachers?" Andrew asked.

"Let me see now, Mr Carollissen, Miss Toefy, Mr Julies, Mr November . . ."

"What exactly happened?" Andrew cut him short.

"This morning some of our teachers decided to enter the school grounds with the pupils. No parents turned up. I advised the teachers not to do so. I knew they were asking for trouble. I tried to reason, but they ignored me." He shook his head despairingly.

"Well, not all of us," Mr October added. "I, for one, felt that we should find alternative methods, other than open confrontation to show our concern."

"So then they marched into the school," Langeveldt said fatalistically. "When the police came they chased the pupils away and arrested seven of our teachers. Then stones began to fly and the police shot off tear-gas and moved in with batons. It was terrible. I'm not sure how much more of this I can take."

"And they were so rude," Mr October said. "You should have seen the way they pushed Mr Langeveldt around."

"They even threatened me with arrest unless I ordered the teachers and pupils to leave the school immediately. Now what else could I do? I am seriously thinking of laying a charge of assault against that lieutenant in charge."

"And then what happened?" Andrew asked insistently.

"The vans left with the teachers. I managed to get most of the children to go home. Then I contacted Mr Solly Cohen, our lawyer. I could not get to my office at school, so had to draw my own money from the bank to pay the admission of guilt fines. We've been waiting here for about two hours. But Mr Cohen says that everything is in order now. I'm just waiting for them to be released."

The teachers appeared, led by a fussing Mr Cohen. They looked grim as they talked amongst themselves. A heated argument broke out between Mr Julies and Mr Langeveldt when the principal tried to join them. It seemed that the group had determined on bail, had wanted to fight the case in court, and were thus opposed to their fines being paid as it seemed to lend tacit approval to their supposed guilt. They brushed past a flustered Mr Langeveldt, ignored Andrew and Mr October, and walked out into the courtyard, greeting their waiting colleagues with clenched, upraised fists. There were cheers and the shouting of slogans. The policemen at the gates watched amused. Andrew hovered around on the periphery of the group.

Lifts were being organised to transport teachers home or to their cars parked near the school. Andrew tapped Eldred lightly on the shoulder.

"I'm very glad you're out, old man," he said. "Could I offer you a lift to Grassy Park or wherever you'd like to go?"

Eldred looked at him steadily for a few seconds. There was something deep and contemptuous in his green eyes.

"In case you wish to know, I can explain where I was," Andrew began.

"I don't wish to know," Eldred replied, turning his back on him as he went on speaking to his colleagues.

Andrew drove back to Elfindale, a lonely and miserable man.

10

Early that evening, soon after 7 p.m., Andrew drove down to Manenberg, still smarting from Eldred's rebuff. Was it necessary for him to tell why he had not been at Eastridge? Maybe he owed Eldred, and only Eldred, an explanation. He could go to Grassy Park the following day and confront him. Certainly some time before the schools reopened, if schools would ever be reopened. He was relieved to have found Ruth at home when he returned from the Rocklands Police Station. Very few pupils and no parents had turned up at her school, and there had been no police presence. He told Mabel nothing about the happenings of the day, nothing about Sinton and Eastridge or the events at the police station. And she in turn had not asked any questions, preserving a tight-lipped silence. He had tried to take a nap, to write down the day's events, to work at his novel, to read, but had been too tense and upset to make much progress. He did not leave his study all afternoon, and found himself counting off the hours and minutes until he felt he could set out for his meeting with Lenina. She must have news about Bradley. Maybe Brad himself would be there. He said to Mabel in passing that he was going out, and she displayed no interest. She was withdrawing more and more into herself.

Andrew drove down Wetton Road and turned left into Manenberg. He cruised down the crowded avenue searching for 464B. The designation *avenue* was most inappropriate. It was anything but an avenue. In District Six they had had streets and lanes, but here they were called avenues, as if that added an elegant touch, the vision of rows of graceful trees shading both sides of the road. Instead it was lined with over-spilling refuse bins, dirty gutters, and double-storey tenements badly in need of paint, rearing up from the dirt and rubble. Stapled to the buildings were spidery staircases, along which children scampered like monkeys. There were too many activities, too many strollers and hangers-on, too many hawkers, too many idle youths lounging around the badly lit entrances to dingy shops.

Andrew pulled up outside a block on which 464 was prominently displayed. So this was it. The flat he was looking for seemed to be on the first floor. He turned up the windows tightly and locked his car securely, realising that he was being watched by many inquisitive and hostile eyes. He was obviously a stranger in an alien environment. He felt his strangeness burning through his skin. But then, what made this so different from the tenement in which he had grown up in Caledon Street? The same sordidness. The same overflowing refuse bins. The familiar smells of poverty and neglect.

But there was a difference. The people in District Six, in spite of their deprivation, had retained their individuality. Here there was an incipient, prevailing sameness. A deliberately created anonymity. As if everything had been reduced to the same common denominator. Even the graffiti, and there were plenty of these on the walls, seemed repetitive. Too many Stalag 17 and Jester and Mongrel gangs flaunting their alleged virtues.

He mounted the rickety staircase to the first floor, negotiating open refuse bins, and then knocked loudly at the door marked B. He heard it being unlocked and then it was partially opened on its ball and chain. A face peered through.

"Yes, what is it you want?"

"Is this 464B?"

"Yes?"

"I'm looking for Lenina. Miss Lenina Bailey."

"What do you want with her?"

"I have an appointment to see her."

"Why?"

He felt like saying that it was none of her business, but instead said, "I'm afraid that's confidential."

"Who are you?"

"I'm an acquaintance of hers."

"What?"

"My name is Andrew Dreyer. She gave me this address. I am to meet her here this evening."

Andrew was getting annoyed at this ridiculous interrogation, at having to reply to a voice, and a face he could only partially see.

He was being carefully scrutinised and assessed. "All right," the voice said suspiciously, "you can come in."

The chair was unloosed and Andrew was allowed to enter into a sitting-room crowded with furniture. The door was immediately locked and bolted behind him.

"Lenina is not here at the moment. She told me nothing about expecting anyone. What time did she say she would see you?"

The speaker was a frail, grey-haired, severe-looking woman. She was obviously unhappy about Andrew's presence. Questions and answers snapped sharply out of her.

"This evening, but didn't give an exact time."

"I'm her aunty, Mrs Hester Bailey. I apologise for keeping you waiting outside, but one never knows who's at the door these days. Take a seat Mr . . ."

"Dreyer. Andrew Dreyer."

She thawed very slightly.

"I know very little about Lenina's movements these days. She tells me nothing. But let me go and find out. I won't be a moment."

Andrew gazed around at the room. Neat, over-furnished and over-polished. A black-and-white television set had pride of place in a corner, the screen covered with an elaborate doily. A display cabinet containing a variety of bric-à-brac. And a dining-room suite, consisting of a highly polished table surrounded by four matching chairs. Vases filled with plastic roses, balanced delicately on their stems. Victorian prints on the walls. A violently coloured Austrian pastoral scene. "The Rock of Ages", showing a woman in a flimsy, see-through garment reaching out desperately for a huge granite cross mounted on an island in a storm-tossed sea.

It all came back in waves of familiarity. Miriam's home in Walmer Estate. Mrs Carollissen's Grassy Park dining-room. The shiny furniture, the cheap ornaments, the same types of prints. A kind of aggressive, showy, decadent, Victorian respectability. The overriding theme was dignity and deference reaching out for the right to exist amid a stormy sea of squalor.

Could this be where Lenina lived? Would the place then not be under police surveillance? As if he transferred it to his own situation, he experienced an uncanny feeling that he was being watched, that he himself was under surveillance. He could hear Mrs Bailey fussing somewhere in the kitchen. But he sensed that there were more than the two of them. There was someone else, another presence.

He looked up to see a gaunt, greying man watching him from the shadow of the inner doorway, watching him. Then the realisation flooded over him and he was on his feet in a second.

Yes, Andrew, yes. It was Justin all right. In spite of the bent frame, the grey hair, I recognised him immediately. He was an old man, far older than his age. His face was dry and parched and showed all the signs of illness and suffering. But the eyes were still lively and amazingly clear. The Justin eyes of our schooldays. He came forward and we met, I had not seen him for almost thirty years. We embraced. A long time ago since last I had seen him, Abe, a very long time ago.

I remember the very first time we met. We had enrolled as Standard Seven pupils at Trafalgar High and were standing in long rows to be guided to our classrooms. Blazers and grey shorts and badges. Per angusta ad augusta. *What balmy, heady days. You must also have been there but most probably standing in a different row. Justin was right behind me. I had come up from Trafalgar Junior and he told everyone around that he was from St Philip's in Chapel Street. I turned around and asked him sarcastically where he lived. He snapped back, "In the slums." I replied, "And so do I." We became instant friends. Once I met you, I must confess that I liked you better, but believed in Justin more. I respected your theories but admired his activism. I knew your stand was more correct, but his was more appealing.*

Then the long walks we used to have home from our school in Birchington Street, along De Waal Drive, past Fawley and Lymington Terraces, and those blocks and blocks of flats in which Whites lived, past Upper Ashley Street School and Zonnebloem to Walmer Estate. Almost all a wasteland now. A District Six of ghosts and desolation, of rubble and half-bricks.

And those heated arguments we used to have, at least you and Justin. The fledgling politics, the facile answers, the enthusiastic analyses. It all came back to me when Justin and I met in that cluttered room in Manenberg.

It was an emotional moment for Andrew, who was usually reluctant to show his feelings, even to himself. Now he was glad that they were alone, that there were no witnesses to their reunion. For him, even with Justin present, it was a moment of solitude. Emotion was solitude. It was being alone in spite of others no matter how close.

They sat down and talked. Hester came in to enquire whether they would like tea or coffee.

"And Braam van Wyk?" Andrew asked. "Do you know what happened to him?"

"It's a tragic story," Justin said. "He was jailed for sabotage soon after I had been, and served ten years. After he was released he went into exile in Tanzania. Then he left for Zambia, I don't know for what reason, and then to Botswana. They say that he always complained that he was being hounded by South African agents. Three years ago he received a letter bomb addressed to him in Gaborone. He was killed instantly."

Andrew listened quietly.

"Remember that place he ran in Long Street?" Andrew added after a long pause. "What was is called again? Cape Town's Only Astrobolic Bookshop, whatever that meant. He had a poster in the window, 'Bring Your Own Wine' . . ."

They tasted the past, savoured it on their tongues, chewed on it, played around with it, and then spat it out in choice bits of reminiscences.

"And you, Andrew," Justin asked gently, "you are well, I suppose?"

What a solicitous question from one who was obviously not physically well.

"Yes, I am as well as can be under these circumstances."

"I hear about you occasionally from Lenina."

"Your daughter?"

"Yes."

"Does she know about our past political involvement?"

"No. Certainly not from me. She only knows that we have met before. That was after I met Bradley."

"So you know my son?"

"Yes, of course. He comes to Lenina."

"Did you tell him about me?"

"No. But he told me about you. He is very proud of you. He gave me a copy of your book."

This was news for Andrew. He had no idea that the boy had even read the book. He had certainly not displayed any interest. The two of them had never discussed it.

Andrew asked, fearing the worst, "Do you know where he is now?"

"I'm afraid not. You'll have to wait for Lenina to tell you. You know of course that they are looking for Brad. He has been on the run for quite some time."

"I suspected that. And Lenina? Is she also on the run?"

"No. But I warned her that they are playing a cat-and-mouse game with her. They are monitoring her movements hoping that they will lead to Brad and the rest. This is a dirty game, but Lenina seems to be indifferent to my advice."

"So when last did you see Brad?"

"Let me see now. Last Tuesday, I think."

"Here, in this flat?"

"No, of course not."

Andrew sensed that Justin would let him know just as much as he wanted him to know.

"What was Brad like when you saw him?"

"Fine, just fine. But Lenina will be able to fill you in with all the details. When did she say she would come?"

"Some time this evening. She wasn't very definite about it."

Andrew changed the subject to hide his anxiety. He realised that he would get no further information on that score from Justin.

"Isn't my being here dangerous for you? What if they come and find you violating the conditions of your house arrest?"

"It won't be the first time. But I have managed to get away with it up to now. If they do come," Justin spoke with great deliberateness, "then you are here to see my daughter because you are searching for your son. You have nothing to lose by telling the truth. My sister-in-law let you in, and you are sitting here waiting. I don't come into the picture at all. One's case is strongest when one is telling the truth, or slightly bending the truth. If you lie, you must be a very strong person to carry it through."

Andrew nodded his understanding.

"You are not in good health, I am told."

"Just a touch of diabetes, that's all. Nothing really to worry about."

Andrew could see from Justin's appearance just how far advanced his illness really was. He was playing down its seriousness. He was painfully thin and although they were about the same age, Justin looked very much older.

Hester brought in a tray with the tea. Her attitude was one of resigned acceptance. She showed no feelings towards Justin and was merely doing her duty. She found him an encumbrance. As she returned to the kitchen after putting down the tray, he nodded his head amusedly at her retreating figure and gave his shy, half-smile. The same one Andrew remembered from his high school days. Justin poured and they resumed their conversation.

"What happened to you over all the years?"

Justin briefly and in a matter-of-fact voice outlined his history. He spoke about the four desolate, barren years of the treason trials, his acquittal and his later joining an underground cell to sabotage soft targets. He got caught when an accomplice gave him away. The long-drawn-out trial, the sentence and the debilitating twelve years on Robben Island, endured with comrades like Govan, Neville, Achmed and Nelson. Island of shame. Island in shackles and chains.

"I contracted diabetes while I was there, and for some time was very ill."

How his fellow-prisoners supported him, watched over him, nursed him during the recurrent bouts of dizziness. The rare visits to a specialist in Cape Town, when, from behind the wire mesh of the police van, he could catch a glimpse of the big city, the crowds and the bustle.

"Then in 1981 my sentence was over at last and I was released. Not a day in mitigation. I served the full twelve years. I was brought here and immediately banned and placed under house arrest. Now I am my own warder, my own jailer. But I am not good at being a jailer and resent being jailed," he said with his half-smile, "so I bend the rules occasionally."

And his relationship with his sister-in-law. Hester had married Justin's younger brother James, who worked on the deep-sea trawlers. He used to be away from home for long spells. She was employed by a firm of nylon spinners in Diep River and spent the rest of her time waiting for her husband to come home on leave. Then

Justin had gone to jail and Florence had dumped their baby on her in Manenberg. For a few years there was something additional in Hester's lonely life. Eight years later James was drowned at sea. Lenina was at that time ten years old and at primary school. She was precocious and practically ran the home while Hester was working. Four years later Justin was released, and since he had nowhere else to go, moved in with his daughter and reluctant sister-in-law. Hester was cold towards him, and Lenina, not a teenager yet, was suspicious about this father she had never known.

The house was under regular surveillance, and the occasional raids were a sore point with Hester. Although Lenina was becoming more involved in politics, this did not mean a softening of her attitude towards her father. Justin loved his daughter but realised that their period of separation had been too long.

He also had difficulty holding down any job. He kept getting sacked even from the most menial positions, when his easily frightened employers were visited by the police. His illness was also an aggravating factor. He was prone to sudden blackouts and it was dangerous for him to be alone. With only Hester's income and a small pension from her deceased husband's firm, the family had difficulty making ends meet. Fortunately Lenina had received a scholarship from a woman's organisation.

"As I said," Justin added, "I have read your novel. It is most revealing. You write very well."

"I am pleased. You know it was banned for a long time and has only recently been unbanned. Do you think it accurately portrays our time?"

"Yes, it does. It told me much about ourselves, and much about you. I recognised many of the incidents and the characters."

"Why did you not contact me when you were released from Robben Island?"

"I didn't think it necessary. I had a home to come to."

Andrew knew that it was the pride of the man. Justin would not accept any charity if he could possibly avoid it. He resented the assistance he grudgingly received from his sister-in-law, and walked the streets during the day when he was allowed to leave the flat, searching for work. More and more he was forced to rely on others. And this was the ultimate humiliation, the ultimate penalty. This was worse than being jailed or placed under house arrest. Maybe this was the only way they could break him, to make him dependent, to force him to rely on hand-outs. To render him impotent.

"And Abe? Tell me about Abe, Andrew?"

So I told him about you. How I received that letter from Canada. And how I replied to it. I told him about our correspondence, about how well you were doing at York. There was not a hint of accusation or resentment from this badly hurt man. He was genuinely interested and delighted in your success. He sent his regards and playfully suggested a reunion on the asphalt playing-field of Trafalgar. The one we helped to build under the supervision of Mr Biggs.

I felt an overwhelming feeling of sadness for this desiccated, bent man who was old and young, broken and unbent, who had suffered and was still cheerful, even offering me advice on how to stay out of trouble. I spent a pleasant, uncomfortable, informative, distressing evening becoming more and more engrossed in Justin as he unravelled details of his story, which he told with an absolute lack of recrimination. Then the phone rang and Hester came in to call him to it.

Justin excused himself and Andrew sat contemplating just how resistant a person like Justin could be. How could they ever hope to break the Justins of the world? What made them even think they could? The dark princes, the exiles in their own land, still making like Fidel and Che.

Justin reappeared and sat down still wearing his quizzical half-smile.

"So then, tell me about your new book," he resumed.

Andrew told him about the novel that was about a writer writing a novel, that it was incomplete because it was waiting for the next section to happen, that it was becoming a blur between fact and fiction. That he could no longer tell the difference. That even the conversation they were having was part of the new novel. Justin listened until Andrew had exhausted the subject.

Andrew looked at his watch and noticed that it was getting late. "Do you think Lenina will still be coming?" he asked anxiously.

"No, I'm afraid not," Justin said quietly. "That phone call was to say so."

"Oh, was it from Lenina?"

"No, it was about Lenina."

"And?" Andrew looked at him with misgiving.

"Lenina has been detained. They took her away from a friend's place about an hour ago while we were speaking. She is being held under Section 29, so no-one has any access to her. There is absolutely nothing we are able to do."

PART THREE

THE TROJAN HORSE

Tuesday 15 October 1985

At 5 p.m. an unmarked, seven-ton railway truck, belonging to the South African Transport Services, slowly drives up Thornton Road. At the back are three wooden crates which each contains two policemen armed with shotguns, rounds of ammunition and tear-gas. The driver and the co-driver, also policemen, wear grey dustcoats to create the impression that this is an ordinary delivery truck. At the corner of St Simon's and Thornton Roads, youths stone the truck. Security forces then jump out of the box and open fire. Three people are killed instantly and many more are wounded. The incident is later known as "The Trojan Horse".

Dear Abe

It is early evening, just after 7 p.m., of a traumatic and eventful day, which is not over yet. If time and the hour run through the roughest day I would hope that that roughest day were now over and gone. Nothing more can happen to me, or am I merely being optimistic? I am sitting alone in my study, trying to recover from an incident that happened in Crawford about two hours ago. I did not witness the event, but came on the scene soon afterwards, and what I was told was harrowing and has left me flat and enervated. It must be the worst incident since the one on that terrible day last month when people decided to march onto their school premises. Since 19 September, we have experienced a mounting number of riots, arrests and detentions. We are back at our schools after a fashion. Sometimes we have children to teach but most times we have no-one. They are always at some rally either at Rocklands, or at Spine Road or at some other, somewhere in Athlone. The situation has worsened to the extent that matters are now chaotic and directionless. The only haven of sanity I have left is my study. I spend more and more time here. But even now, while I am writing this letter to you and writing up the events of the past few weeks, with music playing in the background and a good, stiff glass of whisky at my elbow, I am tense, jittery and disillusioned. How can people do such things to other people?

My mind keeps wandering back to that morning outside the Rocklands Police Station when Eldred (deservedly?) snubbed me. Of course it hurt me. Fortunately it was resolved. Then that business with Justin just two weeks ago. That hurt me even more. Unfortunately it was not resolved. And then also my futile and seemingly pointless search for Brad. I go here and I go there. I follow up this clue and I follow up that one. I go to mass meetings in case I may find him. I haunt the Hewat campus so that my presence is becoming an embarrassment. I know he is somewhere in this ocean, and I am sifting through it with a tea-strainer.

Joe Ismail and Lenina are being detained under Section 29. That's all we know. Where they are at present, we do not know. What is happening to them, we also do not know. Any attempt to get news fails. One shudders to think what might be happening to those detained. Some who have been released speak of beatings, humiliations, insults and threats. Others say that nothing happened to them and that they experienced no physical assaults. But they do add that waiting for something to happen is far worse than knowing that something will happen.

They simply came and took Lenina out of our lives. I have been in contact with Mr Alex Moses, the lawyer, about her and I have just seen him about Justin. The man merely shrugs his shoulders and admits how powerless he is.

131

I find that events happening here resemble fiction more and more. In a superficial way, I suppose it is possible to separate fact from fiction. But are they really different? Are they not different sides of the same coin? Something happens which is so improbable that it defies passing itself off even as fiction, except that it has happened and is a fact. Two of the many ways in which fiction differs from fact are that fiction is manipulable (the omnipotent writer) and is also able to call on the technique of coincidence. The writer has the power to move his characters around at will, can cause events to happen at will, and can come to any conclusion he chooses at will. But once life seems to behave like fiction, once it seems to become manipulative and coincidental, then incredulity sets in, and in the words of Oscar Wilde, "Life imitates Art".

At present, the almost hypnotic regularity with which I experience crisis on crisis, resembles art far more than life. It all seems so structured. Situations are sufficiently regular and repetitive to resemble selective and manipulative art. This is the confusion I am experiencing as an actor in, and a recorder of, these events. At times I feel as if I am not merely writing a novel about life, but that the events are writing themselves. Life writing about life. A novel about a novel. A mirror as it were reflecting not nature, but another mirror. What then is real and what is reflected? Am I writing a novel or is the novel writing me? And in the process is something qualitatively different being created? Can art ever be greater than the artist? Is that fiction or is it merely a fiction?

This afternoon, after school, I drove down to keep an appointment with my lawyer at his office in the Athlone Centre. There were few children at Eastridge during the day as most had gone to a rally at the Samaj Centre. I went to sign a sworn affidavit about the incident concerning Justin on the 28th of last month. It was terrible having to recall that experience, but I had no choice. It had to be done.

Mr Moses warned me that I was not to expect too much. Nothing might come of it, even if we were able to trace those responsible. Already witnesses were afraid to speak and no-one could be found who could identify the car. Justin had queered his own pitch by breaking the conditions of his house arrest restrictions. You can imagine how useless and powerless I felt afterwards.

It was a little after five, that I drove up Thornton Road. Just before I got to Hewat, I was forced to turn down St Athan's Road because there seemed to be crowds milling around near St Simon's Road. I entered the college from the back and parked. Then I walked through to Thornton Road. The scene on the corner of St Simon's Road was one of absolute devastation. Casspirs and vans were parked in the road. A large South African Transport Service truck was also parked there. A house opposite looked as if it had suffered a bomb blast. The wall was smashed and windows all broken. Two policemen were guarding the door. On the pavement about twenty dejected youths were sitting under police guard. They looked very *frightened and one girl was beside herself and hysterical. There were two dead bodies lying on the ground and I saw a policeman covering one with his overcoat. The crowd was in a vicious mood and a small group chanted "Murderers! murderers!"*

Then an ambulance screeched up. The door of the house opened and an hysterical woman led two bleeding little children out. A bystander said that the children had been shot while inside their house. Then another covered body was carried out of the house. Three dead bodies.

Someone tapped me on the shoulder, and a youth in an Arafat scarf asked me whether I had a car. I told him that I did and he beckoned me to follow him. Once we were clear of the crowd he explained that one of their comrades had been shot and was being hidden behind a shop in Camberwell Road. They needed a car to get him urgently to a private doctor in Rylands. Hospitals were no longer trusted. Of course I agreed to help immediately.

1

The youth, his scarf now dangling around his neck, walked hurriedly to the car with Andrew. He mentioned that his name was Jonathan but omitted either by accident or design, to give his surname. He tended to speak in a pained way as if the words were being squeezed out of him, forcing him to concede or agree.

They drove the short distance from Hewat to Camberwell Road where Jonathan told Andrew to stop. The youth got out, deftly skipped a wall and disappeared into a lane behind a small, grimy, grocery shop. He reappeared almost immediately, checked whether the road was clear and beckoned to someone or other who was out of sight. Two youths came out supporting a third who was almost unconscious and covered in blood. They eased him gently into the backseat and one of the youths got in next to him and placed the injured boy's head on his lap. Jonathan, who seemed to be the leader, gave instructions to the other boy. Andrew overheard that the hurt boy was called Shane and that he lived somewhere in Boeschoten Road. The other youngster was instructed to go and inform Shane's parents of what had happened to their son.

"O.K. This is Waheed," Jonathan said as they pulled away. "He's my comrade. So is Shane. The bastards shot him in cold blood. He's only sixteen and in Standard Eight at Ned Doman."

"My name is Andrew Dreyer. I teach at Eastridge in Mitchell's Plain. Tell me where and when did they shoot him?"

"About twenty minutes ago on the corner of St Simon's Road. We had to carry him here otherwise they would have thrown him in jail."

"Tell me exactly what happened," Andrew asked.

"O.K.," Jonathan said, "so we were throwing stones at trucks and vans."

"Why did you have to do that?" Andrew asked.

"We throw stones at any cars or trucks we think belong to white people. We've had enough of their quirts and tear-gas. O.K., so we got no guns, but we can still throw stones."

Shane moaned at the back and Waheed told him gently that they would soon get him to a doctor.

"Is he all right?" Andrew asked looking anxiously into his rearview mirror.

"He's still bleeding a bit," Waheed said, "I think we're messing up your car."

"That's all right."

There was a short pause as Andrew turned into College Road. He resumed the discussion.

"But if you just throw stones at any vans . . ."

"White people's vans."

"All right, at any white people's vans, couldn't you injure innocent drivers in the process?"

"O.K.," Jonathan replied quickly, "O.K. So we injure innocent drivers. But what about the innocent people they injure and kill?" I saw two dead bodies on that corner. They were innocent people. Look at Shane. He was also innocent. If they don't want to care then why must we care?"

"How did he get shot?" Andrew asked.

"O.K. So there was this truck. It was kind of yellow or orange, I'm not sure now. It's the one that was standing on the corner. So we saw that truck going up Thornton Road. Then we saw it coming down again. Then it came up again, only this time it had three big crates on the back which we didn't see before. So we thought that maybe it was a delivery truck that went to pick up the crates."

"And then," Waheed continued the story, "and then we saw that the drivers were white and had on dustcoats. Shit man, white people don't drive trucks in Athlone wearing dustcoats. So we knew something was wrong and we held back. In either case we didn't even have time to throw anything."

Jonathan jumped in quickly, the words tumbling out.

"O.K., so that truck stops on the corner of St Simon's Road, and the police jump out of those crates, and they start shooting, man, they just start shooting."

"Shit, and they are shooting people dead and they wound a helluva lot of others. And then they shoot up that house opposite and there's blood everywhere. And then they carry out another dead body from the house."

"O.K.," Jonathan added, "so we see Shane lying on the ground and he's bleeding like hell, and the police are grabbing everyone. So we carry him away through Hewat to Camberwell Road to that place where I took you. O.K, man, they wouldn't have got away with it if only we had guns."

Andrew was worried because no sound was coming from the boy at the back.

"Wouldn't it be better if we took him straight to hospital instead of to a private doctor?"

"Shit, man, that's the one place where the police sit and wait."

"I find that difficult to believe," Andrew said. "Are you quite sure of that?"

"Yes, man, I'm quite sure. So look what happens. Suppose we get Shane to the hospital as you say. So then they want to know why he is full of birdshot. Maybe they tell the police, or maybe the police already know because they're always waiting there. Then the hospital patch him up and the police take him away. That's how it works, man."

"It can't really be true. I don't believe anyone in a hospital would allow that."

"Shit, man, don't you believe us?"

Shane moaned softly as Andrew turned a corner too sharply into College Road.

"It's all right pal," Waheed comforted him, "we're nearly there."

Jonathan instructed Andrew to pull up outside a house. The name, Dr S. Moodley, was painted boldly on the glass window. The surgery was lit and the door open. Jonathan got out quickly and disappeared inside. He reappeared with a nurse, who directed Andrew and Waheed how to lift Shane and carry him. The backseat of the car was soaked with blood.

They placed the boy on a bed and Dr Moodley fussed in and conducted a quick examination. He was a small, precise man.

"Birdshot again. Nasty business. This is the sixth case since this morning. Tell me, how did it happen?"

"They were shooting at the corner of St Simon's Road," Jonathan explained.

"He's in very bad shape. Nurse, we'll have to phone for an ambulance. We have to get him to a hospital as soon as possible."

"Shit, no man," Waheed remonstrated.

"It's our only chance," the doctor said, "he's lost a lot of blood."

The nurse started phoning. When she had done, she asked them for Shane's particulars.

"What's his name and address?"

"Is that necessary, doctor?" Jonathan asked.

"I'm afraid it is. Have his parents been contacted?"

"We think so. We asked a pal of ours to do so."

"Well, the nurse must have that information."

"O.K., man. His name is Shane Pretorius. He lives at number 164

Boeschoten Road. He goes to school at Ned Doman and he's in Standard Eight."

"Are his people on the phone?"

"I can't say."

"Nurse, we can find that out later," the doctor said while carefully examining the patient.

"Will he be all right?" Waheed asked.

"Only if we can get him to hospital as soon as possible."

"O.K., man," Jonathan said aggressively. "So now you got all the details. Now why don't you do something to keep him away from the hospital?"

"I'm afraid I can't. It's far too risky. He must have a blood transfusion immediately for one thing. Could you please let the nurse have your details in case we need them?"

Andrew immediately volunteered his. The youths maintained an uncompromising silence.

The ambulance pulled up with all sirens going. Shane was carefully transferred to a stretcher and carried out by the attendants.

"You going with?" Jonathan asked Waheed.

"You blarry mad?"

"Yeah man, maybe it's too risky."

There was a brief pause.

"Shit man," Waheed burst out, "I'm going with him. After all he's our comrade."

"O.K., then I'm coming too."

Both climbed into the ambulance.

"And thanks for everything, Mr Dreyer," Jonathan shouted at Andrew. He raised his arm in a clenched-fist salute.

"Viva!" Waheed responded, raising his arm in turn.

"Viva, to you also!" Andrew replied in turn raising his clenched fist.

The doors closed and the ambulance drove off with sirens going and lights flashing.

"Good luck," Andrew said more for himself than for them. "We're all going to need it." He got into his car to drive home to Heathfield. There was blood all over his backseat and his suit was stained with blotches of red.

2

Here we must go back in time to follow another strand of the story. Four weeks before the "Trojan Horse" incident, that Tuesday, bloody Tuesday, 17 September, was the day the people decided that they had had enough and went to open their schools. Rocklands Police Station and Eldred's deliberate snub. Refusing his offer of a lift, refusing his offer of reconciliation. Eldred had never done that before, certainly not during the many, many years they had known each other.

They first met as long ago as 1952. It was Andrew's very first year of teaching and Eldred was in his Junior Certificate class at Steenberg High. A bronze, athletic youngster with laughing, green eyes.

During that year also Andrew realised that he just had to get away from Walmer Estate, away from the claustrophobic atmosphere of Miriam's house, away from Kenneth and James. He seemed to spend his childhood and early adulthood getting away. Always getting away. District Six, then Nile Street and then Lotus River. Only once he was married, once he had his own family, a wife, daughter and a son (he winced involuntarily), only then did he settle down and buy a house in Elfindale. After that he was determined never to move again.

The atmosphere in Walmer Estate had been suffocating and depressing.

One day he stopped Eldred Carollissen in the school corridor and asked him where he lived.

"In Grassy Park, sir," the boy replied promptly.

Andrew asked sarcastically where on earth that was and Eldred, completely confused tried to explain.

"It's actually in Lotus River, sir, in Second Avenue, just off Lake Road."

"And do you have to swim crocodile-infested rivers and fight Zulu impis when you go home from school?"

Eldred smiled broadly.

"All right, young man" (thirty-three years ago), "when you get home this afternoon, you ask your parents whether they know of anyone who needs a boarder. I'm thinking of a spell in the wilds."

The following day Eldred rushed up to him breathlessly and said that his mother wished to know whether Mr Dreyer would like a room in the house or to have the garage converted. Andrew chose a room in the house and regretted it for the next eight years.

The rest of the week he sat in his study and thought about Eldred and that snub at Rocklands. Andrew had looked on Eldred as his protégé. He had followed his career at University of Cape Town with great satisfaction. They corresponded during the two years that Eldred spent at the University of London on a British Council Scholarship. He had been the master-of-ceremonies at Eldred's wedding reception in the Wynberg Town Hall. And when their first child, Chesney, was born, he was asked to be the godfather. He was very pleased when Eldred decided to join the staff of Eastridge. And now this thing had to come between them.

He turned the incident over and over in his mind. He mulled over it, studied it from every angle, analysed it and concluded that he was to blame; no, that Eldred was unfair; no, that it was the damn political situation. He spent the weekend alone and unhappy, emerging from his study only when absolutely necessary. He did not wish to go anywhere or see anyone. A few times he was on the verge of phoning, in fact and actually dialled the number but replaced the receiver before anyone could answer. And when he heard his own phone ringing, he hoped it would be from Grassy Park. But Eldred did not phone and Andrew simmered away until the weekend, occasionally pecking at his novel between long spells of silence and inertia.

Mabel knew when not to disturb him and busied herself with work she was doing for some charity, and attending church services. Ruth was in Fairways for the weekend.

You know, Abe, I am sitting here in my study at Elfindale, this afternoon. I sat like this all yesterday afternoon and the day before that, in fact since Tuesday. The room is hot and it all comes back, those desolate Dutch Reformed Church Sunday afternoons in Lotus River when I boarded with the Carollissens. A heavy midday meal of roast beef, roast potatoes, yellow rice with raisins and stick cinnamon, and blood-red beetroot. And then the dessert (or pudding as we called it), of stewed fruit and custard or canned peaches and custard or jelly and custard. All as rich as possible to fortify one against the sheer boredom of Sunday afternoons.

And then the long, dull hours yawned and stretched themselves. The heat waves beat up from the tarred streets. Not a sign of a movement anywhere. The house dozed and breathed heavily.

I tried to read. I tried to prepare for school. I hoped that Ruth would phone. I hoped that you would call. But no-one phoned and it was too far and too hot to hope that you would visit. Sometimes I would walk down in the hot sun to the Petersen girls in Ottery. At other times I would take the long train and bus journey to Ruth in Rondebosch. Most times I just slept the afternoon away all of that Sunday, bloody Sunday afternoon.

Andrew felt in his Elfindale house the way he used to feel in Lotus River. The same Sunday afternoon boredom and listlessness. Mabel at church. Ruth still away. The house closing in on him. If he remained any longer he realised he would be squashed to death. He must get out. He made up his mind that instant. He got up deliberately, locked the house, got into his car and drove straight to Grassy Park.

Lucille, Eldred's wife, opened the door. She was her usual, pleasant, friendly self. Eldred must have told her about the events at the Rocklands Police Station, but could not have mentioned the incident between them. If he had, she showed no signs of it. Her husband, she said, was somewhere at the back playing with their son, Chesney. Andrew was invited to take a seat while she fetched Eldred.

Strong waves of déjà vu, Abe. Maybe not déjà vu since I had been there before, often before, for eight long years of my life in this very house, in this very room.

The heavy furniture, the heavy, dark, menacing pieces of furniture closing in on one. I could see Mrs Millicent Carollissen holding court on a Sunday evening as she usually did just after the evening service. Her vague, negative husband, happy to be inconspicuous in a corner, hiding behind his white tie, his symbol of office as a deacon.

The englarged photographs on the wall of her parents, posing in all their Victorian prissiness. And in the passageway, garish reproductions of Christ holding his bleeding heart and Queen Elizabeth the Second. Symbols of a devout royalist family in the heart of the Lotus River Bible-belt. And then the after-church guests arrived with their holier-than-thou look, and nasty Charmaine, straight out of Struwwelpeter was instructed to thump out her latest piano exercise for the guests, which she did with malicious relish.

Eldred came in slightly dishevelled. He must have been playing some boy's game with Chesney. When his eyes met Andrew's they went cold and distant.

"Hi!" Andrew said with all the friendliness he could muster.

"Good evening," Eldred said evenly.

"Well," Andrew began, "I felt I just had to come down here to see you. I think we have to speak."

"About what?"

"About last Thursday."

"As far as I'm concerned, there's nothing to speak about."

"I think there's a lot to speak about."

"Well, then, go ahead and speak. I'm listening."

He sat down, every movement correct.

"All right. Firstly I want to explain why I didn't turn up when you people walked onto the school premises."

"That's your prerogative. You don't have to explain anything."

"I will continue nevertheless, if you will allow me."

Andrew spoke slowly and deliberately, sparing nothing. He told of his search for Brad, how he vainly followed up loose ends, how he pursued clues that did not materialise. The meetings he attended in the hope of getting news about his son. The questions he asked, the phone calls he made. Then Lenina had asked him to meet her at Hewat early on that fateful morning. His decision to go to Eastridge. His changing his mind at the last minute, which he couldn't explain even to himself.

Eldred listened carefully, making no comment until Andrew was done.

"So who sent for the police?" he snapped suddenly.

Andrew was taken by surprise.

"I don't understand."

"Who sent for the police on the day the subject adviser came?"

Andrew decided to remain silent.

"It's all right, you don't need to tell me. We already know."

Andrew looked questioningly at him.

"We are also all unhappy about our admission of guilt fines having been paid. We asked for bail on principle."

"I think you are being unreasonable. Langeveldt was only doing his best."

"Doing one's best is like relying on one's sincerity. They are never enough. However that is his problem."

"And mine?"

"You should have been with your colleagues on Thursday morning instead of going off on that wild-goose chase to Hewat."

"Maybe you're right. But I don't regret what I have done. I am not asking you to forgive me. I'm asking you to understand me."

Chesney breezed in from the kitchen. He was a handsome thirteen-year-old with his mother's clear skin and his father's green eyes. He sported a mop of unruly hair.

"Hallo, Uncle Andrew," he greeted his godfather.

"Hallo, Chesney."

"Dad," he said addressing Eldred, "Mom wants to know whether you people are having tea or coffee."

"Both," Eldred said solemnly.

"Oh, come off it. You know, you're turning into a mean old man."

Eldred threw a cushion at Chesney. They seemed to have a teasing relationship. Andrew watched closely. O Absolom, O Absolom.

Having established that both wanted coffee, Chesney returned to the kitchen.

"He's a fine youngster," Eldred said.

Andrew did not reply. He didn't think he wanted to.

"And we're great pals, Chesney and I."

Andrew was sorely tempted to comment but realised that his silence was far more expressive than any words could be. They sat for some time, each wrapped in his own thoughts. Eldred felt his anger dissipating and an empathy creeping in its place, an understanding welling up for this sad man, this father and his fruitless search. The time would come when he also might have to search.

"Hey, Ches," he shouted to the kitchen, "tell your mother not to bother." Then turning to Andrew he said, "What we both need is a good, stiff whisky to calm our frayed and jarred nerves."

They talked between bouts of silence. Chesney went off to some friends. Candice came home, greeted the men and went to her mother in the kitchen. A quiet girl. Lucille joined Andrew and Eldred with coffee.

"Eight o'clock already?" Eldred asked, and switched on the television set. "Let's see what's the new news at the new court."

They sat through dull, uninteresting items. Swiss voters had approved new marriage laws. The French Prime Minister, Laurent Fabius, admitted that French spies had mined and sunk the Greenpeace conservation ship, Rainbow Warrior, in Auckland harbour. The United States would the following day accept the credentials of the South African ambassador, Herbert Beukes, five months after his arrival in Washington.

Then the face of the Minister of Education and Culture appeared on the screen. All educational institutions that were closed on 6 September will be legally opened as from tomorrow, Monday 23 September.

"So that's that," Andrew said, getting up to leave.

"It's been a long time, nearly three weeks," Eldred remarked.

They walked together to Andrew's car, the old intimacy fully restored.

"I notice your late mother approves our re-established friendship."

"How do you know?" Eldred asked.

"I saw her winking at me from her photograph on your mantelpiece."

Andrew realised that Sunday, bloody Sunday, was over at last. It had not been so bloody after all.

3

The following morning, Monday 23 September, schools had been reopened. When Andrew arrived at Eastridge, things looked almost normal — no observable police presence, no security guards, and the gates were wide open. Pupils were standing around talking in animated groups, others were horse-playing, a few Standard Sixes were kicking around a tennis ball and others were chasing one another. Mere school children, Andrew thought, but how quickly they could change into a dangerous, frightening, threatening, mob.

The secretary handed him a pile of mail and he went to his office to sort it out. He had just started when he received a phone call that he was wanted in the principal's office.

"And how are we this morning?" Mr Langeveldt asked breezily as Andrew entered.

"I'm fine," he said. Silently he thought of the principal how difficult it was to keep that bad man down.

"Good. Good. Please have a seat, Mr Dreyer." Mr Langeveldt picked up a letter. "One of the community demands which the S.R.C. brought me, is that we establish a P.T.S.A. at Eastridge. Oh dear, all these acronyms. A Parent-Teacher-Student-Association." He pronounced each of the words separately with distinct relish. "Now I consider that a legitimate request. I have thought about it and am following it up immediately. I am suggesting an interim committee of six elected members, two parents, two teachers and two pupils, and that committee can then elect its own executive from its ranks. I've had Shaun and Gertrude in my office a few minutes ago, and they are

143

at present convening a meeting of their Students Representative Council to elect their two members."

Andrew found difficulty getting caught up in Mr Langeveldt's enthusiasm. He listened quietly without commenting.

"So don't you think it's an excellent idea?" the principal asked looking archly at him.

"Yes, it may even work."

"It must work. The pupils cannot then demand that we publicly declare our political views. It will from now onwards have to be a joint demand incumbent on everyone, themselves included." He chuckled, pleased at his astuteness. "I'm having a staff meeting the moment we have finished here, and will ask the teachers to elect their two representatives."

"And what about the parents?" Andrew asked listlessly.

"Very good question, very good question indeed. I'm thinking of calling a meeting for tomorrow evening in the school hall. Thank goodness we can use it now. The parents can then elect their two representatives. The six committee members can meet on Wednesday evening to choose their executive and draw up their constitution."

Mr Langeveldt seemed proud of his neat arrangements. When not under pressure he was pedantic, patronising and pleasant. He then exercised a kindly condescension thickly larded with references and innuendos to remind the listener of his position as head of one of the largest high schools on the Cape Flats.

"So then, Mr Dreyer, I think we'd better get to the staff-room and get this over and done with."

When the two entered, all activities and conversations ceased abruptly and were replaced by an aggressive expectancy. Mr Langeveldt passed an intimate remark with a junior teacher near the door who seemed embarrassed and awkward at his unsolicited attention.

The principal explained that this was a special meeting. He then complimented the teachers on the way they had behaved on Thursday morning, the way they had maintained the dignity of the profession, and the way they had been willing to sacrifice themselves in the interest of their pupils.

Miss Petersen interrupted him just as he was getting into his stride. "What were you doing while we were maintaining the dignity of the profession? We saw you only when we came out of the cells."

For the first time Andrew learnt that besides himself Mr Langeveldt had also not been present at the demonstration.

"You must appreciate that I cannot answer that question, Miss Petersen. Sufficient to say that I was instructed not to be part of any demonstration of a political nature."

"By whom, if I may ask?"

"Let us say, by higher authorities. I'm afraid I cannot say more. I was warned that I would be risking my job."

"We are all risking our jobs," Mr Evans added.

"Ah, but there's a difference," he said arching his brows, the old Langeveldt once again becoming his patronising self. "I am the head of this institution and you are not. If things go wrong then I must take the rap which you need not."

"Could I ask another question?" Miss Petersen asked, obviously dissatisfied.

The principal winced.

"Who instructed you to pay our admission of guilt fines?"

"Oh that? Mr Cohen of course."

"Are you quite sure? I spoke to him immediately after we came out and demanded to know who had given that instruction. He said you had. He was busy arranging bail as we requested when you overruled him."

"In a way, he is correct. But I only did so under pressure. It was the only way I could get you out immediately. You might have had to wait until today for bail. A weekend in the cells is no joke. I was protecting you people. Your jobs were at stake."

"Our jobs are still at stake," Hermanus Julies cut in. "Technically we have now admitted guilt, we have admitted to breaking the law and committing a criminal offence. We therefore have a criminal record. Teachers can be dismissed from the profession for having a criminal record."

"Oh come, come, Mr Julies. Surely you are not suggesting that the Department would be so spiteful? After all I have your interests at heart. You have me to protect you."

"That is the danger."

There was mocking laughter. Mr Langeveldt joined in to show that he appreciated a joke even if it was against him.

Andrew waited for the attack to materialise and mentally braced himself for it. The principal was cutting a pathetic figure and Andrew was determined not to emulate him. No matter what happened, he would not offer any explanation. He would not give them the satisfaction of beating him down. He had done what he had done and

145

was prepared to take the consequences in as dignified a way as possible.

But the attack never came. It seemed that Miss Toefy and Hermanus Julies were not hostile towards him. If anything they seemed a trifle friendly. Was he imagining things or was it merely wishful thinking?

The principal explained the purpose and composition of the P.T.S.A. The staff debated the suggestion for a short time and then unanimously adopted the idea. They then set about electing their two representatives.

Mr Evans proposed Mr Julies which was accepted. Then in a surprise move, Miss Toefy flashed a quick smile at Andrew and said she wished to propose Mr Dreyer. This was also accepted. The meeting dealt with some other minor business and then adjourned for tea.

Eldred came over to the table where Andrew was sitting with Miss Russell. She was grumbling to herself while knitting furiously. Andrew was trying to read the *Cape Times* though his mind was trying to fathom this new development. While Eldred and Andrew were speaking quietly, Hermanus Julies joined them, cup in hand. Andrew tensed.

"Heard anything about Joe, yet?" Eldred asked him.

"Yes, his son told us that Mrs Ismail was informed that her husband is being held at Pollsmoor. Apparently he has not been manhandled and is well treated. Joe is apparently in good spirits."

"Well, you know, he has been an activist for many years. He participated in the Defiance Campaign in the fifties. He was jailed then already, so he'll survive," Eldred added.

"It's a disgrace the way they lock up people these days. I said that only last night to my sister-in-law, Minnie," Miss Russell said staring aggressively at her knitting-needles. "Mr Ismail is such a respectable person, I said, so what do they want to lock the man up for?"

"Do you think they have anything on him?" Andrew asked.

"One never knows just how much they do know," Hermanus Julies replied. "They may be able to throw the book at him. It is better that they charge him than this waiting and this not knowing. They break you down with time and insecurity."

"And how would you manage if you were detained," Eldred teased him, "and not be able to maintain your glorious Afro hairstyle?"

"There are ways and means," Hermanus replied, looking wise,

146

"there are usually ways and means. I assure you that I will not let my hair down for anyone."

Miss Toefy overheard his remarks, and came over smiling broadly. "You couldn't let it down even if you tried, Hermy. You know, Miss Russell, he irons his hair!"

Miss Russell pursed her lips and was not amused. She did not like types like Miss Toefy who smoked and involved themselves in politics.

"What men don't suffer for vanity," Miss Toefy continued. "Now Hermy, why can't you have short-back-and-sides like Mr Dreyer, here?"

The bantering continued for a short time. Andrew was amused but a trifle uncomfortable. He decided to get back to his office and continue checking the mail. As he was about to leave, Miss Toefy stopped him.

"Any news about Brad, yet? We are all worried about him."

So they knew. Eldred must have told them. That explained their change in attitude. They knew and sympathised. Andrew realised that he had underestimated his colleagues' capacity to understand and forgive.

Later that morning the S.R.C. reported back that their representatives would be the ebullient Shaun Apollis and Neil Ismail, the quiet, self-effacing, lack-lustre son of their detained teacher. He must have got in on a sympathy vote. Neil was most probably in a state of mild shock at his sudden elevation. Shaun added that the pupils were leaving immediately for a "victory" rally at Mondale Senior Secondary School.

Andrew sat in his office staring at the letters but making no effort to read them. He tried to savour this change towards him. He was confused but the overwhelming feeling was one of relief. The sheer comfort and solace of acceptance, of being allowed back into the fold, of being considered as one of them.

I felt I just had to go somewhere, anywhere, I wanted to taste this acceptability, Abe, to relish this feeling of no longer being an outcast, no longer being a political pariah.

So I drove down to Swartklip. I parked under the same Port Jackson trees where I had parked before. Then I took off my jacket and tie, my shoes and socks. I rolled up my trousers and started walking along the shore-line. There was a slight sea-fog as usual and the landscape was as bare and sand-blasted as it had ever been. Then I realised that I was hoping to meet Paai, hoping to see the shabby ball hunched over

147

a tidal pool, playing out a handline. Longing to see the torn, salt-stained, wind-bleached figure grinning toothlessly at me.

But when I arrived, there was no Paai. I went to a clump of Port Jacksons where his shelter had been, but there was no sign of him. A few rusty tins, some broken bottles, a dirty piece of foam-rubber that must have served as a mattress, and a fireplace that had simply collapsed or been blown down by the wind. The place showed all the signs of having once been lived in, but now abandoned. Paai had disappeared. Maybe he was back with his sister, Lucy, in Mitchell's Plain. Maybe the city had swallowed him up. Maybe he was in hospital or even dead. Drowned. Blown away. He was certainly no longer in his crude, uncomfortable, wind-swept hole.

I remember that letter I wrote to you soon after I had met Paai for the first time. I said then, "Sooner or later one must leave the flimsy shelter of Port Jacksons and stand four-square facing the north-wester . . ."

I wonder now whether I had written that about Paai or about myself.

4

On the evening of Thursday, 26 September, the meeting had been held for parents in the school hall. It was poorly attended to the obvious disappointment of Mr Langeveldt, who presided. Andrew had been told that he need not be present. Mr October, however, helped with registrations and told Andrew that after much acrimony (there were both conservative and radical elements present) the two representatives were finally elected. They were a Mrs February who was a member of the Rocklands Tenants Assocation, and a Mr Achmat Daniels, a council worker who was active in a local U.D.F. branch. He had a daughter in Standard Seven. Mr October added that the meeting had not gone as smoothly as the principal had hoped.

The following evening Mr Langeveldt convened the meeting of the six representatives in his office. He was determined to prove how well organised he was. Andrew arrived shortly before Hermanus Julies. The pupil representatives were already present, a bubbling, talkative Shaun Apollis and Neil Ismail, trying his best to shrivel up in a corner. The two parents' representatives were also present. There was something familiar about Mr Daniels. Andrew felt that he had seen him somewhere before. Then it all came back. Of course. At Alexander Sinton the day they had tried to reopen the schools. He had been with Lenina and had then mentioned something about knowing Andrew. Something about District Six. About Caledon Street. Did he mention Caledon Street? Andrew tried hard to recall the exact words but they escaped him. It was more than that brief encounter after Sinton. Somewhere in the murky depths of the long-forgotten past. The eyes, and the unruly, shock of grey hair were far too familiar.

Mr Langeveldt seemed inexhaustible. He immediately convened the meeting and called for the election of an executive. Mrs February was chosen chairperson ("Not madam chair or chairman, *please* Mr Langeveldt"), and Andrew was elected as secretary. The principal agreed to act as treasurer.

They discussed matters of general concern to the school and then appointed a working committee to draw up a provisional constitution. The meeting was adjourned to the following week when it became obvious that the caretaker was hovering in the wings, waiting to lock up.

Mr Daniels came up to Andrew.

"Could I ask you a favour? I need a lift to Beacon Valley. It's the next township."

"Yes, of course," Andrew replied.

Mr Daniels grinned broadly. "I can see that you don't remember me any more."

"I'm afraid not, but I must admit that your face looks very familiar. Didn't we meet briefly outside Sinton in the middle of all that trouble? You were with Lenina?"

"Yes, we met there. But you mean to say you don't recognise me?"

"Other than from that time, no."

"I'm Amaai, man, Amaai from Caledon Street. We grew up together."

"Good God!"

"Yes, I though you would be surprised."

Abe, to say that I was surprised was an understatement. I was completely bowled over. Amaai. Yes, of course. They lived in a house right next door to our building in Caledon Street. Amaai and his brother, Broertjie. And then there was Jonga who lived in a house opposite, next to the C.L.B. Hall. The four of us were close friends.

I remember a mad, March evening, with a crazy south-easter howling down from Table Mountain. I had quarrelled with my mother, one of our usual, silent, frightening quarrels, and miserably joined the trio in the doorway of the Brigade Hall. Amaai and I were both sixteen at the time. Broertjie was a year younger and dirtier. Jonga was a year older. He was a professional pickpocket who had twice escaped from Porter Reformatory. He always had money. He would treat us to a bus ride round the Hanover Street circuit, down Darling Street, up Adderley Street, then along Wale Street until we turned down at Bree Street. Near the docks was one terminus. Then back along Darling Street and up Hanover Street, past Castle Bridge and Star Bioscope, to the other terminus in College Road, next to Zonnebloem. We sat upstairs in the front rows, smoking, horse-playing and teasing any girls who were there. Sometimes, while riding, we would share an expensive box of chocolates which Jonga had pilfered from the O.K. Bazaars. Broertjie would go down the aisle generously treating all the amused passengers.

I remember our huddling together against the cold in that murky doorway, and their speculating on my future because I was already in Senior Certificate at Trafalgar High. Would I become a doctor or a lawyer or a teacher? And their marvelling at the subjects I was doing, Physical Science and Mathematics and Latin. Broertjie said he wanted to go to Paris to learn French, and Jonga said his ambition was to ride the range on a horse and learn to speak American like Charles Starret.

And in the gathering darkness of that doorway, we discussed our situation, our being slum kids, being coloured slum kids in a hostile, white South Africa. Our stunted longings against their avarice and greed. And the growing darkness wrapped itself around us until only the glowing ends of our cigarettes were visible to fight feebly against this depth of hopelessness.

It was a very long time ago, Abe, and afterwards we drifted apart and went, or were forced to go our different ways, except for chance meetings like this one, nearly forty years later.

Amaai lived in Triumph Street, Beacon Valley. Andrew presumed that *triumph* stood for *victory, mastery* or something like that. Some exultation for success or achievement. Something like *triomf* in the Transvaal which name they gave to Sophiatown after the Group Areas Act had replaced the former black inhabitants with working-class whites.

But once Andrew was driving along Cadillac Street, past Peugeot and Chrysler Streets and Volvo Crescent, he realised that these names were the products of someone's bizarre sense of humour. Like Klavier, Sonata and Piccolo Streets which were scattered around Symphony Avenue in Steenberg. Ridiculous but not quite as malicious as Hanover Park or Lavender Hill, which seemed so designated to remind the former District Six inhabitants of their pillaged past.

They pulled up outside a modest, two-roomed council house,

almost indistinguishable from the rows of similar houses on either side of it. The tired uniformity. The wearisome sameness.

Amaai invited Andrew inside. He immediately recognised Amaai's daughter, Gawa, who was a pupil at Eastridge. He was then introduced to Amaai's wife.

"This is Mr Andrew Dreyer, Gawa's deputy principal. We grew up together in Caledon Street. And this is my wife, Galiema."

In spite of her age, Galiema still showed traces of a delicate Eastern beauty. She smiled shyly.

"My wife is from Schotsche Kloof, so she won't know you." Amaai added that he also had four sons, three of whom were married and had their own homes. The unmarried one was still living with his parents in Beacon Valley.

They sat in the tiny, cramped lounge, the walls decorated with a reproduction of the Kaaba in Mecca, a mirror inscribed in Arabic characters with a quotation from the *Koran*, and a poster which read, "U.D.F. Says Hands Off Our Schools".

Galiema asked whether Andrew would like some tea, and retired with her daughter to the kitchen.

"So what happened to your brother?" Andrew asked.

"Broertjie went really bad, Mr Dreyer."

"Please call me Andrew."

"All right, Andrew. Broertjie wouldn't listen to anyone and went from bad to worse. He was in and out of jail. Finally he was killed in a gang fight in Manenberg. We were moved to there after we were forced to leave Caledon Street."

"I'm sorry to hear that about your brother. And what about Jonga?"

"He married and had lots of children. I believe he now lives somewhere in Hanover Park."

"We were very close at one time, the four of us, weren't we?"

"Yes, we were. I still remember the day they buried your mother, when you went missing and everyone was searching for you. We were sitting on Mrs Heidemann's stoep, opposite your building, watching the people coming to the funeral. Then Broertjie told us that Honger's ma drank a Bubbly Cola, so she died. Then Jonga said, "Den she fried." and I added, "An' she cried." And Jonga said, "On her side." And Broertjie repeated, "So his mother drank a Bubbly an' she died." We rolled over on the pavement howling with laughter. People stared at us because we were behaving so badly. And all the time they were searching for you."

"Yes, I had run away."

"We heard so. Your brother James told us. He gave us half-a-crown to try and find you."

"He accused me of having killed my mother. I wouldn't go out for her so she had a stroke." It still hurt. "So I ran away because I didn't dare go to the funeral. Afterwards I went to live with my sister, Miriam, in Nile Street.

"Is she still alive?"

"No, she died four years ago of cancer. I was very close to her."

Gawa brought in a tray containing sweet tea and koeksisters. She was very proud that the deputy principal was visiting.

"Hell, Andrew, man, it's good to meet you again," Amaai said affectionately.

"Yes, it really is good. But tell me more about yourself. What have you been doing all these years?"

"Actually we did meet some time after you left the District. On the Grand Parade in fact, when you made a speech."

"That must have been in 1955. The treason trials. Lenina's father was involved."

"Yes, that's correct, the treason trials. I was working for the City Council on the refuse carts at the time. Later I was transferred to Parks and Gardens where I am now a foreman. I am also on the executive of the Municipal Workers Association and an organiser of the U.D.F. here in Beacon Valley. They raid my house so every now and then. But we manage to survive and stay out of jail."

"You must forgive me that I know so little about you."

"But I know much more about you."

Andrew looked puzzled.

"I know that you're Brad's father."

"You know that?"

"Of course, I do. He's Lenina's boyfriend, isn't he?"

"Do you know where he is now?" Andrew hoped he did not betray the eagerness in his voice.

"Well, I don't know where he is at this exact moment. But there's no problem finding out. I must say that he was very lucky. He just managed to get away when they caught Lenina. They missed him by ten minutes. It was really Brad that they were after. They want him desperately."

"Could you get a message through to Brad?" Andrew asked hesitantly.

Amaai watched, an amused smile playing around his lips.

"Why don't you rather speak to him yourself?"

"You mean that will be possible?"

"Yes, why not. Let me see what I can do."

They drank their tea and spoke about their District Six days, how ineffectual Mr Langeveldt was and what the P.T.S.A. could possibly achieve. Andrew's mind was not on the conversation. He was dying to know more about Brad, but realised that Amaai was not the sort of person who would allow himself to be pressed too hard.

They walked together to the car.

"All right," Amaai said after a moment's silence, "if you like, you can go with me to a small meeting Saturday evening. You can speak to Brad then."

Andrew held his breath.

"Do you know Manenberg?"

"Sort of."

"Pick me up at the corner of Storms River Way and Duinefontein Road at eight-thirty sharp. Not a minute earlier or later. Try and use another car."

"Sure. Certainly. I mean of course. Yes, I'll be there."

"Sleep well. And don't forget Caledon Street, and poor Honger's mother who drank a Bubbly Cola so she died."

"An' she fried."

"An' she cried."

"On her side."

"So his mother drank a Bubbly an' she died."

5

Rain poured down as Andrew drove along Duinefontein Road in Mabel's car. Windscreen wipers slashed away at sheets of water. Tyres squelched along rivers racing over road surfaces. Lights from approaching cars, taxis, minibuses blinded whenever they flashed past. He rolled down his window slightly to try to squint at street names against the side of his face. The second time he drove down the road, he was lucky and caught the name Storms River Way through the drizzle. He smiled at the incongruity of it all. The road was indeed transformed into a river by the storm of water swelling the gutters and gurgling crazily down the drains.

Andrew parked the car and glanced at the clock on the dashboard. 8.35. It wasn't really his fault. He had not allowed for the rain, for the extra time it would take. When he had left Heathfield it had been overcast but fine.

He sat back to wait and turned off the radio in case it should distract him. Ten minutes ticked by. Every now and then he flickered on his wipers to see more clearly, but except for barefooted children scurrying through the downpour, to and from a lighted shop, the rest of the street was deserted. A taxi minibus pulled up in front of him and disgorged six passengers who dashed for the shelter of the shop's foyer. Then, with an agonising screech of wet tyres, it pulled away again.

Another five minutes. Andrew debated whether there was any point in waiting longer. Another exercise in futility. Then someone rapped on his window. He turned it down, but could not make out who it was.

A man wearing a balaclava slipped in. Not Amaai and certainly not Brad, but the voice sounded vaguely familiar. Andrew glanced at the rearview mirror as the person removed his wet headgear.

"It's only me, Mr Dreyer. Trevor Petersen from Eastridge. You still remember?"

Andrew was too surprised to reply.

"Sorry to keep you waiting so long, but I wanted to make sure that it was all clear. I was sent to fetch you and was watching your car from the shop while playing video games. There were two other cars cruising around which looked suspicious. You see them?"

"No," Andrew replied.

"A Beetle and a blue Datsun. But its all right, they seem to be gone now."

"So where do we go from here?"

"We drive down Storms River and turn left into Manenberg Avenue. Follow the bend. I'll direct you from there."

Andrew followed Trevor's instructions. The sharp squalls had given way to a persistent drizzle and he was forced to drive slowly in order to avoid potholes. He thought he recognised Vygekraal Road, the huge open fields squatting alongside it, and the enormous depressing, concrete blocks of flats which reared up out of the damp darkness. He was instructed to turn right, and then right again. Trevor gave these instructions at the very last moment in order to throw off any car which might be following them. By this time Andrew had completely lost his bearings. Trevor spoke only twice other than giving Andrew laconic instructions, once when he asked how things were getting on at his old school, and another time when he commented that he thought that they were being followed.

"O.K.," he said at last, "pull up over there. It seems all clear."

They were in a quiet side street, with a brightly lit café at the far end through the misted plateglass window of which youths could vaguely be discerned playing video games. The rest of the street was deserted. Andrew parked opposite a row of semi-detached cottages.

"Your car will be safe here. A comrade lives in the house opposite. I'll ask him to keep a watch on your car as well as a lookout for anything suspicious. We are going to that cottage down there." He pointed out one indistinguishable and as miserable as the rest in the row.

They walked past four houses in the direction of the shop. A few cars passed but seemed filled with locals. Trevor turned in at a rickety, wooden gate, and knocked softly on the door.

It was opened slightly. They could hear music from inside. Half a face scrutinised them closely. Trevor was recognised and a greying woman, obviously the lady of the house, opened the door sufficiently to allow them to slip through. Inside a small front room crowded with furniture, four children sat glued to a black-and-white television set. The youngsters glanced at them briefly then turned their attention back to the screen. Trevor directed Andrew through to a bedroom running off the kitchen and then disappeared, possibly to alert the comrade about keeping a lookout.

There were about twenty people present, crowding the doorway to the room, sitting on the floor, on chairs, on the bed and standing wherever there was place. There were workers in overalls, about five students, and at least two men in suits and ties who looked like professional persons. The air was humid and thick with cigarette smoke. Amaai sat in a big armchair and was obviously the chairperson. He gave Andrew a wink of recognition.

"I know we are pressed for space, but could we find some place for comrade Dreyer?"

Andrew looked around as cautiously as he could. From his position it was not possible to scrutinise all the faces. But he knew almost intuitively that Bradley would not be there.

He had arrived in the middle of a heated discussion. A two-day strike was being planned for 7 and 8 October. A lawyer who was one of the tie-wearers, warned that it was highly likely that the state of emergency would be extended countrywide. He explained its implications. A bearded man in jeans, a worker or possibly a graduate student, said that the purpose of the strike would be twofold, as a show of economic strength — we must withhold black labour whenever necessary — and to mobilise black workers. The discussion developed around the issue of participation of school pupils in the proposed strike. There were two main points of view. The student representatives maintained their right to be part of the strike, and some older representatives felt that the focus should be on workers.

One pupil, Andrew thought he recognised him from the Rocklands protest meeting, explained heatedly that sacrifices were being called for. Students were part of the struggle. They were the victims of gutter education. If they had to choose between freedom and their academic careers, then they chose freedom. They wanted education after liberation.

"I disagree with you people," a voice said and a greying bent man coughed and emerged from a corner where he had been partially obscured. Justin nodded quickly to Andrew and then turned to answer the youthful activists. He commended them for the role they had played in the struggle, for their political vigilance, and their willingness to sacrifice. But he felt it was unfair to call on all school children to jeopardise their futures. In the process they were jeopardising the future of the society, the future of all the oppressed masses of South African society.

"I agree with you when you call it gutter education, that it is a tool used by the ruling class to entrench its position, but we must learn to use that very education, twisted and warped as it might be, in our fight for national liberation. Our cry should not be 'Education after Liberation', but 'Education for Liberation'."

There was no doubt that the pupils, certainly those present, held Justin in high esteem, but they were not happy about his argument. They claimed that they could bring out all high-school pupils and had the power to shut the schools. If the future was theirs, they wanted some say in the making of that future.

Andrew started to sweat in spite of the squalls of cold rain lashing against the windowpanes. It also drummed on the tin roof and competed against the noise from the television set in the front room. At times it was difficult to hear the speakers. And where in all this noise and arguments was Brad? Had he not come to see Brad? Had he not come to find his son?

Justin dealt tactfully and patiently with his youthful questioners. There was no bullying, no boastfulness about his past involvement. How different from Joe Ismail with his argument larded with quotations from Marx, Lenin, T. S. Eliot, Yeats and Luthuli. Enough to impress and confuse any listener. Joe Ismail now in detention. Rumour had it that during a previous incarceration he had scratched on his cell wall in Caledon Square, *Sic transit nox dolorosa*.

Still, it was reckless and foolhardy of Justin to be there. What a risk to take. If the police raided his flat in Manenberg and found he was not at home, they could throw the book at him. Maybe they knew he was not at his flat. Maybe they were following him to find out where he went. Maybe they were giving him enough rope and waiting for him to hang not only himself but also his contacts. And yet here he was speaking softly, rationally and logically, as if he were in someone's lounge on a Sunday afternoon. Weighing up every argument against every other, accommodating every point of view, even those that differed radically from his, treating his pupils as if they were his political equals, which he indeed considered them as. All this while his daughter was detained. Lenina in a solitary police cell, cut off from any other contact. And where in all this was Brad?

"It is the workers who must be in the forefront of the struggle, the urban and rural workers. We must mobilise them and bring them out. We must create an alliance between the black working-class, the black college and university students, and the revolutionary elements of the black middle and professional classes, the teachers, doctors, lawyers and small businessmen. It is a combination of these elements that alone will guarantee effective change in our country."

"Are you trying to play down the role of pupils in our schools during 1976, 1980 and now?"

"Of course not. I have nothing but admiration and the highest regard for what you have done and are doing, young children and youths from twelve to eighteen years of age. You have faced the armed might of the state with only half bricks in your hands. You have faced bullets with crude, petrol bombs. You have forced the minister to reopen your schools. You have sacrificed and suffered heavy casualties and quite a few deaths. And all this at an age when your white counterparts are busy with rugby, discos and video games. But this is a workers' struggle, a black workers' struggle. If the workers can adopt the courage, tenacity and singularity of purpose of you young people, then I have no doubt that the days of this racist regime are certainly numbered."

Discussion and more discussion. About it and about. Argument and more argument. Discussion and argument. Argument and discussion. Andrew was drawn by the intensity and sincerity of it all. At times he wanted to make a contribution, but then decided against it. Was he really one of them? He knew deep down that he was. Did he really believe in the struggle? He knew deep down that he did. But here he was searching for his son. Was his focus his family or his society? Were the two things mutually exclusive? Could there be any society without a family or the other way round? When searching for Brad, was he not really searching for himself, for his community, for everyone else in this bigoted country?

The door opened and Trevor and another youth came in. This was the first time Trevor had been in the room since their arrival. He spoke intensely to Amaai, who then conferred with Justin and the lawyer. Andrew sensed that something was wrong.

"Comrades," Amaai began, "it has been reported to us by Trevor and Oswald that a suspicious-looking car has been noticed circling around this block? It could be the system. We are not sure but we cannot afford the risk."

"It's a blue Datsun," Trevor said. "It stopped near the shop and then drove off. Some youngsters reported that there were Whites in the car who looked like the system. We then noticed that they had been driving around here all evening."

"We suggest," Amaai said, "that this meeting be adjourned immediately."

A pupil who had not spoken before wanted to know how sure Trevor was of his facts, but Amaai would not allow any further discussion.

"We will contact each of you individually about the time and place of our next meeting. Please leave singly or in pairs. Allow a short space of time in between. And don't all use the kitchen door. Some go through the front door. Try to behave naturally."

The meeting started breaking up. Justin smiled and made the thumbs-up sign to Andrew.

The way he had pushed up his thumb at me, Abe, when I saw him marching off to jail during the Defiance of Unjust Laws Campaign. The Congress salute and that half-smile of his. I remember it all so well.

Then Justin slipped noiselessly out of the kitchen door and was gone.

Amaai came up to Andrew as the meeting thinned out. "Sorry about all this, but I think it is necessary."

Andrew wanted to ask him about Brad but Amaai pre-empted the question.

"Yes, I got a message through to your son, and he sent a reply that he would be here tonight. He is very eager to meet you. But this looks ominous. I hope they haven't got him. I don't like the look of this at all."

Amaai had hardly finished speaking when a shot rang through the house. The children who had been in the front room rushed in screaming and beside themselves with fear. Someone had fired through the front window and the bullet had lodged in the opposite wall. Fortunately no-one was hurt. Almost immediately after this they heard two more shots which seemed to come from lower down the road.

"My God, they mean business this time," Amaai said. "I think we had better get out. They could shoot up the house. Where are you parked?"

They left through the kitchen door. It was drizzling heavily as they quickly turned down a side street, then back onto the road where the car was parked. They saw a crowd gathering outside the corner shop. They rushed towards it and joined it at its edge.

A figure was lying sprawled half-way over the pavement and half in the gutter. Blood was mixing with rain water and pouring down the drain. They overheard snippets of conversations as everyone seemed to be speaking at the same time.

". . . in cold blood."

"I saw how they shot him."

"A blue Datsun."

"No, it was greenish-blue. The number was CY 136 . . . something."

"There were three white men. Two in front and one at the back. It was difficult to see clearly because of the rain. The shots came from the back."

"Yes, it was a Bellville registration. CY 136 . . . I think it was 34 something."

"My God," Andrew said drawing closer, "it's Justin!"

There was a gaping wound at the side of his head, Abe, and another on his left chest. It was drizzling and there was blood all over the pavement. I heard someone saying that they had phoned for the ambulance from the shop. I wanted to kneel down in the rain and help him, cover him, do something. To rest his head on my knee. But Amaai restrained me.

159

"Don't do that," he said sharply, "leave him alone. There's nothing we can do. They've got their satisfaction. They've managed to murder him at last."

The ambulance pulled up with a screech of brakes. A police patrol-van arrived immediately after. Two attendants climbed out of the ambulance with a stretcher. The policemen also got out of their vehicle and examined the body. Then they turned to the crowd.

"Anyone see what happened?" the young officer addressed the crowd in Afrikaans.

He was greeted with a sullen silence.

"Anyone of you see who did it?" The voice sounded threatening.

No-one replied. The ambulancemen lifted the body onto the stretcher.

"Why the hell are you so quiet all of a sudden? You mean not one of you saw anything?"

The crowd continued to stare at him, silently and hostilely.

Amaai nudged Andrew. "Come on, let's get to your car," he whispered.

"But why?" Andrew began.

"Because I'm saying so," Amaai said firmly. He gripped Andrew fiercely by the arm and they walked silently down the street.

6

You can imagine, Abe, what a miserable time I had the following day, a Sunday that yawned from an empty, meaningless afternoon into an empty, meaningless evening. I remained shut up in my study drinking whisky and listening over and over again to Smetana's "Moldau", until it was reduced to a blurred ribbon of sound. I had not told Mabel or Ruth about Justin's death, but they could see from my behaviour that something was seriously wrong. So they left me alone. Mabel sought refuge in her church and Ruth sought refuge goodness only knows where. And I was left to face the huge, gaping void.

Later during the afternoon I phoned the police station, and after my call was shunted from department to department, I finally established that the officer in charge was off duty and expected back only the following morning. I thought of phoning the lawyer, Alex Moses, at his home. I even looked up and found the number in the directory, and then realised that I wouldn't know what to ask him. I did phone Justin's sister-in-law, Hester, in Manenberg, but her phone just rang and rang. At one stage I was on the verge of getting into my car and driving to Amaai in Beacon Valley. Then I changed my mind, thought I would drive to Grassy Park to have a talk with Eldred. I finally decided to remain in my study and wallow in loneliness.

Way back in 1965 I received a seventeen-page letter from a black Durban poet called Pascal Gwala. The letter was prompted by the suicides of Ingrid Jonker and Nat Nakasa earlier in that year. Nat died because he was an exile outside his country, and Ingrid died because she was an exile inside her country.

In his letter Pascal wrote:

"Death is a process and therefore very much relative and objective. Death does not happen with the last pulse of the heartbeat. Neither does it end with the doctor's certificate. Death can be said to begin when a person's will fails to identify itself with life. And will is such a vastness of violent possibilities that to try to understand it we are always pressed on to the understanding of environment first."

He was speaking about Nat and Ingrid and, without realising it, he was speaking about me. My will has also begun to fail for some time now to identify itself with my life. What else is left for me with which to identify? A friend murdered? A son missing? His girl-friend detained? My school in chaos? My daughter estranged? My wife escaped into religion? And I escaping into what Gwala later in his letter described as "the secret enclave of my strangeland mind"?

I realise that in a way I am committing suicide. I am drowning myself in a sea of bitterness and self-pity. I am throwing myself from a skyscraper to be dashed to pieces against the hard reality of disillusionment. I am like Arthur Nortje, another poet who died before his death, consumed and eaten-up with isolation, overcome by ". . . the solitude that mutilates, the night bulb that reveals the ash on my sleeve."

All this time I am thinking that Justin's death is so unnecessary, so needless, so wasteful. I know that at his funeral there will be eulogies, protest songs, slogans and raised, defiant fists. But all I wish to remember is a thumbs-up sign and a shy smile. When Justin lay in that gutter it was the end of a long, although somewhat spasmodic association for all three of us. Justin was already dead; you are dying your Nat Nakasa death in a foreign country, and I am dying my Ingrid Jonker death at home. I feel that my will is fast failing to identify itself with my life. Is yours also slipping?

The following morning at school, Andrew was completely out of sorts. Pupil attendance was improving, and he realised that he must face the daunting prospect of teaching them. He was sitting in his office trying to work up some enthusiasm when he decided to phone the principal to inform him that he must leave school for the day.

"But is it absolutely necessary, Mr Dreyer? We really need you here."

"Yes, it is absolutely necessary."

"Could you be more specific and let me have some details?"

"I don't want to be more specific."

"Your place is here at your school with your pupils, you know."

"Mr Langeveldt, I wish to leave right now. There's some business I have to attend to. Whether I get your permission or not, I'm going. I'm quite prepared to face the consequences."

"Is it about your son Bradley?" Langeveldt was fishing.

"No, it is not about my son Brad."

"But Mr Dreyer, I must have at least some reason, in case the department wants to know. I must be able to cover myself and you."

"Good morning, Mr Langeveldt," he said decisively and replaced the receiver on its rest.

Andrew was hoping not to run into anyone on his way to the car park. Miss Russell appeared out of nowhere as if she had been biding her time in order to waylay him.

"Morning, morning, morning, Mr Dreyer," she said breezily. "But we are off early today."

"Good morning, Miss Russell," he said resignedly.

"Is anything the matter?" She pulled a face to show her concern.

"No, no, nothing's the matter."

"Naughty, naughty, naughty," she wagged her finger, "running off already. But one can't blame you. It's such a fine day after all that rain over the weekend. I was saying to my sister-in-law at breakfast — you know my brother's wife with whom I board in Westridge — I was saying to Minnie only this morning . . ."

Andrew felt he was going to explode. "Good morning, Miss Russell," he said with finality and left her poised in mid-sentence.

Then followed a terrible, frustrating morning, Abe, in which nothing seemed to go right. In a way I was looking for confrontation. I tried to get it with Langeveldt, and behaved somewhat cruelly to Miss Russell. But I suppose I got more than I had bargained for when I met Lieutenant Vosloo of the Special Branch at the police station.

Andrew felt prickly and nervous as he entered the charge office. Policemen chatting over coffee, walking around armed with files, conferring with colleagues. A beaten-up woman was complaining to a bored sergeant behind the counter about another beaten-up woman who was lolling drunkenly on a bench. A young hoodlum, under armed guard, accosted Andrew surreptitiously for cigarettes.

When his turn came at last, Andrew explained the nature of his business. He wanted information about a Mr Justin Bailey who had been shot in Manenberg on Saturday evening. Had anyone been arrested? Where was the body?

"Yes, that will be murder and robbery," the sergeant said almost mechanically. He dialled a number and spoke rapidly to someone at the other end in Afrikaans. Then he clapped his hand over the mouthpiece.

"Your name?" he asked.

"Andrew Dreyer."

"Address?"

"31 Vlei Road, Elfindale, Heathfield."

He conveyed the details, then asked the exchange to put him through to another office and spoke briefly to a second person. Then he turned back to Andrew.

"Mr Dreyer, Lieutenant Vosloo will see you now in room 201. You know where it is? Go down this passage, up to the second floor and it's the first room to the left."

On the way Andrew passed a door marked "Murder and Robbery". So that was not Vosloo's office. 201 had only the number on the door. He knocked, and a sharp, clipped voice asked him to enter.

Lieutenant Vosloo was a small, neat man, sallow in complexion with extremely light-blue eyes, that seemed almost transparent. He gave the appearance of being cold and humourless. He did not look up but went on reading a file he was consulting.

"Have a seat, Mr Dreyer," he said.

Andrew did so.

"Now what is it you want to know?"

Andrew explained as briefly as he could. Vosloo went on reading, then looked up sharply.

"How well did you know the deceased?" he asked.

"He was a friend."

"A very close friend?"

"Yes, I would say so."

"Did you witness the shooting?"

"No, I'm afraid not."

"But you were in Manenberg on Saturday evening?"

"Lieutenant, I've come here to get some information, not to be interrogated."

"You must understand, Mr Dreyer, that this is a complicated case.

This is a political thing. The deceased was a known activist and agitator. He was breaking the law at the time that he was killed."

"That's all very well, Lieutenant, but the reason I am here is to find out why he was killed."

"We don't know that yet, Mr Dreyer. But what we do know is that the deceased was not supposed to be outside his home when it happened. He was under house arrest."

"Is that why he was shot?"

"Are you suggesting anything, Mr Dreyer?"

"I am not suggesting anything."

"We don't know why he was shot nor do we know who shot him. But you still haven't answered my question. Were you in Manenberg on Saturday evening?"

"Yes, I was," Andrew said carefully.

"Why?"

"I was going to meet someone."

"Who?"

Vosloo switched on a tape-recorder. Andrew watched him cautiously.

"Merely routine, Mr Dreyer, merely routine, in case you go running to your lawyer with false information. Now who were you going to meet?"

Andrew maintained his silence.

"Come on, Mr Dreyer. You can't tell me you don't know who you were going to meet?"

"I was to be taken there."

"By whom?" Vosloo showed studied patience.

"Am I obliged to answer all your questions?"

"Not this time. But it would save you a lot of unpleasantness later. So let's start all over again, shall we? Why were you in Manenberg on Saturday evening?"

"I was waiting for someone to pick me up."

"Who was to pick you up?"

"I wish first to consult my lawyer before I answer any of your questions."

"Now that's not being co-operative, Mr Dreyer. So let me then jog your memory. Was it Mr Achmat Daniels, who couldn't make it so he sent Trevor Petersen in his place?"

Andrew was taken completely by surprise.

"Where did you get that from?"

164

"We have our sources, Mr Dreyer, we have our sources. However we did pick up both Mr Daniels and Trevor this morning. They are comfortably in our care. They certainly seem to have no objections talking to us."

"I insist on my right to contact my lawyer."

"But why, Mr Dreyer? We are not doing anything to you. Are we not merely asking you a few routine questions? If we had anything on you, we could have picked you up at any time. We are not going to detain you or beat you up, as you people always claim, even if you did attend an illegal meeting with known subversives who were plotting against the state."

Andrew felt claustrophobic. He just had to get out of Vosloo's presence.

"I wish to leave now, please."

"All right, Mr Dreyer, "you may go if you please. But we'll be in touch, I can assure you. And advise the children at Eastridge that if they want to play with fire and go on strike on the 7th and 8th of next month, then they'll burn their fingers. We are not playing games this time."

He picked up the file and continued reading. Andrew was about to leave when Vosloo delivered his parting shot.

"And don't worry about your son, Bradley," he said without looking up, "we'll find him for you quite soon. We may even allow the two of you to have a pleasant conversation here. Maybe you could give him advice on how to stay out of trouble. But you are not very good at that yourself, are you? How do the English say again? 'Like father, like son, hey?'" He returned to his file.

Andrew gulped down air once he was standing outside the police station. Thoughts whirled through his head. They knew far more than he had expected. Amaai and Trevor had been picked up so quietly that no-one knew about it. Maybe Langeveldt and the rest of the school did know by this time. Of course the police knew about Justin. But about Brad? And what did that man mean by "Like father, like son"? How far back did their records stretch?

He pulled up outside 464B Manenberg Avenue. He raced up the spidery staircase and knocked impatiently at the door. After a wait that seemed interminable it was opened on its ball and chain and Hester peeped through.

"It's me, Mr Dreyer. Open up, please."

The chain was slowly slipped off, and Andrew entered the dim, furniture-crowded front room. The curtains were drawn and he could just make out Hester sitting quietly in a deep chair. He drew the curtains to let the daylight in.

"I'm sorry," she began.

"I am also sorry," he said gently.

"Why did they have to do it? Why did they have to kill him?"

"We don't know why, and we don't know who did it," he explained patiently.

She spoke more to herself than to him. "First they take Lenina away, then they kill Justin. It's not right. But Mr Daniels says that he knows who did it."

"Oh, has Amaai already been here?" he asked surprised.

"Yes, he was the first to tell me about it. He came yesterday morning. I know Justin goes out in spite of the ban, and I always worry about that. But when he didn't come home Saturday night, I knew something serious was wrong. Then Mr Daniels told me what happened. He said the Front will bury Justin next Saturday."

"Did Mr Daniels say anything else?"

"He said I mustn't worry, that the comrades would see to the funeral, that the lawyer, Mr Moses, would see that Lenina is told about her father, and that he would try to get her out for the funeral. Amaai said he would come this morning again. When you came I thought it was him."

"I see," Andrew said as evenly as possible.

"And afterwards the police also came."

"When?"

"Last night. They searched the place and told me that Justin was an agitator and a trouble-maker. And they warned me not to let the comrades bury Justin. There was a Lieutentant or Captain Vosloo who asked about Mr Daniels but I told him nothing. He said there must be no politics at the funeral. He would get a court order. And not more than 100 people at the funeral. Mr Dreyer, we don't even know so many people."

"Where's the body now?"

"The police still got it. Maybe its at the morgue in Salt River."

Andrew sat in silence for a long time not knowing what to say to the grey woman who did not really understand.

"And Florence?"

"Who?"

"Justin's wife, Florence. I think that she must be told. Where does she live?"

"I don't know, Mr Dreyer. Lenina said in Long Street some-where."

"Did Lenina ever discuss her visit to her mother with you?"

"Yes, she told me about it, but said I mustn't tell Justin. And I never did, Mr Dreyer."

"You don't know the Long Street address?"

"Wait a minute. I think I know where I saw it written." She left and returned with the telephone directory. She searched amongst the many names and numbers on the inside back cover. "Yes, I think this is it. I remember now that Lenina wrote it here. There's no name, but this is the address all right, 210 Upper Long Street. That is it, Mr Dreyer. If I remember, Lenina said it was on the third floor."

"Thank you, I'm sure I'll be able to find it." Andrew got up with greater resolution. "We'll keep in touch. If you need any advice or help, then phone me either at Eastridge Secondary School or at my home." He wrote both numbers on the back cover.

"Then I must be off."

"Please, Mr Dreyer."

"Yes?"

"Don't ask that woman to come to the funeral. I don't want her here."

"We need not invite her, but we must inform her. I'll go to see her either today or tomorrow."

"She musn't come to the funeral. It's not right. Not after what Lenina told me about her."

"I am in no position to tell her what she can or cannot do."

As Andrew left, the door was shut behind him, the key turned in the lock, the chain bolt slipped into place, and the curtain drawn. That poor woman, all alone, with no-one left. How long would the Council allow her to stay on in the flat before they put her out? How long before his will failed to identify itself with life?

7

Andrew felt quite jaded and uneasy as he walked up Long Street, past Pepper and Bloem Streets, searching for 210. It was still early evening of the same September day when he had been to the police station and then gone to Manenberg. He had driven straight home after seeing

Hester although he knew that his school was most probably still in session. When he greeted Mabel in the kitchen, he tried to appear as normal as possible, and she in her turn did not question the fact that he was home from Eastridge earlier than usual. There had been a telephone call for him. Langeveldt had left a message that Mr Dreyer should please contact him either at his office or at his home if he had already left. Andrew was in no mood to do so. After a dinner pecked at in uncomfortable silence, Andrew told Mabel that he was going out on some business. As usual she did not question it.

He was still getting into this car, when he heard the phone ringing. Mabel came rushing out to say that Langeveldt was again on the line. Something about Andrew's forgetting to pick up his salary cheque. He felt like telling his principal to go to hell, but instead told Mabel to inform Langeveldt that he would get it the following day.

Twilight made even Upper Long Street look more attractive than it was in full daylight, in spite of derelicts on street corners, emptying Portuguese cafés, closed liquor stores, and badly lit fish-and-chips shops.

Andrew could not see any numbers on some buildings and houses, but had no difficulty recognising Long Street Mansions from Lenina's description of it. He negotiated smelly, over-flowing refuse bins at the entrance, and then climbed the staircase to the dark second floor. The entire building smelt of mould, damp and rot.

He knocked at the first two doors without getting any response. The third was flung open and a man stared enquiringly at him. He was Chinese and wore a dirty vest, rolled-up jeans and was barefooted with a cigarette dangling from his lips. Somewhere inside, a tape-recorder was loudly playing pop music.

"Yes?" the Taiwanese asked him.

"I'm looking for Mrs Bailey."

"Yes?" he repeated without changing his expression.

"Mrs Bailey. I'm looking for Mrs Florence Bailey."

"Yes?"

This was becoming repetitive and tiresome. He was convinced that the man did not understand.

"I want to know whether a Mrs Florence Bailey lives here," he spoke slowly and deliberately.

"What?"

Andrew shrugged his shoulders helplessly and was about to leave to try next door, when a female voice from somewhere inside shouted "Who's there, Charley?"

168

"What you want with Florrie?"

"I wish to speak to her."

"Why?"

A tired, haggard-looking woman in a dirty dressing-gown that hardly covered her body came to the door. The stale make-up on her face had turned sour and showed in blotches. Her most noticeable physical feature however was a shock of violently red hair. She held half a glass of wine in her hand.

Andrew recognised Florence at once.

"May I come in?" he asked her softly.

"Who are you looking for?" she enquired, peering suggestively into his face.

"I'm Andrew Dreyer."

She looked harder. "My God, it's Andy all right." Her face lit up and she grinned broadly, genuinely pleased. "Of course you may come in."

She gently nudged a perplexed Charley out of the way while consoling him like a child. "It's all right, darling, this is just an old, old friend."

The Taiwanese gave Andrew a hostile look and went back to the bed on which he had been sitting or lying, muttering to himself.

The room was dirty and cluttered. The double bed was unmade. A table contained an assortment of partially filled wine and brandy bottles and opened packets of cigarettes. Butts, corks, bottle-tops and used tissues spilled over from the ashtrays. Florence removed a shirt and jacket, obviously Charley's, from a chair and indicated to Andrew that he could sit there.

"By the looks of it, I think your boy-friend does not like me." Andrew tried to speak above the loud noise of the tape-recorder.

"Charley's all right in his own peculiar way. He just looks angry, but underneath it all, he is very kind. Aren't you, my darling?" She went over and pecked him playfully on his greasy, black hair.

"Could you put off that music, please?" Andrew asked sharply.

"Same old Andy," she said smilingly, and turned down the volume. "So what brings you up here to these 'Mansions'?"

"I have something I must tell you."

"What an honour. What a really, great honour. Hip, big schoolmaster visits prostitute in her rooms in Long Street. What has happened to that white girl-friend of yours?"

Andrew felt his temper rising but kept control of himself.

"I heard her daddy took her home," Florence answered him, "away to the Transvaal far from naughty little randy Andy."

"I have some information you must get."

"So you haven't come for entertainment? Florrie is very good at that, isn't she, Charley?" She looked playfully at the Taiwanese, who scowled back. "Maybe the gentleman should wait because Charley came first, hey darling?"

Andrew ignored the taunts. He now realised that it had been a mistake to come. Maybe he should just deliver the information quickly and then get the hell out.

"It's a long time, since we first met, isn't it, Andy," she continued in the same mocking tone. Then turning to her companion she said, "You know, Charley, me and him," pointing to herself and to Andrew, "we go school together. Little boy and girl. Same class."

Charley grinned although it was not obvious whether he understood what was being said.

"Very long time ago, Charley," she said imitating his accent.

And to think, Abe, that this worn-out shell of a woman, standing in front of me, this odious, repellent, mimicking creature, had once been the fresh, young Florence Bailey of Vernon Terrace. Yes, we had been in the same class at St Mark's and Trafalgar Junior. She was an only child, and lived alone with her widowed mother in one of those warm, cosy, cluttered cottages on the cobbled terrace. By the time we were in Standard Five, she had grown into a vivacious, lively bundle of teasing energy, showing the first signs of womanhood.

Annually we used to have a primary schools choir contest, called the Ash Shield Competition, downtown in the City Hall. Maybe you still remember, although I don't think your school was part of it. Choirs came from Berlin Mission, Moravian, Holy Cross, St Paul's and many other schools including our own, Trafalgar Junior.

We sang songs with strong British flavours, such as "Old Father Thames", "Londonderry Air", and "Loch Lomond". How incongruous to think of it now. And "De Little Black Bull Went Down De Meadow".

We boys wore navy-blue shorts, white shirts and red ties. The girls wore white dresses with red sashes and had bows in their hair. Florence was a foam of lace and taffeta, with a huge red bow on top of her flame-red hair.

I stood a little apart from her in the choir, but still our voices seemed to blend and we were full of the lightness and sheer abandonment of childhood. We sang our hearts out but Trafalgar Junior never seemed to win. In spite of that we walked back together up Caledon Street as if we were floating on air. Who can explain the sheer joy and undisturbed bliss of being twelve, carefree and in District Six? Sordid and grimy as it was, the cobbles in Vernon Terrace sang for us, and the south-easter playfully teased our names around corners.

And that was the same Florence, now standing opposite me. This soiled, blemished woman with her half-open dressing-gown showing her flabby, unwashed, overused flesh.

"Florence," Andrew said, realising how platitudinous and precious he sounded, "what on earth has become of you?"

"Are you here to insult me?"

"Of course not."

"You know, the last time we met was over twenty-five years ago, after Sharpeville, when Justin was arrested, and you came to our house in Arundel Street for pamphlets or something. You still see Justin sometimes?"

Andrew remained silent.

"I had a hell of a life after that. First I had to give away my Lennie when she was still a baby."

Andrew forced himself to retain silence.

"We're friends again, Lennie and I. She came to visit me a few months ago. Charley also saw her. She's really a lovely girl now, hey Charley?"

"I know she is."

"You know Lennie?"

"Yes, I do."

"How come you know her?"

"She's a friend of my son's."

"Now fancy that. What a small world. She told me nothing about it."

"They are very close."

"Lennie's still all right, isn't she? Lennie's still O.K.?" She wanted a positive response but he did not accede to it.

"She promised she would contact me again, but she never did. I wish she were not ashamed of me."

"Do you blame her?"

"No, of course not. I only blame myself. I know I've never been a real mother to her. I know I gave her away when she was still a baby. But you must believe me when I tell you that I was forced to do so. It was Tom who forced me. I've never been able to forgive myself for that. I wonder whether Lennie will ever be able to forgive me. When will you see her again?"

"Lenina has been detained. She is in jail right now."

"Oh." It slipped out of her mouth as if she were at a loss what else to say. Her voice dropped to almost a whisper. "Is it politics?"

"Yes, it is politics."

She turned her anger full on Andrew. "Always politics. Always blarry politics. What did I do to deserve this? What are they doing to my baby in jail?"

She sat crying next to Charley and started rocking and crooning to herself as if she still held the baby in her arms. She stopped suddenly.

"You want a drink?" she asked Andrew. He declined. "Charley," she commanded, "pour Florrie another drink."

Charley, who was watching all this, understood immediately from her gestures and filled her glass with red wine.

After a time Florence calmed down and seemed to accept the situation. "So Lennie's in jail?"

"I'm afraid so."

"Just like her father. First I lost my husband, then I lost my baby. Then I lost my self-respect and then everything. Everybody uses me. First Justin, then Tom, and now even Charley and men like him. They all come here to use me."

Andrew felt embarrassed at this self-revelation, but allowed her to indulge herself.

"You know," she continued, "besides my mother, Mrs Hanslo was the only one who was ever kind to me. Then that son of hers, what's his name again? Abe. Yes, Abe, deserted her and was the cause of his mother's death."

"They said that about me too, that I was the cause of my mother's death." Andrew said this more to himself than to her. After forty years the scars still remained.

"But Abe was the cause of his mother's death, wasn't he?"

"That is a very cruel thing to say," Andrew replied evenly. "That's not how it was."

"I just knew that you would defend him. The three of you were always thick, weren't you? Abe, Justin and you. But while the two of you went scot-free, it was Justin who had to pay the price."

Andrew realised it would be useless to counter her accusations. He tried nevertheless.

"That is not true," he said slowly, "I don't wish to go into any details now, but it is not true."

"If Justin were here, I wonder whether he would agree with you."

"Justin is dead."

"What did you say?"

"I said that Justin is dead."

She seemed unable to respond immediately, and sat as if punch-drunk. Charley showed by the worried expression on his face and his open mouth, that he sensed something seriously wrong.

"No, it can't be true," she burst out. "No, no, no." She jumped up from the bed.

Charley also sprang up. "What you do to Florrie?" he asked aggressively.

"It's all right, Charley," Florence said, calming down, "nothing is wrong. Everything all right." She attempted a smile while dabbing at her eyes with a tissue.

"Why you make Florrie cry?" he asked Andrew.

"Sit down, Charley!" she ordered him. He refused to do so. She then vented her anger on him. "Just get out of here. Yes, you," she said when he looked puzzled. "Get the hell out of here."

Charley was completely confused. Florence threw his shirt and shoes at him. "Get out, you lousy, Chinese bastard!"

"What wrong, Florrie, ducky? Charley love Florrie. Nice, nice."

"Get the hell out of here or I'll kill you!" she shouted, pushing him towards the door.

"All right, ducky."

He hastily put on his shirt and shoes, then picked up his jacket. He contemptuously peeled a twenty rand note off a bundle and threw it on the table. Then he picked up a half-empty bottle of brandy, glared at Andrew and then at Florence. "O.K. Charley go now."

"Go at once, you bastard!"

"O.K. O.K. Charley go."

She slammed the door behind him.

Andrew watched all this without reaction or comment. He just didn't have any emotional energy left to interfere. Florence threw herself on the bed and cried until she was exhausted. He allowed her to do so without interference. When she had done, she rose and poured herself another drink. She seemed better after the outburst.

"How did he die?" she asked.

"He was shot. We don't know yet who shot him, but we have a fairly shrewd idea."

"Was it politics again?" she said without looking up from her glass.

"Yes."

"I always knew that he would go that way." She seemed exhausted and all traces of resentment and anger had left her.

173

"Yes, it was all so unnecessary, Florrie," Andrew said as kindly as he could.

She started pacing the floor in front of him.

"So, Lennie's in jail. Justin is dead. And I have no more family left. But it has been so for a long time. Ever since I left Justin. Now this is all that is left of me. This dirty room in this dirty building in this dirty street. I have suffered over and over again in this room. Justin is the lucky one to have died."

Andrew listened without comment.

"Lenina in jail is more free than I will ever be."

This was a different Florence from the woman Andrew had expected to find.

"So, when is the funeral," she asked, "or has it already happened?"

"This coming Saturday. In the afternoon, I think. Say about 3 p.m."

"Where?"

"I suppose from his home. 464B Manenberg Avenue. The flat is on the second floor."

"All right, then."

"Sorry?"

"I'll be there. I'll come to the funeral."

Andrew realised all the implications. He realised that her presence would hurt Hester. It would hurt Lenina if she were allowed to attend. But most of all, it would hurt Florence herself.

"It is most considerate of you. I'll be very glad if you come. I'm sure Justin would want it so. Then I hope to see you there on Saturday afternoon."

8

Early on the evening of 4 October, the phone rang in Andrew's home in Heathfield. Ruth, on one of the rare occasions when she was at home, answered it and called her father who was busy writing in his study. It was from someone who identified himself as the Reverend Simon Abrahamse of the Pentecostal Church of God in Manenberg. He was speaking on behalf of Mrs Hester Bailey, a member of his congregation.

The funeral of her brother-in-law, Mr Justin Bailey was to take place the following day at about 3 p.m. at Woltemade Cemetery in Maitland, gate 12. The priest understood that the deceased and Mr Dreyer had been friends during their youth. Could Mr Dreyer please thank the mourners on behalf of Mrs Bailey after the service? It was her suggestion. No, it did not seem as if Lenina would be allowed to attend the funeral, and permission had been refused by the police. But another urgent appeal was being made, and it was hoped to get a court order for her temporary release. The Reverend Abrahamse did not know whether she yet knew about her father's death. A Lieutenant Vosloo had personally delivered both to him and to Mrs Bailey the conditions laid down for the funeral by the police. The cortège was to leave the Manenberg church not later than 2 p.m. It had to follow a prescribed route to Maitland Cemetery, down Turfhall Road, turning right into Vanguard Drive and then left along Voortrekker Road. The number of mourners was restricted to one hundred. There was to be no-one walking or marching, no display of banners, no shouting of slogans, and no delivery of speeches other than the sermon by the priest and one spokesman for the family. The service had to be terminated at the graveside by 4.30 p.m.

Later in the evening Andrew phoned Eldred at his home. He was told that quite a few staff members, including Eldred himself, the interim Students Representative Council, as well as several other pupils, would attend. Andrew suggested that Eldred contact Shaun Apollis to represent the Eastridge Parent-Teacher-Students Association to show its solidarity with the detained executive member, Mr Achmat Daniels.

Andrew asked Mabel to accompany him, but she declined without offering any reason. Ruth however was eager to go as she knew Lenina through her brother Brad.

The following afternoon the two left for the funeral in good time. They approached the cemetery through Athlone, then drove along Jan Smuts Drive to Sunrise Circle. When they reached Voortrekker Road, they passed a heavy police presence consisting of Casspirs, Ratels, pick-up vans and rows of uniformed, armed men. Strangely enough the police had not erected any road-blocks. A friendly traffic officer directed Andrew where to find the nearest parking. From the size of the crowd already congregating along Voortrekker Road, Andrew realised that the limitations insisted on by the police would prove farcical.

Then the cortège arrived. First the hearse followed by a long procession of cars and buses containing the official mourners. Andrew spotted Hester sitting in the first car, dressed in black with a heavy veil covering her face. Then a procession of clerics, Christian and Muslim, who walked immediately behind the cars. There were about twenty of them, most in ecclesiastical dress. They were followed by two students bearing aloft a huge U.D.F. banner. And then the rest of the procession followed. Thousands upon thousands of people. The sheer number amazed Andrew. School children in blazers, students in T-shirts and jeans, workers in overalls, housewives, professionals, political activists. People of all shades and colours. Men, women and children. Old and young, but mostly young. Here and there a sprinkling of Whites in the long, pouring river of humanity. Banners and placards bearing slogans and the names of organisations represented. Manenberg Youth, Azapo, Pentecostal Youth Movement, The United Women's Organisation, We greet Comrade Justin Bailey, The Call of Islam, black, green and gold of the A.N.C., Unban Cosas. Slogans shouted and repeated. A river of people pouring and pouring from Vanguard Drive into Voortrekker Road. Viva U.D.F. Viva A.N.C. Viva Comrade Justin Bailey. A long, determined, grim-faced, defiant moving mass of humanity.

Andrew explained to a youthful marshal what his purpose was, and he and Ruth were ushered to a place in front near the open grave. Hester saw him and nodded a quiet recognition. The Reverend Abrahamse introduced himself and informed him of the programme for the afternoon. Andrew would be the last speaker and he was to thank the assembly on behalf of Mrs Bailey. The most recent attempt to get permission for Lenina to attend had failed.

The coffin, draped in a U.D.F. flag, was placed next to the open grave by youthful bearers. Then a solitary wreath from Hester was positioned on top of it.

The proceedings began with the singing of hymns and patriotic songs. A choir from Guguletu sang. Another choir from the Manenberg youth. A choir from a high school in Bishop Lavis. Prayers interspersed with slogans. All done with dignity and control.

Then speech after speech. Andrew was standing just behind a row of priests with Ruth a few paces behind him. Hester was supported throughout by two elderly women from the congregation. He saw Florence on the opposite side, partially hidden by some students, dressed in sober black and wearing a scarf and sunglasses. He tried to catch her eye but she either did not notice or chose to ignore him.

Speeches, more speeches, and still more speeches. Speaker after speaker after speaker.

Release Mandela now.
Viva A.N.C., viva.
Release all political detainees.
Viva U.D.F., viva.
Unban all organisations.
Viva Cosas, viva.
Disarm all police and the army.
Viva Azapo, viva.
Scrap all apartheid legislation.
Viva Sayco, viva.
All troops out of the townships.
Viva comrades, viva.

Tribute upon tribute to the slain leader.

He did not die in vain.
Apartheid was responsible for his death.
Viva Justin Bailey.
The struggle continues.
A Luta Continua.

Finally the Reverend Abrahamse indicated to Andrew that all the orations were over and that it was his turn to conclude the proceedings. By now it was well past 4.30. Andrew began slowly and uncertain of himself. His voice sounded hollow over the microphone.

"I speak here as the late Justin Bailey's oldest friend.

"I remember 1947 when he, Abe Hanslo, who is now in Canada, and myself, were friends in the same matriculation class at Trafalgar.

"I remember 1952, when Justin marched off to jail during the Defiance of Unjust Laws Campaign.

"I remember 1955, when Justin, as a Cape Town delegate, was at the Congress of the People that adopted the historic Freedom Charter.

"I remember 1956, when Justin was part of the Treason Trials and spent four debilitating years before his acquittal.

"I remember the many, many years during which he was constantly banned and jailed.

"I remember 1969, when Justin was sentenced for alleged sabotage, to twelve years' imprisonment on Robben Island.

"I remember his final speech from the dock. I remember it because I was there.

"I am going to quote the words of a banned man, which are illegal in this country only for those who dare not listen to them.

"After speaking for over three-quarters of an hour on the occasion, Justin said in conclusion:

"'. . . It is not I who am here in the dock, but the illegal South African government. It is not I who am being sentenced to imprisonment, but the members of the apartheid regime. It is not I who will languish in jail, but the perpetrators of racialism who are in fact jailing themselves. I go willingly to serve my sentence because I know that I represent the future of this country. And one thing you cannot do, you cannot jail the future. Amandla!'"

The crowd at the graveside responded, "Awethu!"

Andrew continued, "I now wish to thank all those of you who by your presence here have shown the high regard you had for Justin. I wish to thank you for your display of solidarity and for your willingness publicly to demonstrate your loyalty. I wish to thank you on behalf of his sister-in-law, Mrs Hester Bailey, on behalf of his only daughter Lenina Bailey, who is detained at present and has been refused permission to be present at her father's funeral, on behalf of his wife, Mrs Florence Bailey, who is also here amongst us, and finally on behalf of a close mutual friend of Justin and myself, Abe Hanslo, who is in Canada, but would have been here if he could.

"To all of you, I wish to quote what I read on a banner when the people marched to Pollsmoor to show solidarity with Nelson Mandela, 'A Nation That Loves Martyrdom Cannot Be Enslaved'."

The Guguletu choir led the assembly in the singing of the national anthem, "Nkosi Sikelel' iAfrika".

Then it was all over.

Andrew went to Hester and exchanged brief condolences with her. Then he moved to Florence, who was standing lonely and neglected.

"I'm very glad that you came," he said.

"I'm glad that I came."

"It was brave but nevertheless the correct thing to do."

"It was very kind of you to mention me. I will never forget the three of you. Abe, yourself and Justin."

She turned and disappeared into the crowd.

Andrew found Ruth, and the two weaved their way to the car. There was now no police presence whatsoever. The Casspirs, Ratels and heavily armed men had all disappeared. They drove slowly in a long queue, directed by efficient traffic officers.

"Dad," Ruth said quietly, "Brad was at the funeral."

"You saw him?" he asked incredulously.

"I spoke to him."

"When was that?"

"While you were speaking to the crowd. He came and stood behind me. He said he was O.K. and that you and Mom were not to worry."

"How can I not worry about my own son?" Andrew asked himself, absolutely frustrated although feeling relief at the same time.

9

After he had seen Jonathan and Waheed drive off in the ambulance with the injured Shane on 15 October, that mild Tuesday evening that had erupted into such violence, Andrew drove straight home to Elfindale. There was blood all over the backseat of his car and his suit was stained red in patches. He went straight to the bathroom and began stripping off his soiled clothes. While he was soaking his shirt in the handbasin, he looked up to see Mabel staring at him from the doorway.

"Are you hurt, Andrew?" she asked as fear shot into her eyes.

"Nothing to worry about, darling," he said, attempting a cautious smile. "I merely helped an injured boy, that's all. I'm afraid my suit is all messed up."

She was relieved at his reply, and started to pick up clothing he had thrown to the floor.

"A youngster was badly hurt in Crawford, and I helped two of his friends to get him to a doctor in Rylands."

Ruth came in and stood next to her mother.

"Did it happen in Thornton Road, Dad? A friend just phoned me about the shooting there. She said that three people were killed. There must have been plenty of trouble."

"There's always plenty of trouble everywhere," Andrew said in an attempt to defuse her statement.

They ate their dinner in silence. Neither Mabel nor Ruth questioned him further. Andrew retired to his study to write up the day's events and compose a long letter to Abe. Things were becoming so confused. Lately he was becoming more unsure whether he was writing to himself, to Abe in Canada, or merely recording the happenings for the new novel. Somehow he hoped it would all finally make sense and fall into place. Truth would merge with fiction, or fiction merge with truth. Reality would fuse with imagination and produce a result consisting of a compact of veracity and fabrication. In real life all that happens *does* happen. In fiction all that happens *could* happen. He was no longer sure whether he could distinguish between truth and fiction.

He began the letter to Abe then gave up. He decided to record the day's events in Thornton Road but didn't get far. He began working them into his new novel but this also would not get going. Then he listed all the happenings since the opening of schools and gave up halfway through sheer frustration. He poured himself a drink. Then he restarted the letter to Abe.

He was still wide awake although it was long past eleven and the house was deadly quiet. He thought about turning in for the night. Both Mabel and Ruth must be sound asleep by now. He was busy packing away his papers when the doorbell rang accompanied by loud knocking. He tensed himself preparing for a confrontation. The bell rang again and there was an urgency about its tones.

Andrew opened the front door.

"My God, Brad."

"It's me, Dad."

"Come in quickly," Andrew said. Bradley signalled to someone outside and a car with the engine running, drove off at speed.

"Two of the comrades," he explained laconically.

Andrew hastily ushered him into the study, locked the front door and turned off all the lounge lights.

Bradley looked tired and worn. He seemed to sag in spite of his athletic build. His dark eyes, dominated by the bushy brows he had inherited from his father, showed signs of extreme weariness.

"I haven't slept properly for the last two days," he explained, attempting a wry smile.

Andrew was not going to prompt his son with questions.

"You look very tired, Brad," he remarked. Then gearing into action he said, "It's not safe here. Let me phone your Uncle Eldred in Grassy Park and I'll run you down there."

"That won't be necessary, Dad."

"Why not?" he asked puzzled.

"Because I have come home. I'm not going anywhere."

"But it's not safe here."

180

"I'm remaining where I am."

"All right, if you say so. I'm glad you're here nevertheless. Let me fetch your mother."

"No, please don't wake her if she's asleep. Is my old room still available?"

"Of course it is."

"Then I'll sleep there."

"O.K. Then we'll have to take the chance. Tomorrow we'll arrange a safer place."

"I don't want a safer place."

"I don't understand you. Your attitude makes no sense."

"I'm staying right where I am, Dad, whether they come for me here or not."

The remark was made casually, but surprised Andrew. He was at a loss to understand it, so to play for time, suggested that they have coffee. Bradley agreed and they went into the kitchen. While he clumsily fussed with the kettle and cups and saucers, Bradley slumped down in a chair, hardly able to keep his eyes open.

"Wouldn't you rather go and sleep at once?" Andrew asked.

"I'll have the coffee first. I need it badly. You know, Dad, I'm tired of running away. I'd decided this evening that I would never run away again."

He told his father how he had slept in different places almost every night from the time he had left home more than two months before. How he had been constantly on the move, sometimes only one jump ahead of his pursuers. Some of the comrades had suggested that he should leave the country, but he had resisted that and refused to consider it. The day they had picked up Lenina, he had escaped their dragnet by just ten minutes.

"I expected you at that meeting in Manenberg the evening of Justin's death. I was told that you would be there, that's why I went."

"I meant to be there, Dad, because I really wanted to see you. I wanted to assure you that we were still friends in spite of the way we had parted. Achmat Daniels gave me your message."

Andrew passed him a hot cup of coffee.

"I also learnt from Justin that he intended to attend that meeting. I went to see him during the afternoon, to warn him against doing so. We ended up quarrelling, which I still regret. It was the last time we spoke. We argued for a long time, that's why he arrived so late at your meeting. I warned him that things were getting hot, that Vosloo was determined to get both of us, that his best bet was temporarily to stick to the conditions of his house arrest order. But he was adamant about going in order to advise some of the youth about the incorrectness of their tactics."

"What happened to you on that evening?"

"I had received a tip-off the same afternoon, that's why I went to see Justin. The noose was definitely tightening. I sent a warning to Achmat to call off the meeting but I believe that he never got it. Then Justin left for the meeting. I had no alternative but to follow but did so about half an hour later."

Andrew listened carefully.

"I saw the blue Datsun I had been warned to watch out for. I had seen it before. Then I spotted Trevor on the look-out in a shop, and told him to get you people to leave the meeting as soon as possible. Trevor told me that you were also inside, and it hurt me that we were so close but could not meet. I was more afraid for you than for myself."

"I believe that you were also at Justin's funeral?"

"Yes, I risked it for Lenina's sake. I hoped that I would not be noticed in that huge crowd. I knew that Vosloo and his men would be there, but I had to go. Justin was a father to me."

"More so than I?"

"I don't want to hurt you, Dad, and we mustn't fight anymore. But you and I were never really close. Somehow I could not get as near to you as I got to Justin. I was very pleased when I heard that you were getting involved and attending political meetings and rallies. But I didn't know just how to interpret that. What were your motives? Was your concern for your family? Was your concern for your son? Were you looking for political credibility? Or were you doing this by conviction? I heard about your speech at Rocklands, but was still not sure. Then I heard your speech at Justin's funeral, and this time I was sure."

They returned to the study, carrying their cups.

"Tell me, Brad," he said once they had settled down again, "why did you come home this evening? You must be fully aware of the risk you are taking."

"Yes, I am fully aware of that. I realise that if they come here there is no escape for me. But I'm prepared for that. I'm tired of running away, Dad."

A faraway look came into Andrew's eyes. "I know how you feel, son. A long time ago I also felt like that and I wrote about it." He leaned over, took a copy of his novel from the bookshelf, paged through it and started reading.

You know, Abe, all my life I've been running away. I ran away from District Six. I ran away the night my mother died. I ran away from Miriam's place. I've been running away from the Special Branch. Now I'm hiding in Lotus River like any common criminal. Maybe I've been running away from myself. But that's all over now. I am determined to stay.

"I don't know whether I am the one speaking, or whether it is the character in this novel, or whether it is you now, or the fictional character in my new book. Maybe we are all the same person saying the same things in the same voice."

"I never knew you like this, Dad."

"Yes, I am like this."

"You know, I am really beginning to understand you."

"I am at last beginning to understand myself."

Brad was struggling to keep awake.

"Go to bed," Andrew said. "I'm not sleepy, but you go. I still have a letter to finish. Use your old room."

"If it's all right by you, Dad. Please don't wake me unless they come."

"I won't wake you, even if they come."

Brad went into his room and shut the door. Andrew sat for a long time just staring. Then he poured himself a stiff whisky and continued his letter to Abe.

10

15 October 1985 (midnight)

Dear Abe

I have spent a large part of this evening trying to complete this letter to you. I wrote the first few pages before dinner, and am now near to completing it. I know it is a long letter, but it is more than a mere letter as I'm sure you will notice. I shall most probably send it off within the next few days with the last chapters of the new novel. I am pleased that you have received those sections I have sent off previously. In spite of all the happenings today, the shooting in Thornton Road, rushing that injured boy to a doctor, Brad's unexpected but welcome return, I am now feeling calm although a bit tired. But don't you worry. I shall not go to bed until I have finished your letter.

Maybe my son's arrival proved to be something of a catharsis. Maybe the weeks of searching coming to so abrupt an end, proved something of a purgative. Whatever it is, I am more composed and relieved now than I have been for a very long time.

In between I have been steadily working at the novel which is very near completion. How will it end, or rather, how will it end itself?

I could use a Brechtian "alternative happy ending" to make readers feel better. I could get Brad to escape from South Africa with Lenina, get to Canada and marry in a picturesque church outside Toronto. You could give the bride away. Brad could become the official athletics coach to the Canadian Olympic team and the doyen of the local anti-apartheid movement. I could retire and be given an emotional farewell reception in the Eastridge Civic Centre where Mr Langeveldt could make an impassioned speech before presenting me with an inscribed gold watch. You could publish the definitive work on Nigerian poetry and thereafter become the valued confidant of Wole Soyinka.

Or better still, I could use a Dickensian ending with all the loose threads tied together. Lenina could be acquitted and go off to the Seychelles with Brad, after their marriage in St Mark's Church, District Six. Vosloo could come to a nasty but deserved end. You could arrive back in South Africa to accept an English chair at a great, liberal university. And it could all end up not with a bang but with a contrived, manipulated whimper.

In the preface to one of the editions of The Story of an African Farm *Olive Schreiner calls such endings the "stage method" because, as she says, this is what happens in fiction.*

But in real life it is not so. Real life is unpredictable and less dramatic. Brad is at present alive (thank goodness), but frightened in spite of his display of bravado. Lenina is languishing in a lonely cell, most probably ignorant of her father's death. I am sitting in my study outwardly calm, but waiting for the tell-tale knock at the door. We are made of flesh and blood, Abe, not of printer's ink.

But Olive Schreiner also describes this other method, the method of the life we all lead.

"Here nothing can be prophesied. There is a strange coming and going of feet. Men appear, act and re-act upon each other, and pass away. When the crisis comes the man who would fit does not return. When the curtain falls no one is ready. When the footlights are brightest they are blown out; and what the name of the play is no one knows."

It is quiet outside as only the suburb of a busy city can be quiet. One hears no cars screeching, no transistors blaring, no children screaming. A calm settles which suppresses all extraneous noise. It is far quieter than the midnight quiet of a Boland hamlet, where the silence is a continuation of the sounds of day, not in contrast to it.

Brad is sound asleep in his room. Outside of the drama of his sudden appearance, and the melodrama of his decision to stay until his captors come (what a familiar ring there is to that), he is temporarily at rest.

My mind drifts back to a mild, March evening in 1960 when the two of us parted. I remember we had quarrelled because I refused to leave South Africa with you, and you shook hands reluctantly outside Ruth's flat in Milner Road. Then you walked to your car and drove out of my life for years. Ruth and I went up to her rooms. For a short time we stood self-consciously together, and then I started to open the French windows.

After Ruth left me and went back to her family in the Transvaal, I deliberately shut all the windows of my life. I continued doing so even after I married Mabel and we had two fine children. But both my son and my daughter showed me how wrong I had been and, by their example, forced open those windows for their sakes, for my sake and for the sake of our people.

Of course the police may come for Brad at any time. I expect them tonight. They may come tomorrow. They may never come. When he wakes up he might have a change of mind and decide to leave South Africa. I shall give him every assistance, and encourage him to stay with you in Canada. He deserves an additional father.

I am metaphorically tired. I still have to end this chapter of my life. I do not know how to do so because chapters of one's life don't just end, they spill over into the next chapter, and the next and the next. Maybe the confusion of fiction and fact is a deliberate one. Maybe it will paradoxically clarify matters. Maybe fiction does create a clearer insight into reality. Maybe life does, in its own peculiar way, imitate art.

I am finished with this letter and have said all that I wish to say at present. I am now going to pour myself a stiff whisky. I am then going to open all my study windows and break the silence of my suburban night by playing a recording of Rachmaninov. Then I am going to sit and wait for what might happen next. Go well, my friend, go well.

Yours sincerely
Andrew